His passionate kisses and tender caresses put Kelly nearly out of her mind with need.

He let go of her long enough to pull his sweater over his head. It was hot, even though the air conditioner softly hummed on and off at timely intervals. The prickly heat he felt had more to do with his body temperature than anything else.

Kelly had a hard time sitting still on Houston's lap. His sex was hard as stone and every time she moved a muscle a part of her lower anatomy rubbed against it. The strong desire to see and touch what felt larger than life had her thinking all sorts of naughty girl stuff. If it were Christmastime, she'd get only coal in her stocking. And Saint Nick would give her a good scolding!

Houston had no idea how much of a bad, bad girl Kelly could be. Under the right circumstances, she could absolutely give him something he could feel.

His next fiery kisses had Kelly fidgeting. She hadn't thought she'd ever be the aggressor, but she was ready to become just that. She slowly got up from Houston's lap. "Excuse me. I'll be right back."

"Is something wrong?"

"Very wrong! But I'm about to make it right."

Books by Linda Hudson-Smith

Kimani Romance

Forsaking All Others
Indiscriminate Attraction
Romancing the Runway
Destiny Calls
Kissed by a Carrington

LINDA HUDSON-SMITH

was born in Canonsburg, Pennsylvania, and raised in Washington, Pennsylvania. After illness forced her to leave a successful marketing and public relations career, she turned to writing as a healing and creative outlet.

Linda has won several awards, including a Career Achievement Award from *RT Book Reviews*. She was also voted Best New Writer by the Black Writers Alliance, named Best New Christian Fiction Author by *Shades of Romance* magazine and a Rising Star by *Romance in Color* in 2002. She is a recipient of the 2000 Golden Pew Award and the 2004 winner in the romance category for the African American Literary Awards Show.

For the past seven years Linda has served as the National Spokesperson for the Lupus Foundation of America.

The mother of two sons, Linda lives with her husband, Rudy, in League City, Texas. To find out more go to her Web site, www.lindahudsonsmith.com.

Kissed by a
CARRINGTON

LINDA HUDSON-SMITH

ESSENCE BESTSELLING AUTHOR

This book is dedicated to my loving sister,
Donna Jean Brinson. Your staunch support in
my personal life and writing career means the world to
me. Thank you for the loyalty! Thank you for the love!

KIMANI PRESS™

ISBN-13: 978-0-373-86153-8

Recycling programs
for this product may
not exist in your area.

KISSED BY A CARRINGTON

Copyright © 2010 by Linda Hudson-Smith

www.kimanipress.com

Printed in U.S.A.

Dear Reader,

I sincerely hope that you enjoy reading
Kissed by a Carrington from cover to cover. The
Carrington triplets are back by popular demand
from the countless readers who desired more of
the Texas dead ringers!

I am very interested in hearing your comments and
thoughts on the romantic liaison between the NBA's
Houston Carrington and the Texas Cyclones' sports
medicine physician, Kelly Charleston. These beautiful
people will once again touch your hearts and quench your
thirst for exciting and sizzling romance.

Please enclose a self-addressed, stamped envelope
with all your correspondence and mail to
Linda Hudson-Smith, 16516 El Camino Real,
Box 174, Houston, TX 77062. Or you can e-mail
your comments to lindahudsonsmith@yahoo.com.
Please visit my Web site and sign my guest book at
www.lindahudsonsmith.com. You may also read
my newsletters and meet other published authors,
aspiring authors and other creative spirits at
thewritersworld.ning.com.

Linda

came easy. The first time he'd met her was nothing more than a

Chapter 1

On a lovely day in early June, wild screams, overzealous whistling and hand clapping thundered through the cavernous restaurant. There didn't appear to be a single woman—young, middle-aged or elderly—who didn't find handsome, toffee-complexioned Houston Carrington sinfully sexy. The NBA's Texas Cyclones' power forward, a confirmed bachelor, couldn't help but smile at the wild reactions as he made his way to a reserved table inside the popular restaurant All About Appetites, an upscale eatery in downtown Houston, Texas. He was used to this.

The ladies' instant recognition of the hometown sports hero made Houston feel good. He was a man who enjoyed women of all types, shapes and sizes.

The moment the hostess seated Houston, a male waiter approached him with caution and obvious reverence. "Good afternoon, Mr. Carrington. Welcome back to All About Appetites. It's a pleasure to serve you. Interested in starting with a drink, sir?"

Recognizing the waiter's nervousness, Houston extended his hand to the young guy while reading his name tag. "Thanks, Alex. Please bring me a bottle of mineral water. I'm expecting another party, so we'll order appetizers and meals once my companion arrives."

"Right away, Mr. Carrington," Alex said, quickly backing away from the table.

Houston drummed his fingers on the table, looking back and forth between his watch and the entryway. His date wasn't late; he was early by fifteen minutes.

A bad case of nerves could knock a man off his normal course, he thought.

As Houston thought about his beautiful luncheon companion and how the date had come about, his drop-dead-gorgeous smile came easy. The first time he'd met her was nothing more than a brief introduction by a friend at a Christmas party six months ago. The second time he saw her was at a charity auction to raise money for Haven House, a foster-care home. Both sightings had remained crystal clear in his mind.

Looking like she belonged on the front cover of a fashion magazine, a stunning female, with rich, dark sienna skin, had stood to make a bid. Thick, glossy, reddish-brown hair swept her shoulders. She was clearly intent on winning the auction entry when she'd lifted her hand as high as her bid of twenty-five hundred dollars.

The fabulous-looking male being auctioned off for a celebrity lunch date was Houston's brother Austin, who was the Texas Wranglers' quarterback. The toffee-complexioned dead ringers were only two members of the Carrington triplets, who played different professional sports in front of their hometown Houston fans. The other brother, Dallas, played shortstop for the National Baseball League's Texas Hurricanes.

Houston recalled the audible gasps that had swept through the room over the amount bid. The smug look on Austin's ex-fiancée's face had quickly changed to an expression matching her evil, hateful ways. Clearly, Sabrina Beaudreaux was not a happy participant. Determined to win, Sabrina had tried topping the last bid by another five hundred dollars, but to no avail. Kelly Charleston, the stunning beauty, was not to be denied.

For the next few minutes, Sabrina and the model-type, five-foot-seven Kelly held a private bidding war. The numbers had gotten so high no else dared to bid on Austin, though the ladies thought he was priceless. Since other gorgeous bachelors were to be showcased on the auction block, some women figured they'd save their bids for then.

The next time Houston saw Kelly after the auction was at a Karamu feast held at Haven House on the last day of Kwanzaa. Each encounter was crystal clear in his mind.

Houston glanced at the entry again. With no Kelly in sight, he sat back and recalled how this luncheon had been arranged. The details were ingrained in his mind.

Austin had approached Houston. "I need a big favor."

Houston had been skeptical. "What's on your mind?"

Austin grinned. "I need you to swap places with me for the celebrity luncheon date. I don't want to hurt Ashleigh. Sabrina knew

I wasn't among the celebrity auction participants when she pulled this fast one."

Houston wasn't too thrilled. "And you went along with it because the cause is too important. Haven House needs all the money we can raise, right?"

"What would you say if I told you the lady requested the swap? She says she met you at a Christmas party."

Houston nodded. "We were merely introduced. No conversation occurred between us. As for us swapping places, we haven't done that since high school."

"The beautiful lady bid on me but I think she'd like lunch with you, Houston. Please accept it. I don't want to risk losing the funds. It's all for Haven House."

Houston had agreed to take the date in his brother's stead. He could hear Austin's plea as though it was happening right now. Due to home games and the hectic away schedule, this was the first chance he'd gotten to make good on his promise.

Houston turned his thoughts from the past to the present. It was now *Kelly time.*

Lovely Kelly Charleston slid out of her sand-colored Porsche sportscar and handed over her keys to the valet parking attendant. She had the top up even though the June day was warm and pleasant. She didn't want to mess up her just-been-to-the-salon waves and curls. Dressed in a hip-hugging heather-gray dress, showing off all her eye-catching curves, she was a delightful and marvelous vision. The shiny gray-and-black patent stilettos added a couple inches more to her already graceful height. She was vivacious, beautiful and sexy—a total knockout.

Kelly didn't want to be late for her date with Houston Carrington, the sexy power forward for the NBA's Texas Cyclones. A pretty hostess immediately escorted Kelly to the table where Houston awaited her arrival. His breath caught, causing him to swallow hard. She looked sensational. The kind of reaction he had to her wasn't so unusual, but remaining his normal cool and aloof self in her presence might be difficult. It was the first time any woman impacted him so profoundly, and they'd only known each other a short time. Wrenching his eyes from her sexy figure wasn't easy. Ladies didn't come any more beautiful than this one.

As Kelly arrived, Houston practically leaped to his feet. Lifting her hand, he gently kissed the back of it. "We have to stop meeting like this," he teased. "You look stunning!" Pulling out a chair, he waited for her to sit before reclaiming his chair.

"Thanks for the compliment. You're quite handsome yourself," she said flirtily. Kelly wasn't worried about coming off as too forward. She smiled, revealing sparkling white teeth. "Hope I haven't kept you waiting long." Her voice was soft and smooth as silk, yet the rich, slightly husky intonation sounded seductive to him.

Houston glanced at his watch. "You're actually on time. I was a bit early."

Kelly nodded. "I like punctuality. It's a great quality to possess."

He liked her candor and self-confidence. "I agree. I'm also a stickler for punctuality. Yet I hang around with a group of guys who habitually run late."

"Good friends of yours?" Kelly asked, raising a perfectly arched eyebrow.

"My teammates. I can't tell you how often our travel plans are delayed because of tardiness. Good thing we travel on the franchise's private jet."

"Most professional sports teams do travel that way," Kelly asserted. "My friend is an air traffic controller. He only handles corporate jets and privately owned aircraft."

"Interesting gig," Houston remarked, wondering if Kelly was romantically involved with the man she'd just spoken of. His quiet thought had him annoyed. This was a first date—and by all accounts of his past history, a final one.

If Austin hadn't said Haven House might not get the bid monies unless he accepted the date in his stead, Houston wasn't so sure he'd be here.

Houston picked up two menus and handed one to Kelly. He opened his despite his knowledge of what food and dessert items were offered. "Hope you brought along a decent appetite. This place is appropriately named. My teammates refer to it as Triple A."

"All About Appetites," Kelly said on a laugh. "Cute! I like it. I was here once, but not for dinner. I came around the same time they started offering live music."

"Surprised I didn't run in to you. I love the music entertainment they bring in. My teammates and I frequent this place."

The couple quietly began discussing the menu. Kelly asked Houston questions about the entrées and he recommended several items he'd ordered before.

"The tender, juicy mesquite grilled steak and jumbo shrimp is one of the best combination entrées," Houston praised.

"I love steak and shrimp."

Once Houston and Kelly selected their meal choices, he summoned the waiter and wasted no time in making their preferences known.

As if Houston had suddenly recalled something, he snapped his fingers. "Please bring the lady a glass of white zinfandel." Austin had overheard Kelly's wine order at the auction and had passed the information on to Houston.

Kelly looked at Houston with skepticism. "How in the world did you know?"

Houston winked. "I make it my business to know." He laid his forefinger against his temple. "By the way, my brother never told me why you wanted *me* to come on this date versus him. Care to enlighten this old curious George?"

Color stole into Kelly's cheeks. Although she already knew the answer she pondered Houston's query, the million-dollar question swirling around in her mind.

Did Houston need to know the truth?

Kelly cleared her throat. "I bid on Austin because I utterly love to annoy Sabrina Beaudreaux, whom I hadn't seen in a while. She and I are old college roommates. The lady treated me horribly the first semester. I eventually ended up changing roommates."

"I heard there was tension between you. Members of our family felt it at the auction. We tried to accept Sabrina in our lives. Austin was going to marry her, but the Carrington family was never comfortable with his decision or with her. She was rude to us and she constantly showed an unattractive spirit of selfishness and heartlessness."

Kelly snorted under her breath. "I'm sure your family didn't see the half of it. People Sabrina dislikes, fears or is just plain jealous of are the ones who feel the full brunt of her meanness. She often made me the butt of her downright crude and unkind jokes." Kelly cringed at the painful memories.

"I'm sorry for whatever you endured." Houston closed one eye and peered at Kelly through the other, letting her know she still hadn't answered his question. "I've heard what you've said, but I'm also aware of what you haven't said. Why me?"

Amused by his persistent line of questioning, Kelly smiled softly. "Why not you?" she asked straightforwardly.

"That's what I want to find out," he said, eyeing her inquisitively. "You're the only one with the answers."

"Although Austin was the most popular male athlete on the auction block Sabrina wasn't the only reason I bid on him. I simply had a desire to check out the chemistry I felt the first time I saw you in person. So I asked Austin if he was willing to make a switch for the luncheon." She'd told Austin not to reveal her agenda, like she thought that would really happen between brothers.

The famous triplets, Austin, Dallas and Houston, born to Angelica and Beaumont Carrington, were tall, toffee-brown-complexioned, sinfully handsome, athletically built and buff beyond imagination. The brothers' sexy, athletic physiques, Southern accents, sparkling ebony eyes and silken curly hair had women all over the nation swooning. Kelly had found out she was no exception on her first glimpse of Houston.

Leaning forward, Kelly made unflinching eye contact with her date. "I find you attractive and sexy and I wanted to see if the first unbelievable reaction I had to you was real." She trilled off the sweetest, most heart-stopping laughter he'd ever heard. "It was."

Feeling good about Kelly's remarks, Houston laughed jovially. "You've hit a tender spot in my heart. The compliments are so sweet." His gaze strayed momentarily. "You're not alone in your reaction. I confess I was also enamored with you on each of our quick encounters. It's nice to share lunch with you, Kelly Charleston—very nice."

While extending her hand to Houston, Kelly felt the heat rise in her cheeks.

The meals were delivered in a timely manner. Once the waiter found out everything was to his patrons' satisfaction, he promptly disappeared.

Kelly didn't know if Houston was into blessing the food or not so she took the lead and said a short supplication. Following his enthusiastic amen, he looked up at her, approval shining in his dark eyes.

The next look Houston gave Kelly was odd. "I know this is just a celebrity charity date, but I try to let people know who and where I am regardless of the situation. As for the women I date, rarely is there a second one. Because of my profession and lifestyle, I have a lot of platonic female relationships, but I'm not the type to commit. I only date one woman at a time, but even that is never serious."

Kelly was totally surprised at Houston's pointed remarks. He'd been up-front on sharing his views on relationships, but she wasn't sure the timing was appropriate.

The look on Kelly's face let Houston know he'd caught her completely off guard. "You may think I shared too much information for a first-time get-together, but that's the way it is with me, Kelly. I'm direct and up-front, pulling no punches. Big problems arise for me when I don't lay my cards out in plain view."

Taken slightly aback by how painfully direct he was, Kelly took a sip of her drink. "It is a bit much, but only because I'm surprised by the timing. Are you perfectly clear from the jump with every woman you meet? And why *aren't* you the committing type?"

Houston ran steady fingers through his dark curls. "I love meeting all kinds of women, love them in all shapes, sizes and colors. My career keeps me moving at full speed. I think it'd be unfair to tie someone down, especially when I can't be there on a consistent basis. Commitments come with a certain amount of demands. I have a house but I'm also in love with a new condo…commitment is not my middle name."

"Hmm, those are interesting and commendable edicts. I like a man who is straight and to the point, yet it's unusual for stuff like this to come up in a discussion during a casual first lunch, don't you think?"

"You don't strike me as the kind of woman who kids herself. We've both mentioned our wild reactions to each other so I think the things I've said *are* appropriate."

Shrugging, Kelly chuckled nervously. "Put like that, I'd have to agree. How do you define yourself and manage your life as a superstar athlete? And how *are* things for you out of the spotlight of superstardom?"

Giving several moments of intense thought to her queries, Houston pursed his lips. "I define myself as a man, Kelly, a simple man who tries to live an uncomplicated life. I try not to give out false hopes and I don't go through life with unrealistic expectations from others or myself. No expectations equal no disappointments."

Though fascinated by his philosophy, Kelly tried hard to hide her feelings. "Why don't you believe in commitment?"

"It's not that I don't believe in it, because I do. I commit myself to important issues every single day of my life and I work hard to fulfill them. My job has me on the road a good bit. Personal relationships often suffer badly under that type of scenario."

"So, do you just love women and then leave them behind in your traveling dust?"

Houston peered over at Kelly in a slightly scolding way. "Hardly! I'm up-front about my position." He explained to her the number of women out on the road doing their best to distract a man from his good intentions. "I've seen marriage after marriage fail because of cheating, allegedly due to the numerous absences. I've also seen a number of successful ones, yet it's the failed ones I seem to focus on. As for superstardom, that's a label my brothers and I have inherited. We don't see ourselves as such, in or out of our professions. Taught by our father to be the very best at everything we do, we are merely extremely hardworking men who relish success."

As Kelly thought about how to turn away from their current conversation, she toyed with the idea of whether or not to tell Houston she had signed a contract as a sports medicine physician with his NBA team, the Texas Cyclones. Thinking it was better to wait until she was formally introduced to the entire team and the other staff members, she marked it off as a nontopic of conversation. After exposing her attraction to him, she didn't want him to think she'd taken the job just to be around him. That wasn't the case.

Feeling it was best to get off the subject he'd foolishly started, Houston summoned the waiter. Kelly requested another zinfandel and he ordered a glass of pinot grigio for himself.

While Houston waited for the orders to be filled, his mind flipped back to the constant taunting from his brothers over the phone last evening. He didn't understand why Austin and Dallas stayed up in his personal business. Just because they'd both fallen madly in love didn't mean he had to. He covertly took another look at his date. Curvaceous in all the right spots, Kelly only stood five foot seven compared to his six-foot-three-inch frame, but she was one tall order for any man to try and fill.

The waiter delivered the drink refills and promptly disappeared. Kelly reached out to accept the wine from Houston.

Hoping to lighten the dark mood he'd created, he pulled the drink back. "I forgot to taste your wine earlier, but I can't let this one get by." He took a small sip. "In case Sabrina paid the bartender to poison you, I want you to know I'm willing to die for you."

Kelly felt the pain of her sharp intake of breath. Laughter bubbled within and broke loose. This gorgeous jock had said the sweetest thing, even if it'd been uttered in total jest. She could only imagine how wonderful she'd feel if he'd actually meant it.

Smiling brightly, Kelly accepted the drink. "So you'd die for me, huh? I hope we never have to find out." She raised her glass. "Cheers."

Houston gazed intensely at Kelly. "Would you die for me?"

Kelly's eyes met his unblinkingly. "Of course, but please don't quote me on it. I'd first want to know how I'm expected to lay down my life. Not so sure I'd step in front of a bullet or a fast-flying dagger intended for you or anyone else."

They both laughed.

Houston was too much of a challenge for Kelly to walk away from.

"I liked the interesting way you've defined yourself. You've left me with no doubt about your character. I'm impressed with how you live your life. It's commendable. I hear you saying you walk through your existence being true to self. I like that." Nothing of what he'd said about his view on romantic relationships had been disrespectful or despicable. In fact, he had been up-front and rather sensitive about it.

She liked integrity and sensitivity in a man. Kelly didn't know for sure, but she felt strongly Houston possessed both—and probably a wealth of other fine characteristics.

Houston was pleasantly surprised by Kelly's assessment of his character. "I've never heard anyone interpret me the way you just did. Very few people get me right off the bat. It seems that you have. Thanks for the generous sizing up."

"You're welcome. Does it scare you that I'd love to learn more about you?"

"I don't scare easily, Kelly. But I have to warn you. You might not like everything you learn. Things you hear about me might not exactly be the truth, either. When in doubt about who I am, simply ask me."

"I'll do that. Thanks for being so transparent."

Kelly had seen Houston's remarks about being a confirmed bachelor and his inability to commit as interesting challenges, something she was always up for. He'd be surprised to know how competitive she was. However, this was the first time in her life she'd ever entered into a competition to win a man's heart.

If Houston truly believed he'd never commit to any one person, she'd accepted the challenge to show him otherwise. Proving him dead wrong wouldn't be easy, but she had already decided to pick up the gauntlet he'd thrown down.

If Kelly had her way, Houston would come to want her in every way a man wanted a woman. Yet it didn't look as if there'd be another encounter for them. But all was not lost. Kelly was an eternal optimist.

Time flew by with the speed of lightning while Kelly and Houston enjoyed the delectable food and learned a few more interesting tidbits about each other. Humor and seriousness had been a part of the conversations, leaving each to wonder what exactly made the other tick. If nothing else, they both knew how to ride out the choppy waves. Despite Houston's rules on personal relationships, he found it difficult to deny himself a chance to learn more about Kelly. She had first exposed a nerve then she'd pressed on it relentlessly. He'd been intrigued by a woman before but never to this degree. No one had ever made his heart race with the force of hurricane winds.

Glancing at her watch, Kelly got to her feet. "This has been one interesting meeting." She wrinkled her nose. "I'm sorry it has to end, but I've got a few important matters to tend to before the day is done." Kelly couldn't let Houston know how deeply she feared seeing him only through her television set.

Houston stood, towering over Kelly. "*Interesting* is just one of many words that describes our luncheon. All good things come to an end. I have had a great time with you." *And I'm no longer sure that this is the end of us, as I was in the beginning.*

Kelly and Houston appeared enthralled with each other as he walked her out.

Chapter 2

Not one to easily give in to bouts of nervousness, Kelly was surprised at the annoying tremor in her heart and at how dry her full, generous lips and mouth felt. The Sahara Desert was an adequate description for the dusty-tasting, cracking condition of her tongue. In spite of the juicy berry-wine lip gloss she wore, her lips felt parched.

Meeting the entire Texas Cyclones team and its owner and management staff wasn't a nerve-racking occasion for Kelly. Yet knowing Houston was among the group had her regretting the decision she'd made not to reveal to him the legal contract she'd signed to join the franchise as a team physician. Houston had imparted a fair amount of his personal history to her, but she hadn't given up nearly as much.

For the auspicious occasion Kelly had worn her favorite red power suit, simplified by a soft, silky white blouse. The dressy business attire, a perfect fit on her slender, well-toned body, was visible proof of her belief in the benefits of exercising regularly. Red patent-leather heels, almost the exact color as the suit, weren't as hot as the stilettos she'd worn on the luncheon date with Houston.

As the professional basketball team filed into the room, Kelly ran her fingers lightly through her reddish-brown tresses. Bouncing with full body, her hair shone with the glossy product her stylist had sprayed on generously after a wash and blow-dry.

A few deep breaths helped to calm Kelly. Then her eyes engaged with Houston's ebony ones. The expression on his face was totally unreadable, like a mask put perfectly in place to hide the true image behind it. Her breath suddenly felt tangled.

Houston didn't look a bit surprised or particularly shocked to see Kelly standing there. His gaze was hot and unwavering, swirling all about her, tampering with her calm demeanor.

Smile, she quietly commanded him. *Smile that beautiful smile for me, Houston Carrington, just long enough to ease this web of confusion I feel.*

"Well, men, this is Dr. Kelly Charleston, the newest player added to our team roster. She's the highly qualified sports medicine physician I just briefed you on," Maxmillian Sheffield, the franchise owner, announced. "Is she not as beautiful as I said?"

"Hear, hear," someone shouted from the middle of the room.

As the team did "guy things," wolf-whistling and pumping fists, Kelly blushed, her sienna cheeks glowing. So Houston *had* known about her contract before he'd walked into the room, she thought. Yet his expression hadn't given it away.

Maxmillian Sheffield, simply referred to as Max, filled any room he entered with his greatness. Kelly's few encounters with him had put her in the middle of what his staffers had said about him. He was kindhearted, considerate and wore on his shirtsleeves the incredible humility and humanity he also carried inside his heart.

One of the wealthiest men in the country, Max lived modestly, comfortably, but fully, sharing his overflowing coffers with the less fortunate. Max was a giver. Kelly had heard it said many times by others; only God could beat Max at giving.

"Kelly is on board to take care of our team's medical needs," Max said, "mainly the orthopedic-related ones. I brought her to us on the highest of recommendations, but no need to repeat all that. Even though our season is over and we're not in the playoffs, we hired Kelly to help with our summer league, preseason training and our future seasons. Without further ado, I present to you Dr. Kelly Charleston. Let's give her a hearty round of applause."

Enthusiastic hand clapping and warm smiles of approval appeared genuine.

Kelly stood in the center of the room, as opposed to timidly hiding behind the podium. "Hello, guys! It's a pleasure and a privilege to sign on with the champion NBA Texas Cyclones. I'm grateful for this opportunity of a lifetime. I won't travel with the team, but I'll be prepared to meet all your needs at home."

Kelly went on to let the team know that besides their own marvelous facilities, they'd have full access to the same state-of-the-art equipment her orthopedic practice had installed in their downtown medical/athletic facility, Houstons Sports Medicine Center.

"One of my partners in private practice, Dr. Jacoby Quinn, is also under contract with the team. I'd also like you to know I've been a staunch Cyclones fan for many years. Now that we're slightly acquainted, I'm open to any questions you might have."

Houston's left eyebrow lifted. "Any questions?" he asked pointedly, giving Kelly a mere sample of just how incorrigible he could be.

Kelly licked her lips in a stirring manner, a provocation intended solely for one Mr. Carrington. "*Any* questions that have to do with sports medicine or my credentials," she shot right back, her killer smile knocking him totally off-kilter.

Many of Houston's team members had attended the charity event for Haven House. As far as anyone knew, Austin was the only triplet bid on. Houston would like to keep it that way. Never in a trillion years would he intentionally give away his recent association with Kelly, yet he relished a little harmless fun at her expense.

Laughing inwardly, Houston quietly conceded round one to Kelly.

Kelly happily answered all the astute questions the players asked her. Her demeanor was professional, but she was savvy enough to allow her sensational sense of humor and effervescent personality to ooze. Her desire was to win the team's support, but she also wanted the guys to trust and like her. It would definitely make her job easier.

Max slid his cupped hand under Kelly's elbow. "Instead of the partial tour you had the day of your interview, I'd like to give you a full one of the facility and also show you where to hang up your stethoscope during the paperwork portion of your workday. I hear chart entries and signings are the least popular part of your profession."

Kelly laughed at Max's great sense of humor. "That's for sure. Cramped fingers and hands are occupational hazards, but I wouldn't trade it for anything. I'm ready to go if you are." As Kelly left the room with Max, she waved at the players, smiling broadly.

Instead of Max showing Kelly areas of the training center she'd already seen, he took her to the various sections she hadn't toured, in the interest of time. The Texas Cyclones' training facility was an amazing architectural structure. It was also a massive building, with a number of elevators and escalators provided for easy access from one point to the next. Lots of marble, brass, stainless steel, ceramic tile and an abundance of glass and textured walls could be found throughout.

Upon reaching the area Max had saved for last, he opened the door with a key and allowed Kelly to precede him. With his fingers already on the light switch, he quickly flipped it. "This is your personal hangout, Dr. Charleston."

The loud gasp from Kelly pleased Max. His employees were important to him and their happiness was also. He was one of the youngest owners in the NBA, but he was known as having the wisdom and charisma of someone far older than his thirty-eight years.

The red-and-gold welcome banner hanging high above the desk made Kelly smile. "Oh, my goodness! This is so unbelievable. Look at the size of my office. It's like an apartment inside here. Every piece of office equipment imaginable is installed."

Kelly had another fit when she discovered the private bathroom. "For me, this is equal to the fabled executive washroom. Does it get any better than this?"

Max's expression suddenly sobered. "It can always get better, Kelly. That's what our franchise is about. Making things better is our never-ending goal for all concerned in this business and for the city of Houston and the community at large. In keeping with President Obama's message, I'm willing to do anything I can to bring about change, change for the better good of our country and her citizens. Adding you to our staff is one of those remarkable changes. Again, welcome! We're blessed to have you."

"I can't thank you enough for everything you've done for me." Holding emotions in check was sometimes hard for Kelly.

A warm hug was warranted—and Kelly would have loved to give Max a big one. She thought it was too forward of an action for now, yet she believed it'd happen one day. Max was truly a wonderful individual and he genuinely cared about his players, his staff and all the others he'd mentioned. Kelly was beginning to see his heart of gold.

"I have one more surprise for you. Then I'll set you free," Max told Kelly.

The reception Max had planned in Kelly's honor was another nice surprise for her. As her eyes misted again, she turned to the owner. "This is very special. Thanks, Mr. Sheffield. I appreciate how you've gone out of your way to welcome me."

Max waved a scolding finger. "'Mr. Sheffield' only works for me in the boardroom. Even then, most of my associates call me Max. Please, Kelly, if you don't mind, I prefer Max. You'll soon find out I'm a staff-friendly boss."

Kelly reached for Max's hand and held it briefly. "Max, I'm honored!"

Max smiled broadly. "Glad we have that settled. Now let's go get a couple of plates and hit the buffet tables. If we don't hurry, there'll be nothing left. My guys love to eat. We'll also pop the corks on a few bottles of celebratory champagne."

"I'm all for that," Kelly enthused. "Everything looks so appetizing."

Kelly felt both tired and rejuvenated as she ran for her car. She had stayed at the reception until the last person had cleared the room. In her opinion, everything had gone extremely well between her and the attendees. Even though her official duties wouldn't begin until the summer league got under way, she was looking forward to it and the preseason and regular season games. She would be in-house periodically to set up her office and familiarize herself with the team's training facilities and procedures.

A few of the guys had dubbed her Dr. C. The majority of the players simply called her Dr. Kelly by the time the festive reception was over.

As Kelly buckled her seat belt, a light thump on the driver's window caused her to look up with a slight start. It surprised the daylights out of her to see Houston's mesmerizing eyes peering back into hers. Dazed by his sudden appearance, it took her a minute to realize she had to turn on the engine before lowering the window.

"Congratulations and welcome aboard," he stated, sounding quite genuine.

"Thanks. I'm excited about working with and getting to know the team before the official season." She paused a moment. "I apologize for not giving you a heads-up on my professional role with the team. I now know that I should have."

"You aren't obligated to tell me anything about your personal life. I was there to fulfill my obligation to help Haven House collect the bid you made. That's done now."

Kelly looked nonplussed. "What do you mean by that, Houston?"

Houston shrugged. "It was my understanding you might not cough up the funds unless I agreed to the luncheon date in place of my brother."

"Excuse me!" Kelly felt terribly affronted. "There's nothing further from the truth. That's thinking I may be a thief. Who in Hades did you hear that from?"

"Afraid I can't give up my sources." Houston was now wondering if Austin had lied to him just to get him on the date. His two brothers would never stop the irritating attempts at matchmaking. "We've met the perfect woman for you," Austin and Dallas had crooned to Houston.

"Then you shouldn't repeat what you *thought* was said. It is a bold-faced lie. I rendered the entire bid amount in a check made out to Haven House before I left the event. Have a nice life!" Angrier than she'd been in a long while, she smashed her finger against the button controlling the driver's-side window.

Houston reacted quickly to the unexpected rising glass in an attempt to avoid decapitation. For several seconds, he just stood there, looking after Kelly's car, which sped through the parking lot like it was on the track at a NASCAR racing event.

It looked as if he owed the vivacious Dr. Kelly Charleston an apology. If that *was* the case, Austin was guilty of putting him in an unattractive position. As he thought back on his comments about collecting on the bid, he realized he hadn't exactly been sensitive in how he'd phrased it. It was so unlike him.

Houston knew he had to see Kelly again, at least one more time. An apology was necessary, no matter who'd misrepresented the reason for the date. Her thinking he was an insensitive jerk didn't sit well with him, not when he wasn't like that. As he conjured up the stunned, wounded look on her face, he felt a sharp ache of deep regret.

Why do I act so out of character when I'm around Kelly? Houston wasn't sure he wanted to know the answer, since he probably wouldn't like it.

By the time Houston made it to his Porsche, which was a different color and model from Kelly's, he had his mind made up about seeing her again. As he settled onto the driver's seat, he thought about how to apologize. No one had to tell him he'd hurt her feelings and no one had to advise him to make it right.

Houston turned the key in the ignition and revved the engine for a few seconds. The car shot out across the lot, slowing as it turned out of the parking area and onto the street. He looked ahead to try and spot Kelly's car. By the way she'd sped off, he wasn't surprised she was nowhere in sight. Just as he came up on the next exit, he saw her car moving slowly down the ramp. Following the Porsche off the freeway, he kept her in sight until he could signal her to pull over. Then he recalled they'd exchanged cell-phone numbers in case either had to cancel the luncheon date.

With his Bluetooth earpiece in place, Houston used the phone's voice-command capability to get Kelly on the line. She responded on the first ring, sounding irritated and a bit disgusted. "Hey, Kelly, think you can pull over for a minute? I need to talk to you."

"Who is this?" she asked, knowing full well it was Houston.

Houston didn't believe for a second Kelly didn't recognize his voice. If she'd stored his number in her cell, his name had also shown on the viewing screen. "It's Houston," he said, tolerating her petulance. "Let me have a word with you, please."

She sucked her teeth. "You've said enough. Frankly, I don't want to hear another remark coming out of your mouth."

Houston chuckled under his breath. She was red-hot and he found her little temper tantrum bold and sexy. "Suit yourself, but you don't know what you're missing out on."

"Like hell I don't!" Kelly pressed the end button on her cell phone just to show him she didn't care about anything that had to do with him. It hurt her to know he believed she'd withhold the promised donation. The reason she'd supposedly reneged on the deal hurt her more than anything else.

His mood turning somber, Houston repeated the voice command. It rang several times before he realized she was refusing to take his call. He understood her anger and could appreciate her feelings. However, he aimed to apologize…and his intent was steadfast. One way or the other, he planned to let her know how sorry he was.

Minutes later, Houston caught up to Kelly again, leaning on his horn to get her attention. As she glanced over at him, he gestured for her to pull over. *Please,* he mouthed, hoping she'd comply. If not, he'd follow her to her destination, wherever that was. She'd either park somewhere or eventually run out of gas. His tank was full.

Houston had pretty much shown Kelly how persistent he could be during their lunch date so she wasn't surprised by his actions. If she didn't pull over, she didn't believe for one second he'd give up. Houston was no quitter.

Slowly, Kelly steered her car over into the right-hand lane so she could turn up into the Walgreens discount store parking lot. She had her choice in slots since the area was near empty.

Houston pulled his car in right next to hers and got out.

Kelly's hands began to tremble. As Houston tapped his fingers lightly against the passenger-side window, she suddenly realized he intended to get into her car with her. She certainly hadn't bargained for that. The idea of him seated so close to her, in such tight quarters, made her sweat. Yet she popped the lock open.

While easing his body onto the seat, Houston felt cramped in her car because his Porsche was custom-designed for his tall, athletic physique. He looked over at her and smiled gently. "I was an absolute horse's behind back there. I was insensitive to you. I was at lunch on behalf of Haven House, but I've never enjoyed myself more. I know you are an honest person and would never skip out of a commitment, financial or otherwise. Can we please get past the bad start? I take full responsibility for it. I'd love to be forgiven."

The soft and sincere way in which Houston had spoken had Kelly reeling. Her head was going around and around. The man made her dizzy. She didn't even want to deal with her desire issues. Wanting him in a way she hoped he'd one day want her made her feel mental. "Why should I forgive you?"

"Because I asked you to and 'cause I really want you to. I don't want you upset with me. Just the idea of you mad at me is upsetting. The reason why I feel this way is that I like you, Kelly. You're fun to be with. I'd love for us to become friends."

Friends. She both liked and disliked the sound of the meaningful noun. *Friend* was too tame for what she wanted. Sharing in fire and brimstone and hot, breathless passion was more to her liking. Envisioning his beautiful body naked and steamy, stretched out on her mattress, his manhood hot, hard and ready for her, made her wish she was anywhere other than in the confines of her car. Imagining eating ice chips from his body and lapping the melting water with her tongue only heated her up more.

Kelly turned slightly in her seat and looked directly at Houston.

"Why did you insult me like that? What you heard about the bid, do you believe it?"

"I didn't intend to affront you. I believe you and what you told me. I plan to find out the truth. I don't like being lied to, especially if it was intentional."

She sighed with relief. "I believe in forgiveness and I'm a forgiving woman. That doesn't mean I have to be your friend, but I like you and I want to be." Leaning in, she kissed him gently on the cheek. "Thanks for believing in me. The donation to the home was never a condition of the date. I was always going to pay. I simply wanted the date to be with you. Remember?" Kelly had wanted to go out with Houston for the reasons she'd cited. She had wanted to find out if her bombshell reaction to him was real.

"I'm glad that's settled. Think you'd like to hang out with me again?" he queried.

"Based on your commitment rules, I'd think you'd be the one to shy away."

"We've already discussed that. You know where I stand. There's nothing wrong with a man and woman becoming friends. Is there?"

There is when one is hot as Hades for the other. "You're right." She looked at the clock on her dashboard. "This has been interesting, but I've got to go."

"Hot date?" Houston instantly wished he hadn't asked such a personal question.

"Red-hot," she remarked. Her hot date was with a steaming bath.

Houston reached for the handle and opened the door. Just before sliding off the seat, he leaned his head back in, catching her off guard as he kissed her. "Friends."

"Friends," she repeated, bewildered by the airy, fleeting kiss to her mouth. It was one of the sweetest kisses ever, though his lips had barely grazed hers.

Removing the cell phone from his belt, Houston handed it to Kelly. "Please store your home number for me so I can call. I'll also give you my contact information."

Taking hold of his phone, Kelly suddenly felt giddy inside. Wishing he wasn't watching her so intently, she punched in the ten digits, hating the trembling in her fingers. Feeling shook up inside,

Kelly inserted just her initials—*K.C.* Worried he may not find it like that, she erased it and put in her full name, adding *M.D.*

Kelly handed the phone back to Houston. Their hands touched. Then their eyes connected in a fiery way. As the heat of seduction emanated through their bodies, concentrated gazes held steady for several seconds.

Staring into Houston's eyes was like looking into a midnight sky. It was too easy for Kelly to get totally lost in his dark gaze, too effortless for her to forget the world existed when he could draw her into his with a mere glance or a lingering one.

While making her way into the beautifully decorated master bathroom of her home, with its fancy gold and brass fixtures, Kelly stripped out of her clothes. An entire wall behind the dressing table was mirrored. Black-and-white wallpaper with red-and-gold trim adorned both the spacious bathroom and the large but cozy bedroom.

A plush, downy-soft white comforter, matching sheets and pillow shams were adorned with a pattern of large hand-stitched black roses and an intricate edging done in Christmas red. The oversize master suite, her favorite space of all, was open and airy.

An oval-shaped tub, surrounded by a step-up black-and-gold-veined marble apron, was adorned with red, black and gold candles in every size and shape. The window nearest the tub looked down onto an in-ground pool/spa amidst a stone deck. Two majestic Magnolia trees stood watch over a lovely evergreen garden. The custom-built Clear Lake home, amidst a forestlike setting, was less than a year old.

It was nowhere near dark, but Kelly closed the slats on the plantation shutters. Filling the tub with water before turning on the strong pulsating jets, she lit cranberry- and jasmine-scented candles. Before she could step up and down into the tub, the phone rang. Dashing across the room, she quickly reached for the portable extension on the dressing table.

"Is this too soon for you?" Houston asked.

"Soon enough," she sang out, laughing softly. "Where are you?"

"I'm on the road leading to my place, which is so unlike the large spreads my brothers own. Austin had his before he got married. Both are staunch cowboy ranchers."

"Cowboys, huh? What about you?"

"I'm the urban cowboy in the family. We grew up on a ranch with hundreds and hundreds of acres of land, where our parents still live. Daddy taught us all he knew about ranching, but it's more in Austin's and Dallas's blood than mine. My home is surrounded by plenty of forested acreage in South Shore Harbor off 518. What I love most are the innumerable trees and lake access, yet the trees can be hazardous during hurricane season. I'll have to invite you over. The landscaping alone is worth the trip."

"I'll just bet it is," she said, her tone seductively taunting. Exploring the landscape of his hot body would be more than worth it. "Tell me more about the urban cowboy."

"I appreciate the land, while Austin and Dallas love to work it. I enjoy planting the occasional shrubs and flowers, but I don't have stables to muck or fences to mend. My brothers have qualified personnel to tend to the vast acreage and the horses and other animals. I have a gardener and a pool man. My housekeeper, Aleigha Swan, comes once a week. She cooks for me on occasion, but mainly handles the catering for parties and other special events I host quite frequently. I love to entertain at home."

"So, there are some big differences between you and your brothers. You look so much alike I imagined you also thought and acted the same way. Silly of me, I guess."

"Not really. Lots of folks think that way. And we are very much alike. Our parents did a great job in raising us to become our own individuals. There are a host of things that set apart Austin, Dallas and me. We grew up with the same values and principles, hung out together constantly, but each triplet has our own patented personality and our own special way of doing things and living our lives. We all have problems, but loving each other isn't one of them. The Carringtons are a devoted crew. I'd love for you to come to one of our family dinners. They're off the hook and so is the food."

Kelly looked surprised. "Is that an invitation?"

Houston thought about what Kelly had asked. "Yeah, it is. We do dinner once a week when everyone is in town. Let me know when it's a good time for you."

Kelly nodded. "I'll do that. Sounds like a nice evening. Thanks."

Houston smiled as he opened the remote-controlled gates

securing the lavish homes. "Thanks for pulling over earlier today. I'm glad we had the conversation. Again, I'm sorry."

Kelly closed her eyes. "Me, too. It's all good."

Houston parked in the long circular driveway. Instead of getting out of his car, he just sat there, thinking hard about what he'd said and done. Only a short time ago he'd been spouting off his commitment speech to Kelly. Today, he'd asked her for date, a real one, a first date with one of the most intelligent women he'd run across, not to mention one of the most beautiful. His idea of spending time with the opposite sex was supposed to be fun, honest and uncomplicated, without any game playing on his part. "Keeping it real" was his favorite mantra.

As much as Houston hated to admit it, he was more than merely intrigued by Kelly. There were many things about her that blew him away. He was taken with her in a big way, feeling things he'd never allowed himself to indulge in. The lady doctor was intellectually, socially and physically correct. She appealed to him on every important level he could think of. Her wit was sharp, but oh, so sweet, which required him to be on his toes and his best behavior. Kelly made him laugh, made his heart dance.

Was it possible for one woman to have it all?

As Houston thought about a beautiful lady named Angelica Carrington, he knew it was a definite possibility. His mother, a rare gem, was one woman who had it all.

Then there was Austin's wife, Ashleigh, and Dallas's girlfriend, Lanier. Both brothers had chosen women who had many attributes mirroring those of their mother. Houston had always known that when he went for a lifelong partner she'd have to possess the same qualities as the beautiful, spirited woman who'd raised him, the wonderful lady whose heart overflowed with kindness and love. His wife had to be the same kind of person Angelica was, a woman whose husband and children absolutely adored her.

Was Kelly Charleston that woman for him?

"God only knows," Houston whispered shakily.

Inside his beautifully appointed lakefront home, decorated by one of the finest interior design firms in the greater Houston area, Houston headed straight for the huge, delightful kitchen, which featured dark cherry-wood cabinets and every modern piece of stainless-steel appliance and complementary equipment available for purchase. The high table with high-back bar stools was large enough to seat eight. Above the center island hung a built-in rack holding a variety of copper pots, pans and other cooking utensils.

Opening the door of the two-sided stainless-steel refrigerator, Houston pulled out a bottle of water. Twisting off the cap, he tossed it in the garbage can and then walked through the spacious one-story home, which had a formal living room, a more open casual great room, a family room, a dining room, built-in bookshelves lining the rooms and halls and several fireplaces.

Once Houston reached his massive master suite, decorated in gray, red and navy blue, he plopped down on the humongous mattress, which had been custom-made to accommodate his size. A ceiling fan/lighting fixture hung directly over the center of the bed. Two more fans hung from the ceiling in the attached retreat.

Works of Black and Asian art graced every single wall, along with a variety of shiny wall sconces holding appropriately sized candles. The majority of the bedroom featured recessed lighting, with the exception of several brass lamps positioned around the room. His home was equipped with the finest in office equipment and the latest state-of-the-art audio and visual components. Several glass bookcases were filled with books in a host of genres. CDs and DVDs were stored in a built-in cabinet.

Deciding to take a shower before lying down, Houston rushed into the bathroom and opened the glass door leading to the largest stall architectural plans would allow for. The shower was equipped with four separate showerheads, two fixed and two handheld. Each head adjusted to the user's desired water temperature.

Houston hastily tore himself out of his clothing and stood under the jet stream of steamy water. The moment the hot liquid hit his body, he felt his muscles relax. His mind then went straight to Kelly.

Chapter 3

Freshly showered and naked as a jaybird, Houston slid under the blue, gray and red comforter and lodged two king-size down pillows under his head. As his thoughts of Kelly continued, he recalled the icy tone of voice she'd used earlier. Some guys might've called her frigid because of it. He had to laugh at that.

The layers of heat he imagined on the surface and beneath the tiers of Kelly's soft but firm flesh belied such. His body had sizzled at the slightest touch from her. Her skin had to be silky soft and pliable because it looked that way. The idea of caressing Kelly everywhere on her shapely body caused his manhood to respond.

Since turning off his wondrous thoughts was impossible, Houston phoned Dallas. Once he got his brother on the line, he dialed Austin's number. This situation called for a three-way.

Austin answered the phone, sounding drowsy. "You sound out of it," Houston remarked. "Dallas is on the phone, too. I initiated the call, but we can do this later."

"No, man, it's cool," Austin assured his brother. "I've been awake a few minutes. What's happening in your world, Houston? What're you up to?"

"Up to my neck in thoughts of Kelly Charleston! You won't believe this…" Houston said.

"What?" Dallas asked, yawning.

"The beautiful lady is under contract with the Cyclones," Houston revealed.

Austin whistled. "Signed on in what capacity?"

"A sports medicine physician. When Max announced it just before we met her, I nearly fell out of my seat. Did you know she was a doctor, Austin?"

"Not a clue. Sounds like you're cornered, my brother." Austin chuckled under his breath.

"That's not the half of it. I asked her out on a date, after I hurt her feelings."

Dallas gave a disgruntled snort. "What did you do or say to offend her?"

Houston told his brothers about the offensive remark he'd made about fulfilling his lunch date obligation for Haven House.

"Ouch," Austin exclaimed. "That's my fault. I guess you know by now I lied to you about why you had to accept the date."

"It's a little too late for regret now, don't you think? I told her I'd been lied to, but not by whom. She took serious offense to my comment."

"Houston, you're way too sensitive to do something like that," said Dallas. "This girl is already getting to you."

"I agree," Austin seconded. "Asking her out on an official date, especially after putting up such a fuss about the lunch, is also very telling."

"A classic sign of falling hard," Dallas remarked. "I suggest you go with your feelings."

"Who said anything about feelings or falling hard?" Houston shouted.

"You just did," Dallas responded loud and clear. "There are definitely some feelings happening here, whether you want to admit it or not. I can't recall the last time you had a follow-up date with any sister. Maybe you did in high school or college but certainly not lately."

"I like her, Houston," Austin confessed. "She seems like a nice person. She's real, man."

"Very real," Houston said, blowing out a breath of frustration. "I mentioned taking her to our family dinners."

"Make it happen soon," Austin recommended. "Is she under contract to travel with the team?"

"No." Houston was quick to respond. "I can't say I'm sorry about that. Things could get complicated under that scenario. I don't want my teammates getting wind of this. If they do, they'll ride me like a bucking bronco."

"The guys will definitely find out if this relationship progresses into something serious," Dallas advised. "You know how our team-mates sniff out any hint of rumor or innuendo."

Houston sighed hard. "There you guys go again, always jumping to conclusions. We haven't had a next date, but you're both talking like we're already deep into something."

"I hate to let you in on this, bro, but you *are* in deep," Austin cautioned Houston. "You just won't let go of the tight control on your silly commitment notions. Let yourself feel this woman. But we won't harass you. Just don't take too much time to make up your mind."

"Yeah, man, we're with you," Dallas assured, knowing they'd harass Houston at every turn, more so if he decided to keep Kelly at arm's length. "Make sure you know what you're doing. You don't want to hurt her. Maybe it's time to let loose the Doberman inside you, the one guarding your heart. No one ever knows the beginning from the end, but finding out what's in between can be a beautiful experience."

"Dallas is right, Houston. Now that I have you two guys on the phone," Austin said, "there's something important we need to discuss."

Seated in the cavernous kitchen inside Austin's ranch-style home, Houston looked tired. He had gotten up earlier this Saturday morning than he'd intended. It had been hard to get out of bed. After talking with his brothers about Kelly last night, he'd lain awake until the wee hours of the morning thinking of the lady doctor.

The conversation had ended with Austin calling a meeting to discuss plans for Angelica's birthday. The brothers wanted to do something extraordinary for their mother, their biggest supporter. It was a daunting task since they showered her with special gifts all year long.

"Dining in a fancy restaurant is old hat," Houston drawled lazily. "We do it all the time."

Dallas's fingers raked through his dark, satiny curls. "We need to do something original, something we haven't done for her yet. Mom deserves the best."

Pushing his coffee cup around in circles on the table, Austin looked thoughtful. "We know that much. We've given her everything but the sun. This gift has to be extraordinary."

Houston's eyes lit up. "What about a cruise?"

Austin pumped one fist in the air. "Great idea! She's talked about going on one but hasn't done it yet. What do you think, Dallas?"

"Works for me. Dad would love it. Old Beaumont will have a

fit if we send Mom away without him. They're extensions of each other—where one goes the other follows."

Austin and Houston laughed at Dallas's *old* reference to their dad. They all did it from time to time, but never in his presence. They had the utmost respect for their father. He was the man who'd named the triplets after various cities of his native Texas, the person who'd taught them to become strong, independent, upstanding black men. Beaumont led by example. His boys had followed along in his footsteps without getting lost in his oversize footprints.

Looking a bit concerned, Austin stroked his chin. "We can't be gone for too long. Since Ashleigh's in her third trimester, a three- to five-day cruise will work best for us."

Dallas nodded. "The time frame is cool with me, big brother. We can sail to Cozumel right out of the Port of Galveston or the Port of Houston."

Austin, the firstborn triplet, was a born leader. Houston and Dallas looked up to Austin and also went to him for sound advice on personal guidance and growth and life in general. Dallas was the money man, sought out for discussion on financial issues and relied on heavily for his recommendations on various investments. Houston was the knowledgeable one, referred to as a walking encyclopedia. Black history was his favorite subject and he researched it relentlessly, sharing with the family the unusual things he'd learn. Each brother supported the other in individual and joint ventures.

Austin nodded. "Great suggestion. Ashleigh's not keen on flying until after she delivers. I don't want her isolated from proper medical care, either."

"Maybe we'd better come up with a good backup plan," Dallas suggested.

"If all of us can't go on the cruise, we'll just send Mom and Dad," Houston said.

Liking Houston's suggestion, the guys nodded in agreement.

Ashleigh, Austin's golden girl, suddenly appeared in the doorway. She was a beautiful woman with a fiery copper-colored mane of thick, unruly curls and a sun-kissed champagne-gold complexion. "Did I just hear my name?"

Dallas and Houston rushed to Ashleigh's side, giving her warm hugs. The guys genuinely loved their sister-in-law, who was once a foster sister. As a foster child, Ashleigh had resided in the Carrington home for many years. Years later the family had been reunited on a Valentine's Day cruise.

Houston always noticed how mesmerized Austin was by his wife's gentle beauty. He kept his eyes on her as the brothers made their normal fuss over his adorable wife.

Smiling brightly, Ashleigh waddled into the room, her stomach clearing the doorway first. The brothers followed along behind her, reclaiming their seats at the table.

Ashleigh plopped down on Austin's lap, kissing him passionately. "Talking about your favorite subject, huh?"

Austin kissed Ashleigh back. "You know it!" As his hands rubbed her stomach tenderly, he couldn't take his eyes off her. "How's our little one today, Mommy?"

Ashleigh smiled sweetly. "Just fine, Daddy. No kicks yet from our future star punter. I'm sure he or she is just gearing up for the day. We haven't been awake very long."

Houston loved the way Ashleigh referred to herself and their child as one body. He was also enamored with the fact that his sister-in-law thought a girl was as capable of being a star athlete as a boy. Male or female baby was just fine with the couple. A healthy child was the daily prayer. Wanting to be surprised, Austin and Ashleigh had refused to learn the baby's gender.

Ashleigh sniffed the air. "Who fixed coffee?"

Houston laughed. "Who else, Ash? We used to get our coffee from McDonald's restaurant in the mornings. Glad you took time to teach us how to brew, but Austin is still selective about when he makes coffee for us."

Austin tossed Houston an intolerant glance. "I already do enough for you and Dallas. You guys eat and sleep out here at the ranch almost as much as Ashleigh and me."

Houston grinned guiltily. "You shouldn't have built those fabulous guesthouses. Ash, would you like a cup of herbal tea or a glass of orange juice or milk?"

Feeling a tad uncomfortable, Ashleigh moved over into the chair next to her husband's. "Orange juice would be nice. Thanks, Houston. Has anyone eaten breakfast?"

All heads shook in the negative.

Slowly, with extreme caution, Ashleigh arose. "I'll rustle up something real quick. We're ravenous this morning," she said, rubbing her stomach.

"Not a chance, Ash. I'll do it." Austin leaped out of his seat then helped Ashleigh back into hers. "Be still. Just sit there and look beautiful for me."

Ashleigh playfully swatted Austin's behind. Pulling his head down, she gave him a flurry of gentle kisses. "Husband, I'm not disabled. I'm merely pregnant."

Austin kissed her forehead. "That's why I wait on you hand and foot. Enjoy it, babe. Once the baby comes… Well, we already know what'll happen around here, Mommy."

Ashleigh laughed heartily. "Yeah, we do, Daddy. Sheer pandemonium!"

Everyone laughed.

"Has anyone talked to Mom and Dad this morning?" Ashleigh inquired.

Houston raised his hand. "They were fine last night around nine."

Ashleigh glanced at the clock. "I'll call them after we eat. Everybody's coming for family dinner tonight, right?" Ashleigh chuckled. "Like I really had to ask. Of course you strapping Texas boys will be anywhere food is involved." She laughed. "Just kidding. You guys are so loyal to the family. I love that about each of you."

"Family is all we've got. No one knows that better than you, Ash, because of how you were raised. Speaking of family, Mom can't wait for the new addition to arrive and to become a grandmother," Houston remarked. "That's all she talks about these days."

Busy at the stove, Austin grinned. "Tell me about it! Mom and Dad are already goners over their first grandchild. You bringing Lanier, Dallas? What about inviting Kelly, Houston?"

Dallas rolled his eyes back. "I try to get together with my girlfriend every possible chance. With you no longer working full-time at Haven House, Ash, she has her hands full. If only she'd trust the employees more, but she has to do it her way."

"That's Lanier Watson for you. Her way or the highway," Ashleigh commented. "Since she lives in the house, everything falls on her. It's actually a twenty-four-hour gig."

"Lanier thrives on doing it all," Dallas remarked. "The woman's a workaholic."

Houston wanted to avoid the question about Kelly so he was glad Austin hadn't come back to him. He hadn't called her to confirm a date for a family dinner night, but he still planned to. Only a couple of days had passed since the meeting and reception at the training facility. He was still too busy running away from commitment to act upon his feelings. Kelly wouldn't travel with the team, but he already knew how hard it'd be to resist her indelible charms right here at home.

Houston didn't know why he felt this way, but he was afraid he'd met his match in Kelly. He couldn't say his days as a liberated man were numbered, but she had him wanting her and running scared at the same time. He had no clue how to conquer his fears. Whether to invite her to dinner or not had him frustrated. Houston was glad when Austin set out the food. A meal placed in front of the brothers was a surefire distraction.

Scrambled eggs, hash browns, turkey sausage and bacon were stacked high on colorful platters. The pan-fried steak smelled delicious. A loaf of oven-toasted bread was piled on a small plate. Butter and jelly filled small, round serving bowls. Apple butter, a family favorite, was on every Carrington table.

Austin gave a humble prayer of thanksgiving. "Okay, dig in. Don't forget the tip jar." Austin always reminded his brothers and their teammates to leave a gratuity. At restaurants, the small monetary token was in addition to a bill. No check had to be paid at Austin's home.

The tip jar kept on the granite counter was half-filled with cash. No change was allowed. Austin had started the tipping jar long before he'd married. Since his brothers and teammates ate a lot of meals at his home, he thought his cook/housekeeper, Stella Hanson, should be rewarded. Once Austin married Ashleigh, Ms. Stella only prepared meals on special occasions, yet her paycheck wasn't affected. The tip jar remained and the guys continued to fill it with cash to invest in a money-market account for the triplets' future kids.

As the Carrington family ate their breakfast, the room was as quiet as falling snow.

Houston looked from one brother to the other, his eyes flickering with amusement. He could see Ashleigh was still fascinated by how much the guys ate. The vast amount of food gobbled down was outright astonishing. If daily exercise wasn't a part of their lives, Houston feared they'd all blow up like the Goodyear blimp.

A wry smile playing at the corners of his mouth, Austin captured Houston in his gaze. "Say, bro, aren't your feet tired yet?"

Houston looked puzzled. "What're you talking about?"

Austin laughed at Houston's frowning expression. "You never responded to me about inviting Kelly to dinner. I guess it means you're still busy running hard and fast. Thought you were ready to be caught. That's the impression I got during recent conversations."

Sighing heavily, Houston scowled. He should've known his family hadn't let him off the hook. They never did. "Man, my feet are just plain cold. One minute, I think about getting up close and personal with Kelly. Then I start using the same excuses to avoid getting involved."

"Little brother," Dallas said to Houston, "you keep this up, you could lose out. What if Kelly Charleston *is* the one? She's hardly a member of the little groupies out there in force in every city our teams visit. You'd better go for it before some other man snatches her up."

Houston shot Dallas a dagger-thrust look. "You haven't made the ultimate commitment to Lanier, yet you've been with her awhile. Kelly and I aren't even dating."

"Everybody here knows Lanier's the holdout, including you," Dallas countered. "She's just like you, man, scared to death of commitment, terrified of forever after. I've been ready for the next level. I'm a patient man but it gets hard. You don't want any woman you care about to feel any doubt. If I didn't believe Lanier truly loved me, I would've been long gone."

"She does love you," Ashleigh assured Dallas, "with all her heart. In her defense, we know she grew up amidst a bad marriage and a volatile household. The verbal and physical fighting between her parents was how she landed in foster care. Lanier wants forever with you, too, Dallas, but she just doesn't have a good grip on her fears. Please remain patient with her."

Dallas gave Ashleigh the thumbs-up. "I plan to. Love is patient."

Uncomfortable with the direction the conversation had taken, Houston excused himself from the table, promising to return in a few minutes.

On the back patio, seated at the round glass table, surrounded by the unbelievably serene atmosphere Austin had created for himself and Ashleigh, Houston pulled out his cell phone. After three indecisive starts and stops, he finally punched the code for

Kelly's home number, hoping she was in. Houston hadn't talked to her in a couple of days.

The Cyclones team had made it into the playoffs but had been ousted in the second round, right after their unstoppable center was badly injured. The official season had ended at the end of May, but the preseason wouldn't get under way until late summer. Houston wasn't fond of the lengthy downtime, though he welcomed the break.

Houston's heart skipped a beat upon hearing Kelly's sweet, sultry voice. "Hey, lady, how's it going this morning?"

Savoring the delicious sound of the sexy bass voice on the other end, Kelly closed her sable-brown eyes. Had her constant thoughts of Houston somehow gotten through to him? "Morning, Houston. I'm fine. What about you?"

As though Kelly could see him through the phone, Houston moved his hand in a so-so gesture. "I'm good. I miss the game, of course. Once the finals are over, sometime in June, I'll play in a summer league. Have to keep the skills honed. What're you up to?"

Up to my elbows in missing you like crazy. "Staying busy. Office hours at my private practice, Houston Sports Medicine Center, make my days crazy, especially with so many new patients. I'm not complaining, though, 'cause I'm blessed. I could use a nice long break, but my schedule is packed right now. Just calling to say hello or did you have something specific in mind?" She hoped for the latter.

Sucking in a deep breath, Houston slowly released it. "I'd like you to join us at Austin's tonight for our family dinner. Are you free by chance?"

Kelly suddenly felt the insanity of this crazy liaison with Houston. The boy was here today, but would he be gone tomorrow? Did she dare dance with a man who had no proclivity for commitment? She didn't want to start wondering if she'd see him again. Nothing romantic had occurred between them, yet she had no stomach for the bitter taste of disappointment she might be signing on for, wittingly so. She wouldn't be able to yell she'd been blindsided, not when he had exposed so much of who he was and how he felt about commitment.

Although Kelly wanted to accept Houston's invitation to the Carrington family dinner she was hesitant. But what would it prove to deprive herself of time in his company? Not a thing. She had already decided to accept Houston just for who he was. He'd been honest and right up-front about how he chose to live his life. No sane person argued with candor.

"Are you still there, Kelly?"

She sighed. "I'm still thinking about the invite."

Kelly wanted to make the right decision. There was no doubt in her mind about her desire to be with Houston. Besides, she didn't want to thwart the chance of them becoming at least friends. Despite the minor run-in, they *had* enjoyed each other's company.

Houston chuckled. "Have you come up with anything yet?"

"As a matter of fact, I haven't. Do you have any suggestions, Mr. C.?"

Intrigued by Kelly's taunting remark and follow-up question, Houston propped his feet on a nearby chair. "Well, let me see if I can help you out. What about the fact we could have a great time together? Our conversations will definitely be intellectual bombs and there are endless things to laugh like crazy about. Those are very good reasons for you to accept. Also, my family would love to meet you."

Kelly gasped inwardly. "Oh, you play so dirty. You just couldn't resist tossing in a bit of irresistible bait." She already knew she'd enjoy his family from the things Houston had said about them. She'd even mentioned how nice it'd be to spend time with the Carrington crew.

Being estranged from her own family was hard on Kelly. The unresolved issues standing between her and her parents were difficult to bring to a close.

"What time should I get out to Austin and Ashleigh's ranch?" Kelly asked.

"Seven is the magic dinner hour for us. I'd love to pick you up. It won't be a problem."

"Thanks but no thanks, Houston. If I drive myself, I won't have to wonder if I'll ever see you again." Without further comment, she rang off.

Sorry she'd disconnected rather rudely, Kelly stared at the phone, trying to decide if she should call back and apologize. Instead, she sat back in the recliner in her bedroom and reflected.

Kelly hadn't personally met Houston when the sports medicine position had first become available, but he was one of her favorite basketball players. She had closely followed his career and had developed an infatuation with him via the television and the home games she attended.

Houston Carrington intrigued Kelly both on and off the court. She was now more intrigued than ever before. His superstardom wasn't at the heart of her desire to get to know him. It was the sexy flesh-and-blood man who turned her on and flipped her heart inside out. She wasn't sure she knew how to deal with it.

Feeling the prickly heat from Kelly's last remark, Houston clipped the phone back onto his leather belt. By the tone of her voice, he couldn't help wondering if she already felt a bit of disillusionment with him.

Up to this point, Kelly hadn't said if she was in a romantic relationship, which made him unsure of where she stood. He couldn't blame her if she was a little concerned with how things might go between them. He himself was on edge over it. Thinking of how he and Kelly had come into being was outrageously intriguing. No other woman had paid for a date with him. Of course, he knew the donated money was for Haven House, but indulging in silly flattery every now and then never hurt anything.

Houston got up from the chair and went back inside the house. The moment he entered the kitchen, all eyes instantly turned on him. "Ash, you can count on one more mouth to feed for the family shindig. I invited Kelly…and she accepted."

"Way to go, bro," Austin and Dallas shouted simultaneously.

Dropping back down in his original seat, Houston looked embarrassed. "Give it a rest, guys. You have no clue how hard it was to make that call. I can't seem to figure out what I want with and from Kelly. I'm confused about her. Pray for me," Houston joked. "Unlike you two muscular, hardheaded jocks, I know I need Jesus."

Everyone laughed.

"Boy, you need the holy Trinity," Dallas shot back like a crack of thunder.

Laughter erupted again.

Even Houston had to laugh at Dallas's comment. "I can't top that one so I won't try." He looked down at his watch. "I need to get going here shortly. This day has sprouted wings."

Austin eyed his brother closely. "I guess you have to go get all primped up for your big date with Kelly," he teased. "Word of advice, you could sure use a haircut."

Houston tore Austin to shreds with a glaring look. "Save it, man. Not trying to hear it."

The Carrington triplets were used to good-natured ribbing with each other. No one ever took it seriously. It was simply a part of their extremely close brotherhood.

Dallas leaped to his feet. "I could use a haircut, too, but I need to make sure I have a date for tonight. Ash, I'm run on over to Haven House for a minute to check on my favorite girl. Want to come along? The girls would love to see you. They miss you like crazy."

"I miss them, too." Ashleigh looked to Austin. "Mind if I go along with Dallas?"

Austin shrugged. "Not at all. I'll drive you so he won't have to come back out here until this evening. I'd like to see the teenagers, too."

"Let's all ride together," Dallas said. "You two can drop me off at my place after the visit and drive the SUV back here. I'll use my other car this evening."

Knowing they did this sort of thing all the time, Austin nodded. "Works for me."

Houston scratched his head. "Maybe I'll drop by Haven House with you guys. I haven't been over there in a while. I'll just meet you there 'cause I know Dallas drives too slow to keep up with my fast-moving wheels."

"Don't go there," Dallas warned. "There's nothing you can do I can't do better."

Austin saw the two egos about to clash. "Can it, fellas! Let's just go. Driving fast isn't something either of you should brag about. Too many people die in major car accidents for you two boneheads to get out there and drag race like a couple of teenagers. Besides, it's a breach of both your contracts. Your limbs are insured for way more than either of you are worth."

Austin's ranch was less than twenty miles outside downtown Houston. The area was beautiful, appearing to spread out far enough to meet up with eternity. Summer hadn't been ushered in yet, but it was already hot. Houston drove along the road feeling at peace with his surroundings. The top was down on his shiny, metallic black

Porsche Boxster, but the heat was unbearably muggy, causing him to turn up the air conditioner's fan.

The breakfast conversation had Houston wishing his brothers would stop bringing up Kelly's name. Austin or Dallas always had something flattering to say about her. He knew Kelly was a beautiful, smart woman—and he didn't like hearing that some other man might snatch her up. It could happen, but he didn't allow himself to dwell on it. Only he or Kelly would know if anything romantic or long-lasting would happen for them. Everyone else should butt out.

If he had no desire to change the way he lived his life, why did his family?

Houston saw that Dallas couldn't stop smiling at the stunning five-foot-eight siren Lanier Watson. By the soft, loving expression on her pretty mahogany face, he knew she was no less enamored with him. Dallas never could get enough of being with her. When Lanier had the occasion to act a lot like "the renegade brother," what Dallas referred to as Houston, Dallas did his best to remain patient with her. Lanier feared long-term entanglements with good reason.

"Welcome to Haven House, best friend," Lanier greeted cheerfully, hugging and kissing Ashleigh, openly displaying deep affection. "Girl, I can't tell you how much I miss you not being here full-time. Hey, Mr. A.! How's it going with the proud poppa-to-be?"

Austin brought Lanier into his warm embrace. "This poppa *is* proud and he's just great. Every day with Ashleigh is like reliving Christmas morning as a small child. You see how our girl's stomach has grown. Is she beautiful or what?"

Tears popped into Lanier's eyes. "As beautiful as ever."

Houston looked between Dallas and Lanier, wondering if they'd ever end up like Ashleigh and Austin, who were only one of the happiest couples on the planet. Lanier's eyes easily conveyed her love for Dallas.

Houston suddenly appeared in Lanier's line of vision. "What's up, Hou? I'm really happy to see you. Yours is definitely a rare visit."

Houston walked up to Lanier and hugged her. "Hadn't seen you and the girls in a while so I thought I'd tag along with the family. I promise to do better with visits. How are you?"

Lanier took in her surroundings, her eyes beaming with sweet sentiment. "I couldn't be better. I'm still as happy as a lark. The residents of Haven House and Dallas have truly allowed me to experience a more exciting and joyous existence."

Houston easily interpreted the expression of love and desire he saw in Dallas's eyes. It was obvious his brother thought the world of Lanier.

Before anyone could say another word, four teenage girls came bounding into the living room. The girls went ape as soon as they spotted Ashleigh and the guys. Animated greetings and heartfelt hugs were exchanged. Then the teenagers left the room the same way they'd entered.

Ashleigh was moved to tears by the genuine expression of love she'd just received. "Kathy, Tina, Willow and Gina look good, Lanier. You're doing a great job. They seem so happy. But where are Stephanie and Lauren?"

"The sisters are with their aunt for the weekend. The girls are happy, Ash, but they also have you to thank. The young ladies were an absolute emotional mess when we first got them. Your love and patience brought them through. You know how many times I felt like kicking their young butts to the curb. I don't easily deal with smart mouths and bad attitudes. Man, did those girls have nasty vocabularies and short tempers when they first arrived. Things are much better now. We've become one big happy family," Lanier enthused.

Ashleigh smiled. "I can't take all the credit for how these kids have grown. The numerous times you sat up all night with one or the other, calming their fears, drying the endless tears, made them feel wanted for the first time in their lives. We've accomplished it all together, Lanier. No one person is responsible for the success of Haven House. Ours is a joint triumph."

"Okay, girls, ease up on the sentiments," Houston said. "You've got me and my bros frowning up to keep from weeping. That wouldn't be a pretty sight. You ladies have done a miraculous job with the kids," Houston said sincerely. "We're proud of you both."

Lanier cast Houston a sweet smile. "Thanks. You always know just the right thing to say. So what's up with everyone? Any special reason for the surprise visit?"

Dallas looked hopeful. "Carrington family dinner is tonight. I need a date. Can you hook this brother up?"

Lanier crooked her finger at Dallas, her eyes flirting wildly with him. "Let's discuss this in private. Excuse us for a minute. We'll be right back."

Houston laughed at the look on Dallas's face. His brothers were whipped and neither of them cared who knew it. His father had also lost his mind over a woman. No man loved his wife more than Beaumont loved Angelica.

Houston was starting to get it, but he knew he had a ways to go before personally meeting up with a storybook ending. Some people did live fairy-tale romances. He had seen the magic with his own two eyes, growing up around it for twenty-eight years. After thirty-two years of marriage, his mother and father were still crazy in love. As Kelly's image came into his mind, he closed his eyes and let himself indulge in a bit of romantic thinking.

Chapter 4

Houston stood in the driveway of Austin's home to wait for Kelly. She had already called from the front gates, which Austin had opened via the telephone. The cameras installed above the massive black wrought-iron gates, designed with a huge *C* in the center, allowed the residents to view approaching visitors. The electronic security equipment at the ranch was extensive. Unlike Houston's posh housing community, Austin didn't have private gate guards.

As Kelly got out of the car, Houston walked over to greet her. She looked beautiful dressed in a casual, lightweight khaki-colored pantsuit and an indigo silk shell. Brown low-heel sandals and shoulder-strap purse completed the look.

Houston gently kissed Kelly on the cheek. "Glad you made it. Any problems with the directions I gave you?"

"None, but my GPS tracking system comes in handy. How are you?" She liked how relaxed he looked clad in perfectly pressed blue denim jeans and a crisp white shirt, open at the collar. He wore no socks and his casual navy leather shoes were fashionable.

Houston slid his hand under Kelly's elbow. "All the family has arrived. Ready to officially meet the rest of the Carrington crew?"

Kelly nodded. "I'd like that. If they're anything like the great things you and Austin have said about them, I'm sure I'll be comfortable."

Houston put his arm around her shoulder. "You will be. No doubt in my mind."

He knew his family would treat Kelly respectfully and make her feel welcome simply because they were kind, loving and generous people, yet he really had nothing to compare this experience to. His brothers had made a big deal out of the invitation he'd extended to Kelly because he hadn't ever brought any woman to family functions.

When it came to physical needs, his got met, but long-term relations never developed. It was a mutual agreement.

Walking alongside Houston, Kelly suddenly felt nervous about meeting the family, yet she expected to be shown kindness. According to Houston, he belonged to the most wonderful family in the world. She found herself groping for his hand just before they entered the house. She let go seconds after receiving comfort.

Houston had a huge grin on his face. "Carringtons, I'd like you to meet Kelly Charleston." He then introduced her to each of his family members by name.

Kelly smiled beautifully. "It's nice to meet all of you. It may take me a minute to remember each name, but I'll eventually get it right."

"We're sure of that," Ashleigh said. "Come on in and have a seat, Kelly. We recall seeing you at the auction, though Austin was the only one you met."

Austin extended his hand to Kelly. "Good to see you again. Welcome to our home. Ashleigh and I are honored."

Kelly wasn't sure about the nature of Ashleigh's remark, but it hadn't sounded mean-spirited. She *was* Austin's wife—and she'd probably been a bit curious about her famous husband privately meeting the woman with the winning lunch bid. "I remember seeing everyone that evening. I'm glad we're meeting officially. Houston talks a lot about you and has put you on very high pedestals," Kelly joked.

"Probably way too high for us not to break something on the way down," Angelica said softly, smiling warmly. "Houston tends to exaggerate about how wonderful his parents and brothers are, but never over the deep love he feels for his family."

A closer look at Angelica let Kelly see how elegant this woman was. Petite in stature and weight, she looked as if she took really good care of herself. Although she only wore casual designer attire Kelly saw that she had exquisite taste.

"Would you like something to drink, Kelly?" Beaumont's brown eyes twinkled with merriment. The kindness of his soul had a way of shining through his entire being. An impressive-looking man, Mr. Carrington was as handsome as his three six-foot-plus sons. He stood every bit as tall.

Kelly nodded. "A diet cola would be nice. Thank you."

"One diet cola coming right up," Beaumont responded in kind.

"You can sit here if you'd like, Kelly." Patting the seat cushion, Lanier moved over to make space for Kelly to sit next to her. Dallas was on the other side of Lanier.

Without hesitation, Kelly took the offered seat, thanking Lanier as she sat down. The kind gestures were endearing and felt personal. She felt warmly welcomed by the entire group. Dallas hadn't said anything to her directly, but his kind, friendly smiles appeared to show approval.

Beaumont stepped back into the large family room, immediately drawing the attention of everyone present. "Okay, Carrington crew and guests, the food is ready. The patios tables are set. You folks can head on outdoors. Kelly, your cola is inside the cooler by the outdoor bar. I didn't bring it in to you since we're heading outside."

"That's fine. Thank you, sir." Kelly got up from the sofa.

Houston nudged Kelly with his shoulder. "I'm hungry. What about you?"

She enjoyed his playful gesture. "I could use a bite or two. I hear your dad cooked dinner. That's so unusual. I can't imagine my father or mother lifting a single finger to do anything domestic. Maybe that's 'cause they didn't have to. We had servants, of course," she announced, heavy on the sarcasm.

Houston unwittingly squeezed her hand. Then he wished he hadn't. "My father does the majority of the cooking. He loves to grill. Most meats and a variety of vegetables are grilled at their house. The man is insane over barbecuing."

Houston thought it best not to feed whatever disdain Kelly might carry for her parents. He had a hundred questions to ask about her family, but he was content to wait on her to tell him what she wanted him to know.

Kelly stopped in her tracks and turned to face Houston. "You're so blessed and lucky. If I had a family like yours, I'd live on a cloud. I don't even know why my parents bothered to have me. I was probably an accident. No siblings ever arrived after me."

Houston jumped out in front of Kelly. "Stop it. Don't ever look at yourself as an accident. From what little I know, I think you're a good person, a beautiful spirit and a brilliant physician. Our whole team is totally taken with you. I saw that for myself. One thing I love about you is that you don't seem to define yourself by your prestigious M.D. label. You're the best damn accident I've ever run in to."

Kelly wished she didn't feel the way she did. "Thanks, Houston. Jared and Carolyn were so busy working and making money, I often accused them of forgetting they had a daughter. Although my parents didn't send me off to boarding school my upbringing was largely left up to the hired help paid handsomely to live in."

Feeling her pain, Houston pulled Kelly in closer to him and gave her a tender hug. "You sound so sad. I'm sorry for whatever you've been through, but please give yourself a break."

"Much like you triplets, I grew up in a very wealthy, prominent family, but ours is nothing like the totally amazing group of folks I've met this evening."

Houston nodded, giving her a compassionate smile. "The Carringtons thrive on being together and loving each other unconditionally. An unbreakable bond exists, an endless circle of loyalty and constant togetherness. If one of us has a problem or a need, the entire family rallies around to own it and deal with it collectively."

"Mama Tilley and Papa Joseph Rose are like parents to me. I stay in constant touch with them. My mother and father are successful heart surgeons and they're partners in a thriving practice. By design, I see very little of them, socially or otherwise. They're receiving an award for their lifetime medical service to the Houston communities they serve, but I'm not sure if I'll attend the event."

Smoldering sparks of anger flared in Kelley's sable eyes. Then the flames died down as quickly as they'd appeared. This wasn't Houston's problem. It was hers—and she'd deal with it privately, like she always did. "I'm sorry. Talking about my parents gets me riled up, but I don't want to take it out on you. Forgive me, please."

Houston kissed Kelly's forehead. "Lighten up, lady. No forgiveness necessary. Let's just have a good time. No problems allowed at the Carrington dinners. Okay?"

"Your wish is my command, Urban Cowboy."

Loving how sexy she made the name sound, Houston smiled broadly. "Looks like I've got a new nickname. I'm the only one who's ever called me that. I like it coming from you. It sounds hot and seductive," he teased.

"That's 'cause it totally befits the sexy man behind it. You're one of the hottest cowboys I've ever met." Kelly giggled. "In fact, you're the only cowboy I've met."

"That's not true. You've met three others. Dad, Austin and Dallas are true-blue Texas cowboys. You can see firsthand what I'm talking about later. That is, if you're interested in taking a walking tour around Austin's ranch."

Kelly smiled sweetly. "I look forward to it. I guess I've met more cowboys than I'd confessed to. This is also the first real ranch I've visited." She paused for a moment. "I just made another false statement. I went to a ranch in Wyoming with my college friends on spring break one year."

"How'd you like it?"

Kelly shrugged. "Everyone thought they wanted to experience life on a dude ranch. That is, until after we got there and the staff made us get up at 5:00 a.m. We were under the impression it'd be all fun and games. It was hardly that, yet it was an adventure I'll almost never forget."

Houston laughed. "Five is about the time most ranchers come to life, if not earlier. I've known my father to start working as early as four in the morning."

Kelly frowned. "I must admit my girlfriends and I found a way to dodge some of the required duties occurring right after the early wake-up calls. We got up but later snuck away from the group and climbed up into the hayloft and went back to sleep. We didn't come up with that idea until a couple of days after the torturous schedule began."

Houston threw his head back and laughed. "Charming story. I like it."

The laughter vibrating from somewhere deep in Houston's belly held Kelly spellbound. The sound of his joy was captivating. It was a true but simple story, but he seemed to enjoy it like it was a bestseller. He had mentioned how uncomplicated he liked his life. Was it this easy to please someone, knowingly or unknowingly? Kelly hadn't even been trying to please him. She wasn't sure she knew how to please a man.

The family had waited for Houston and Kelly to make an appearance. Their conversation had kept them rooted to one spot longer than planned. He felt guilty for holding up dinner. When he apologized, he was told by the family not to sweat it.

The host passed the blessing. Making it short and sweet, Austin held on to Ashleigh's hand all the while. It was actually a ritual for the entire family to join hands during prayer. Austin knew everyone was ready to get into what had been dipped up from the pots and pans. The huge redwood table was laden with goodies.

Kelly was amazed by the amount of food prepared. "The dinner menu is something else, Houston. I can't recall ever seeing this much food."

"The Carringtons know how to put out a big Texas spread. Like I said earlier, just about every meat entrée is grilled. Steak, brisket, beef ribs, shrimp and chicken are slow-cooked. 'Meat eaters' would best describe the Carrington men's voracious appetites."

Baked potatoes, fresh asparagus and corn on the cob, both white and yellow, were also roasted on the grill. The baked beans had been prepared in the oven and Ashleigh had baked the yeast rolls and chocolate cake, according to Houston. The creamy red potato salad, a Texas favorite, was one of Angelica's specialties.

Once everyone began eating, the room quieted down considerably. Pass me this, that or the other were the only remarks uttered. The guys began shoveling in food as soon as it landed on their plates. Loss of appetite probably never occurred among the triplets, Kelly considered. These guys knew exactly how to put it away, all in record time.

The Carrington family was magical to Kelly. Looking around the table, from one to the other, she saw how tuned in they were, as if they knew each other's every thought and next move. Their laughter carried contagious joy. She was sure problems existed, just like in any other family, but she had a pretty good idea they weren't exposed or discussed outside their inner circle. It seemed the Carringtons coveted their private lives.

Whatever was in the Carrington mix, Kelly suddenly wanted to be right in the thick of it. Was this fun, animated group of people what real families were made of?

Sensitive to Kelly's mood, Houston brought his mouth close to her ear. "Are you okay, Kelly-Kel? It seems as if you're somewhere in outer space," he whispered huskily.

Kelly loved the nickname Houston had dubbed her with. He had made it sound endearing and sweet. "I was just thinking about you and your family."

Houston frowned slightly. "Good or bad thoughts?"

Kelly cast him a dazzling smile. "I'm not telling. A woman has to keep some secrets locked away in her heart."

Intrigued by Kelly's uniqueness and her charming personality, Houston loved the interesting comments she tossed at him. He smiled back at her, unable to help himself. If only he could let himself go with her, he'd probably be a lot better off than constantly fighting to keep himself at a safe distance.

Fleetingly, Houston wished he'd dated one person consistently so he'd know for sure what it was like and what he should expect. He operated from a blind spot, but he now realized he'd put himself at a terrible disadvantage.

Kelly wished she could resist the charming Houston, yet she was happy to be at Austin and Ashleigh's home with him. Being in the company of the entire Carrington family was an awesome experience.

The other two tough sports heroes and their handsome father were so attentive to the women they loved. Kelly closely observed how Dallas kept his eyes fastened on Lanier and Austin couldn't keep his hands off Ashleigh. Beaumont and Angelica conversed with each other through flirtatious language. Theirs was a love etched in stone. These couples only had eyes for each other.

With all the love and romance Houston was constantly around, Kelly couldn't understand how he managed to stay so unaffected. He was attentive enough to her, but it was nothing in comparison to how the other Carrington men reacted to their significant others.

Therein lies the problem, Kelly mused.

I'm not Houston's significant other. I'm not even his girlfriend. Will he ever look at me the way Austin looks at Ashleigh? How many more times would the very same question come to her mind in one evening? Kelly had to wonder.

The cool evening air was a nice change from the muggy heat of the day. Several ceiling fans hung from the rafters of the covered porch cooled things off. Strung with colorful Chinese lanterns and Tiki torches, the vast area reserved for dining was well lit.

The deep shades of ever-changing colors lighting up the pool provided a peaceful, romantic ambience. The majestic trees surrounding the vast property appeared to dance in tune with the stirring winds. It was just before sunset and the stimulating sounds of nightfall could be heard in the distance.

Quiet conversations and frequent trills of laughter permeated the outdoor atmosphere for the next couple of hours. A father and his three sons took turns telling jokes, keeping the dinner party lively. Beaumont was the biggest comedian of all. He had a cache of off-color jokes about any subject a person could possibly think of.

Angelica's eyes lovingly scolded her sons. "Guys, please don't encourage Beau in his charming but incorrigible ways." She knew it was all to no avail. As a mother and wife, she had to make an attempt. This was what her men did when they got together.

Dallas and Lanier were the first couple to excuse themselves from the table after the dessert had been consumed. Houston and Kelly followed suit only moments later. The two guys had given farewell affections to their parents, who were about ready to leave the ranch. Austin and Ashleigh stayed behind to see the elder Carringtons to their car.

It was a fine Texas evening for a romantic moonlit stroll around the ranch.

Houston was eager to show Kelly around the place. It was too big to see all at one time. It might take a couple of days to tour the entire property.

"Let's walk down to the stables first." He pointed out the white-washed buildings to her. "I'd like to introduce you to Austin's pride and joy, Q.B. and T.D."

Kelly lifted a brow. "Horses! Quarterback and Touchdown, right?"

"Yeah, but how'd you guess?"

Kelly laughed heartily. "*Stables* might've given it away. As for their names, they're a perfect fit for Austin's career."

Houston chuckled. "I didn't stop to think about what I'd said. You're right, of course. Austin loves his Palominos. The other horses on the property are used by the hired hands. There's also been a new addition to the stables. My brother purchased a beautiful Appaloosa for Ashleigh before they found out she was pregnant. She named the frisky horse, with the beautiful, shiny spots, Sundance. Although she's only gotten to ride Sundance a few times she visits her every day. She'll ride again after the baby comes."

Kelly got a far-away look in her eyes. "I used to want a horse when I was little. I received a flat-out 'no' when I asked. I never brought it up again. Do you ride?"

"There isn't a Carrington who doesn't. We were taught to ride at an early age."

Kelly took off running toward the area Houston had pointed out, surprising him. She couldn't wait to see the horses. She hadn't learned to ride, but she was now thinking it wasn't too late for her to take lessons. Maybe one of the guys could recommend a good teacher. She made a mental note to ask Houston about it later on.

After catching up to Kelly, Houston steered her into the stables and over to the stall where T.D. was housed. The horse greeted the visitors with a loud whinny, making them both laugh. "This is a friendly one, but we still have to be careful. Here," he said, taking her hand, "let me show you how to handle her without getting injured."

"Her? T.D. is a girl?"

Houston cracked up. "She's a girl, a very beautiful one. Stroke her mane gently. That's the way. She loves to be cuddled."

"What woman doesn't?"

Their eyes met and held for several engaging seconds. Kelly wasn't sorry about what she'd said. If Houston didn't like it, that was too bad for him. She wasn't going to monitor every word she spoke for his comfort. She was used to speaking freely.

"Men like to be touched, too. I already know you have soft hands. I've felt them."

Kelly was glad he wasn't bothered by her comment. "They're soft but strong. I know how to minister one hell of a deep-tissue massage."

Houston's eyes locked with hers. "Is that something I can look forward to?"

"We'll have to wait and see. I pray that you don't get injured during the off-season, but if you have one that calls for a massage, I'll see to it or have one of the therapists take care of you."

"I set myself up for that one, didn't I?"

Kelly shrugged, feigning ignorance. "Set yourself up for what?"

Houston laughed inwardly. "Okay, so it's going to be like that. I'm cool. Let's move two stalls down so you can meet Q.B., who is not a girl."

Q.B. was also a beautiful animal, whose light-colored coat glowed like sunlight. The horses' coats were so healthy-looking. Kelly was careful to gently touch Q.B., the same way Houston had shown her how to handle T.D. The horse gently nudged her shoulder with his nose, causing her to giggle. She'd seen people kiss the noses and foreheads of horses, but she wasn't going that far, though Kelly would like to hug Austin's pride and joy. Texas and Wrangler were also favored by their owners.

"Let's move on down to the lake before it gets too dark to see anything." Houston grabbed a checkered blanket from a wall rack. "There are a lot of fish in the lake, but we don't catch them. Austin's not willing to reel them in to fry up in a pan. They buy fresh fish at the seafood market nearby."

"Are all the Carrington men that sensitive?"

"Every one of us. We don't hunt wild game, but we do purchase deer steaks and pheasant and other wild game from the neighbors who do."

Kelly scowled. "It sounds utterly barbaric! But I guess it's no different from eating any other kind of meat. Slaughter is involved no matter how it's performed."

Houston looked uncomfortable with what Kelly had said, but it was the truth. He didn't like the idea of harming animals, but men had been acquiring meat that way for countless years. It was the way of the world, whether it was right or not.

Down at the lake Houston spread out the blanket and prompted Kelly to sit. He followed suit. While taking off his shoes, he urged her to do the same.

Kelly was happy to free her feet and let the air rush through her toes. Setting her shoes aside, she stretched out on the blanket, propping her head on one elbow. "This is nice. It's much cooler by the water's edge. This is some Texas ranch. I spotted a white gazebo during our journey. I have a fondness for the structure. Do Austin and Ashleigh use it?"

Houston nodded. "Boy, do they use it. Austin had it wired with speakers and hundreds of tiny white lights when it was built on that slope. It has a wooden dance floor and built-in seating around the inside perimeter. There's also a bar and bandstand. One can see for miles and miles from up there. It's a pretty romantic setting."

"It sounds lovely. Have you ever taken anyone there with romance in mind?"

Houston chuckled. "I've been up there hundreds of times but not for romance. Austin throws old-fashioned hoedowns and uses the gazebo for social events. We love country and western music, but we're kind of selective."

"Austin Carrington thought of everything, didn't he? It sounds like Ashleigh gets her fair share of romance from her loving husband. By the way, I like CW music, too."

"They are a very romantic couple. We always tell them to 'get a room.'"

Lanier and Dallas, hand in hand, came upon Houston and Kelly, but they just waved, smiled and moved on.

Houston waved back at the couple. "I wonder if they're leaving already. They usually stay a lot longer. What about you, Kelly, are you ready to go home?"

Kelly sighed with deep contentment. "Not yet. It's so peaceful out here. But if you're ready, I'm okay with leaving. Is it getting late?"

Houston slipped his hand into hers. "It's not that late." His eyes softened. "I like being here with you this way. I agree that it's quiet and peaceful. I love the outdoors as much as you seem to. I wish our basketball games could be played outside. Austin and Dallas have the best of both worlds. Occasionally they play in indoor sports stadiums, but for the most part they're out in the elements. I wish. NBA games are always played inside as you know."

Kelly leaned over and kissed Houston on the nose. "You poor, millionaire baby," she cooed. "I feel so sorry for you."

Houston chuckled. "You love messing with me, don't you? I have no complaints. I know I'm blessed. How many people get paid megabucks to do what they love?"

"You *are* right about that." Kelly lay back on the blanket and looked up at the dazzling stars. Locating the brightest one, she closed her eyes and made a wish upon it. "Starlight, star bright," she chanted softly, "please make my wish come true tonight."

Enchanted by her soft melody, Houston stretched out and drew closer to Kelly. Turning up on his side, he looked down into her beautiful sienna face. As his manhood instantly gave rise, he moaned inwardly, discreetly repositioning his privates to a more comfortable position. "Care to share your wish with me, Kelly-Kel?"

Kelly stroked Houston's face with the pads of her fingers. Looking at him was pleasurable. "It won't come true. I'll only tell you my wish if it does."

Houston kissed Kelly's forehead tenderly. "Fair enough. I love helping people fulfill their dreams. Maybe I can help make your wish come true if I know what it is."

Doubting Houston's last statement, as it applied to her, Kelly angled high an eyebrow. His statement did not pertain to any kind of committed relationship. Kelly knew it to be a bold fact, one that had come from his lips.

Kelly openly stared into Houston's eyes. "I hate to differ here, but I don't think that is a true statement when it comes to you and me. Yet I've decided to meet you right where you are. So it's okay if you can't make my wishes come true."

Houston appeared stunned by her candid comment. "How can I do that if I don't know what they are? I'm not a mind reader, you know."

Kelly didn't think Houston had to be a mind reader to know what she wished for most. All he had to do was feel her vibes. Her body language should give him some clue.

She was hot for him, but it wasn't merely a sexual thing. Kelly burned inside and out for his affection. His brilliant mind also set hers afire. Their conversations were stimulating, sparkling with humor. He was a superstar on and off the basketball court.

Kelly was terribly infatuated with Houston. If he hadn't gotten all the subtle signals she'd been firing off, she didn't know what else to do to make him feel her.

Houston lowered his head until he felt Kelly's breath on his lips. Lightly, his mouth flirtatiously skirted hers. Keeping his eyes fastened on her lovely face, his tongue teased and deliciously taunted her lower lip. A slightly passionate kiss came next, shocking and delighting him and her. The next few tender and sweet kisses put Kelly in a state of want, making her feel as if she was slowly coming unhinged.

Lowering his head farther, Houston's mouth explored the exposed flesh on Kelly's throat. He knew he probably shouldn't be doing this, but he couldn't seem to keep from fulfilling his desire for her. She was sweet and had so much sex appeal.

As Houston's lips dotted moist kisses onto her bare arms, Kelly felt her heart skip several beats. While her body grew rigid with need, biting down on her lower lip was all she could do to keep from falling into him. Her breasts already heaved with the pain of her hard-to-control breathing. Her body had heated up rather rapidly and was responsible for the moisture between her legs.

Houston gave Kelly one last tender kiss before he brought things to a complete standstill. The short-lived moments of utter ecstasy were over and done with. They both fought against the deep disappointment. He was aware he'd moved the liaison up a notch. The surprise for him was that he hadn't tried to battle what he felt for her. Kelly was *that* irresistible to him. Keeping her at a safe distance might not be possible, he conceded.

"I guess I'd better let you get home." Houston sat upright on the blanket. "I'm sure Ashleigh and Austin are ready to hit the bed. Let's thank them and say good-night."

The couple didn't have to go through the house to get off the property, but Houston was as well-mannered as he was taught by his parents. Leaving without thanking the host and hostess wasn't how etiquette was handled in his neck of the woods.

Kelly saw his desire to leave the premises as an excuse for why he'd cooled things down with her. However, the Houston she'd come to know didn't make excuses for himself. The man knew exactly who he was, and what he wanted and didn't want. *It is what it is,* she thought, yet she felt good about how he'd let himself go with her, even if it had only lasted a few minutes. Maybe he'd soon see a need to cut himself loose from all the rules binding him. She'd love to be the one to set him free.

Kelly was the most vivacious woman Houston had ever known. She certainly kept him on his toes. Dr. Charleston was one woman he'd love to know everything about, yet he was still abnormally worried about getting in too deep. For sure, he knew he couldn't and wouldn't play with her emotions. The level of intensity didn't matter in the fact he had kissed her, repeatedly. That alone had shown his vulnerabilities where she was concerned. Houston knew he had a lot to come to terms with regarding her.

Kelly wanted to scream away her frustrations, but it'd do no good. Houston was simply who he was because he didn't know how to be anyone else. He hadn't made love to her, though she felt as if he had. The light but arousing romance had ended abruptly, much too soon for her. It wasn't something she'd ever want to get used to.

Without looking in Houston's direction, Kelly slipped her feet back into her sandals. The trembling of her hands didn't concern her. She knew it was the result of her emotions. Houston had worked her and her body to a fever pitch, only to leave her sanity hanging by a thread. There were so many intimate zones Houston hadn't touched on her body, but her imaginative mind had taken her there anyway. It was hard as hell to turn off erotic thoughts, especially when they involved the sexiest man she'd ever met.

Kelly wouldn't wish away a single moment they'd spent together, but she had to wonder if this was the end of the road for them. It wasn't the end, she told herself, allowing her confidence to take control. It couldn't be.

What Houston and I shared this evening was only the beginning.

Chapter 5

During the drive back to his South Shore Harbor lakefront home, Houston reflected on the evening. He felt relieved things hadn't become noticeably awkward between him and Kelly. Just as she'd done with his teammates, she was a hit with the rest of the Carringtons and Lanier. He was extremely pleased with his family and hadn't expected anything less than warmth and kindness from them toward his date.

Still physically and emotionally fired up over their slightly sensuous tryst, Houston already knew it hadn't been the smartest move on his part. Yet nothing could make him regret the romantically charged experience. Some things weren't easy for him to ignore. His feverish body was one of them. He still felt overly heated. If his throbbing manhood had gotten any harder, it might've broken in half. Granite was indeed hard to break off. Houston had to chuckle over such a silly, ego-driven thought.

Romancing Kelly had him feeling very tender-hearted toward her. She was a sweet and gentle lady and her feistiness enchanted him, too. Kelly had also made it known she wouldn't hesitate to put on the boxing gloves when personally slighted.

After backing the car into the garage and cutting the engine, Houston lowered the doors from one of the coded remote buttons located on his rearview mirror. He entered the house and went straight back to his bedroom, where he rapidly got out of his casual attire. Carrying the worn items into the master bathroom, he tossed his shirt and underwear into a dirty-clothes bin. Then he neatly hung up the jeans in the walk-in closet.

A steamy shower was tops on Houston's agenda. As he stepped inside the glass stall, he turned on the hot water. Pouring a generous amount of shower gel into his hands, he lathered it over his entire body, massaging it into his skin with a bath sponge. He left the suds on his skin until after he had washed and conditioned his curly hair.

Minutes later, Houston stood under the spray of water and rinsed out the conditioner and the foamy suds from his body. Instead of drying off, Houston tossed on a thick, hooded robe. Feeling energized and squeaky-clean, he entered his bedroom and immediately checked the time on the cable box.

Giving himself no chance to talk himself out of making the call, he picked up his cell phone and located Kelly's home number. Once the number popped up on the screen, he dialed it from one of the four phones stationed in his bedroom, bathroom and retreat. Extensions were kept on the nightstands on both sides of the bed.

"One, two, three, four," he said, counting the rings.

Kelly rolled up on her side and picked up the on the fifth ring, just before the answering device kicked in. "Hey, Houston, didn't expect to hear from you so soon."

"Tsk, tsk," he scolded lightly. "Did you really think I wouldn't call to see if you'd made it home okay?"

"I won't compare you to some other folks I know, but I really didn't think about it. At any rate, I'm glad you were concerned enough to find out if I'm safe. I've been home long enough to shower and dress for bed. I'm all settled in for the night."

Houston didn't like being compared to anyone. He was happy she hadn't done so. "Great minds think alike. I did the same thing. I know what'll happen the minute my head hits the pillow...and that's why I'm sitting up in bed, with my back against the headboard. What're you wearing?" He didn't believe for a second she'd tell him.

Thinking about Houston's enticing question, Kelly gently stroked her lower lip with her thumbnail, remembering the soft feel and sweet taste of his kiss. "Use your imagination, sweetie. You might find more pleasure that way."

Kelly loved beautiful lingerie. She owned lots of silk, satin and lace, yet preferred loose-fitting attire to wear to bed or just lounge around in. Jockey sportswear made the kind of intimate casual apparel she was most comfortable wearing. She also favored oversize T-shirts and colorful nightshirts, especially for sleeping alone.

Houston loved her spontaneous responses. "That was a hell of a beguiling answer, but maybe a little too much mind work for me. It'll be easier for me to imagine you in nothing at all."

"In that case, you'd definitely be pleased," she responded playfully.

Houston grinned at her confident statement. "Maybe we'd better change this conversation. It has the potential of getting a little steamy, don't you think?"

"Afraid of a little heat, Urban Cowboy?" Kelly asked in a low, teasing tone.

"Girl, you have no idea how much heat I can stand. Sure you want to go there?"

"Maybe not." Guessing it was time to back off, Kelly laughed heartily. "If it gets too hot, my soft flesh has the tendency to incinerate pretty easily. I grant you the victory on this one. You let me have the first round before."

"You're a little vixen! You knew exactly what you were doing. What if I don't want you to concede? I'm enjoying this conversation tremendously. It's a real turn-on."

Kelly couldn't believe Houston had confessed to being turned on by her. It felt good. "I'd admit to setting you up if I'd done that. But if I recall correctly, I wasn't the one who started this whole thing. What if we both concede and call it a draw?"

Houston growled low. Then he laughed. "I'll accept a tie, but it comes with a serious 'beware' warning."

"Beware of what?"

"Use your imagination," he responded, unable to contain his laughter.

"I see I'm not the only naughty one. You were also incorrigible at the team facility during my initial meeting with the administrative staff and players."

"I know. Sorry about that. One more thing…and I'll let you go. You mentioned your parents getting an award but you weren't sure if you'd go. If you need an escort, I'll do my best to make myself available. I'll need you to provide me with a date and time."

Kelly's stomach grew tight. Unpleasantness often caused her belly to knot up. She still didn't know if she'd attend or not, but she knew she should. Her parents had come to every important event in her life. Houston was full of surprises. Compared to the things he'd revealed about himself, he wasn't acting or sounding like a man who didn't like to get involved. He'd taken her to meet his family and now he was willing to meet hers. However, he did say he wanted them to become friends, though his slightly romantic behavior belied an "only friends" theory. "That's a grand gesture. Thank you. The awards ceremony is this Saturday evening at the downtown Hyatt Regency on Louisiana Street. I promise to make up my mind by tomorrow, one way or the other."

"I'll block the evening just in case. That is, if my calendar is clear. If it's not, I'll see if I can find any juggle room. We'll talk soon. Have a good night."

"You, too, Houston. I'm grateful for the thoughtful call. Sleep well."

Houston hung up the phone, tossed off his robe, slipped between the sheets and pulled the comforter up over his nude body. He had meant to tell her he'd be willing to escort her to the awards event earlier, but he'd forgotten. Conveying his suggestion to her in person would've been better than handling it over the phone. It would've made it more personal and she could've seen the sincerity in his eyes.

As Houston thought about their spicy conversation, he grew still. Wanting Kelly with burning passion was one thing, but he had to remain responsible. He held himself accountable for his actions. The feelings of others mattered to him. And hers did, too.

If Kelly's heart got deeply involved with his, Houston didn't want even a minor fracture to occur. His heart was seriously rebelling against his rules, but his mind hadn't surrendered yet. No way could he make love to Kelly and then stay away. She had him thinking hard about what it might be like to seduce her without putting on the brakes. Letting himself go with her was a serious and sensitive matter to consider.

Would he be able to let go of the stringent rules governing his personal life?

Houston's thoughts quickly turned to the nationwide groupies he encountered in every city. He'd seen women stand in wraparound lines just to get a mere glimpse of popular sports figures. One bunch of innocent ladies ran the gamut from college students to housewives. These women were content to just see their superstar idols up close.

Then there was the group of chicks who'd do just about anything to get an athlete's attention, acting out the part of "girls gone wild." Flashing breasts or lifting skirts was no big deal. Houston could easily ignore their kind and stay clear.

Sophisticated ladies of independent or parental wealth could afford to get into the posh sports clubs in their cities, where they lived and played. These interesting debutantes, many of them very beautiful, dazzled and dangled themselves in front of what they considered top-shelf superstars. Dressed in skimpy attire and exhibiting the latest hairstyles and stilettos, these particular ladies made sure jocks got more than a mere glimpse of the sexy bodies they loved to flaunt.

While neither of the latter two groups minded sharing their new or used treasures on the first, second or third night, Houston felt safer with the more mature sophisticates. However, he never took anyone back to his hotel room, nor did he visit personal residences. Whatever the evening brought forth always occurred in a neutral setting.

Most athletes were aware that some of the more clever ladies were interested in only money and fame, rarely caring about a man's heart. Some of the guys played it smart and some didn't, but everyone learned the game, sooner or later.

A few big-headed rookies got caught up in the madness of aggressive women because of their sheer vanity, thinking they were all that. Even some of the veterans ended up learning tough lessons from ladies with premeditated purposes, eventually finding out the truth the hard way. STDs, paternity suits, theft of personal property, stalking and false accusations happened a lot in the unpredictable world Houston lived in.

Houston was hardly a virgin. During his college years and in his rookie season he'd been wild and crazy, yet always responsible enough to use protection. As he grew older, he also became wiser. His brothers and he discussed the perilous situations that existed at home and on the road. They'd grown up in an era where men and women were aware abstinence was the only foolproof method of birth control. Each brother was aware of the numerous false paternity suits slapped on athletes, superstars or otherwise.

Because Houston wasn't interested in fathering a child before marriage, he had at one time considered a reversible vasectomy. His mind had switched gears after he'd seriously thought about all the risks involved. Houston wore condoms religiously, though abstinence was the only guaranteed protection against STDs or pregnancy.

Houston remembered he needed to check his calendar. Leaping out of bed, he walked over to the dresser and picked up his PalmPilot. After surfing through his personal appointment listings, he saw that

Saturday evening was open. He was free to escort Kelly to the awards event *if* she decided to go.

Back in bed, Houston turned off the nightstand lights and laid his head back on the pillow. He soon found out it wasn't so easy to turn off the torrent of thoughts running through his head. As he pondered the plans for the birthday cruise for his mother, he wondered if Kelly might be interested in sailing with the family. Although he was unable to believe he was actually entertaining the thought of inviting her to go with him Houston undoubtedly knew an extraordinary change was taking place in his life.

Houston didn't know what this all meant, but he had made up his mind not to fight against whatever was happening. Let it go and wait and see, he quietly told himself.

Wearing a three-quarter-length white lab coat over her slim navy blue skirt and red silk blouse, Kelly walked into treatment room three inside the suite of offices she shared with three other physicians. She had already read the nurse's notes about one of her regular patients, sixteen-year-old Kevin Maize, a high school track star. She looked at the young man and smiled. "Hello, Kevin! How are you this morning?"

Kevin shrugged. "Not too good. The same painful swelling I had in my right knee six months ago is back. That's why I'm flossing these denim cutoffs."

Laughing at his remark, Kelly retrieved a pair of plastic gloves and slid them onto her hands. "Sit over here," she said, pointing to the treatment table. "Scoot all the way back and then raise your leg. Carefully bend your knee and make sure your foot is down flat on the table."

Checking his knee for unusual swelling, Kelly closely eyed the area. Puffiness was present, but it didn't look infected. She pressed lightly. He winced simultaneously. "On a scale from one to ten, ten being the worst, how bad is the pain?"

Looking worried, he frowned. "I'd say about a nine, Dr. Charleston. What do you think it is? It went away and now it's back."

"Don't know yet. X-rays were negative the last time. Brace yourself so I can recheck the knee." Using as light a touch as possible, her fingertips felt all around the lumpy flesh. "Did you somehow fall on your knee or possibly twist it?"

Kevin shook his head. "Not that I'm aware of. Everything with my knee is the same as it was last time."

"That's what has me stumped. I don't want to do another X-ray unless it's absolutely necessary. Who came with you today?"

"My dad's out in the waiting room."

"Okay. We'll get him in here. I'll be right back. Lie back and stretch out as much as you can. Try to relax your knee and be careful to keep the emphasis on comfort."

Outside in the hallway, Kelly summoned Anthony Wheeler, a dedicated male nurse who'd just come out of another treatment room. "Anthony, please bring Mr. Maize back to room three. Also ask Anna to pull Kevin's last X-ray for me. I want to take another look at it. I'll be in Dr. Quinn's office." Anna Lockart ran the front office.

"Stat, Dr. Charleston," Anthony said cheerfully, giving her a bright smile.

Kelly walked to the end of the hall and lightly knocked on the open office door belonging to Dr. Jacoby Quinn. "J.Q., I want to confer with you. Is now a good time?"

"Sure, Kelly, come on in. What's on your mind?" Jacoby gestured for Kelly to take a seat.

Kelly sat down in one of the leather wingback chairs located in front of his beautiful desk. She got right into the dilemma she was faced with, sharing with her colleague all the important details she had on Kevin Maize's past and present medical history that pertained to his knee. "He was in here six months ago with the exact same symptoms. I thought tendonitis may be the culprit, but I'm not sure what it is. I'd like a second opinion. You're one of the best orthopedic surgeons in the house."

"I need to review his records and X-rays before I come in and take a look-see."

"You'll have them shortly. I already requested his last X-rays to be pulled."

"I like the way you work. You're very good at anticipation, Kelly."

"Thank you." A light knock on the door kept her from saying anything more.

* * *

Freshly showered, seated in the leather recliner inside the master retreat, Houston flipped through the *Houston Chronicle*. He was saddened by the vast increase in crime. The thriving city had grown by leaps and bounds and people from all over the world were making Houston their home. Growth was more than likely responsible for the rise in crime. He also remembered a time when the fourth-largest city in the United States had suffered an economic meltdown, causing crime to increase then, too. As of late, things had really changed for the worse in the Bayou City.

Looking over at the phone on the end table, Houston stared at it like he wished it would finally ring. He had put in several calls to Kelly, phoning both the residence and cell phones. She had yet to return a single one. Five days had lapsed since the family dinner.

Feeling disappointed surprised him. He also felt a bit of desperation, a totally foreign emotion for him. Houston had phoned Kelly back to let her know he was available to escort her to the awards dinner. After much serious thought, he had also made the decision to ask her to join the birthday cruise celebration.

According to Austin, passage on the cruise needed to be booked very soon. With only a few premier cabins left, and the trip just a couple of weeks away, the travel agent needed a final cabin-count as soon as possible. The group was interested in balcony accommodation/suites so they had to move pretty quickly. If Kelly declined the invitation, Dallas would then have to book a single-supplement for Lanier.

Houston was very much aware that Kelly might not think it a good idea since she'd already made comments about his offer to escort her Saturday evening.

Although Kelly had told him she'd let him know her decision regarding the event, he hadn't heard from her. Maybe she had decided not to go. It wasn't like her not to return his phone calls. Houston hated to admit it, but he was starting to feel like some women probably felt when he was direct about his lifestyle.

Seconds after Houston thought of calling Kelly one last time, before he could pick up the receiver, the phone rang. He sighed when he heard her voice. "You finally got my messages, huh?"

"Only minutes ago. I've been too busy to check my voice mail.

Before we get into why you phoned me, I plan to go to the awards ceremony. Are you free to attend?"

"That's one of the reasons I phoned. I'm all yours that evening."

Kelly chuckled softly. "You mean to say you have other reasons? I'm all ears."

Houston swallowed hard. "I have something pretty important to ask you."

Kelly was positive no proposal of marriage was forthcoming so she simply nodded. If it were to happen, she'd never make it to the altar. Dying from a state of shock over Houston's desire to get engaged would definitely make it impossible for her to walk down the aisle. *Knock off the sillies,* she quietly told herself, laughing inwardly.

Houston wished Kelly was there in person, but she wasn't so he'd have to try and effectively make his case over the phone. "Mom's birthday is just around the corner. My brothers and I decided we'd surprise her with a cruise to Cozumel. No specific dates are pinned down yet, but we're looking at sailing within the next couple of weeks. To get the kind of cabins we prefer we have to book right away. I'd love for you to join us for the celebration. Do you think it's a possibility?"

Kelly's immediate reaction was to stick her finger into her ear to see if she'd unwittingly allowed a wax buildup. She couldn't possibly have heard Houston right. Either her ears were clogged or the brother had suddenly taken ill.

Houston dealt with dead silence for several seconds. "Kelly," he said softly, "did you hear me?"

"Heard you talking but didn't quite comprehend the gist of your message."

"My mother's birthday, four-day cruise—and I invited you to join us."

A cruise with her and Houston sharing the same cabin? Utterly unbelievable.

There had to be a catch somewhere, Kelly mused. Houston wasn't into second dates, let alone serial dating. Yet he'd already invited her to dinner. That alone made her sure they wouldn't share a cabin. In his mind, they were working on becoming friends. Despite all of that, Kelly wanted to accept his offer. She saw being at sea with

Houston and the other Carringtons as a magical holiday in the making.

Perhaps she should take some time to give more thought to his proposal, but she saw no use denying herself anything she wanted. Intentional or not, Houston's guard was coming down. She hoped it would up and disappear altogether. "I'd love to go."

Shocked but delirious with Kelly's response, Houston smiled broadly. "Great! You and Lanier can share a cabin if you don't mind, out of respect for our parents. Dallas and I are bunking together."

Kelly battled hard to hold back her derisive laughter. It didn't surprise her that she was so right-on-the-money about the cabin. *Was Houston getting too predictable?* She hoped not. Predictability could bore her to tears. Even as the thought passed through her head, she knew boredom with him would hardly occur. There was nothing humdrum about him. Houston was the most fascinating man she'd ever made the acquaintance of.

"The trip is on me, Kelly. I'm happy you're coming along."

Kelly turned her mouth down in a slight frown. "I'll pick up my own tab, thank you. That way, neither of us has to feel obligated. Who knows, you and I just might meet our soul mates aboard the ship. At the very least, we may run into someone attractive, interesting or possibly both. It's good we keep our options open."

With no intention of responding to her maddening remarks, Houston thought it best to ignore them. The cruise was an exclusive event and that bit of information would be made crystal clear to Dr. Charleston long before they sailed off into the sunset.

"I'm going to e-mail you the details about the awards event. My schedule is crazy for the entire day, but I'll do my best to get everything out to you shortly. I'll meet you at the Hyatt on Saturday, but I don't recall the time. I'll include it in the note."

Taken aback by Kelly's remarks, Houston had to bite down on his tongue to keep from blasting her with a sharp retort. "From your front door to the Hyatt and back to your door is my plan. I'm your escort from the beginning of the evening up to the end. Hope to talk with you later on. Have a great day." Without waiting for the counterprotest he was sure she was ready to launch, he disconnected the line.

Kelly trying to meet him at the Hyatt bothered him terribly. He attempted to dismiss it from his mind, along with the remarks she'd made about them possibly connecting with soul mates. As he got up and went into the media room to watch film from an old basketball game, he fought hard to smother the inward seething.

Thoughts of Kelly with another man, especially on something as romantic as a cruise, weren't the least bit pleasant. In fact, Houston suddenly realized he'd have trouble thinking about her with any man, period, intimately or otherwise. His brothers' remarks suddenly rang loudly in his ears again. Austin and Dallas had warned him about the possibility of someone snatching her up if he didn't get his act together.

The entire basketball team thought Kelly was superhot, so Houston had hard evidence that other men found her sexy and beautiful. It wouldn't stun him if she was asked out by one of his teammates. Max Sheffield was gone on her, too. If Max wasn't in a long-term relationship, Houston wouldn't put it past the wealthy entrepreneur to try and wine and dine Kelly. The owner loved beautiful, intelligent women. Kelly stacked up.

The players called Kelly the Sienna Splendor behind her back, but it was done with admiration and affection for the woman who'd already softened hardened male hearts. No one had approached her on a personal level, but the facility gym had buzzed with her name the day the players had come in to clean out lockers.

If the team ever saw Kelly with him at a social function, he knew his teammates would automatically assume they were in a relationship. Since Houston hadn't been seen with the same woman twice, it would be an easy call to make. He hadn't clarified his short-lived liaison with Kelly to any member of the Cyclones, yet he was positive they'd respect him enough to steer clear of her if they began dating exclusively.

Houston leaned in and landed a soft kiss on Kelly's cheek. Standing back, he allowed his eyes to rove over her full length, glad Saturday had finally arrived. He hadn't seen her for an entire week. "You look marvelous, lady. Love the dress, love the color… and I absolutely love how it accentuates your well-toned body. It's a sparkling winner." He extended his arm for her to take. "I'm honored to be your escort for the evening."

Kelly looked beautiful and enchanting. Very chic and sophisticated, the floor-length, low-backed, plunging neckline, midnight-blue sparkler was designed by Maggy London. Dark blue and silver evening slippers and matching clutch were nice accents. Diamond oval-shaped studs sparkled on her ears and a one-carat oval solitaire on a nearly invisible gold wire graced her neck. Houston felt completely bowled over.

Kelly smiled up at her handsome date. "I'm pleased you initiated it." Her eyes drank in his elegance—his scrumptiously gorgeous body was draped in a Ralph Lauren designer traditional black tuxedo and complementary accessories. "You look similar to how I've imagined you all day long. But I have to admit that you've far exceeded the sensational images I'd conjured up. What cologne are you wearing? The delectable scent is manly and hypnotic. So seductive. I like it."

"Thank you. I'm Ralph Lauren all the way this evening, from head to toe. It's Polo Black. Since I dressed in the same color, I thought it was a good fit."

Houston opened the car door for Kelly and stood there until she was seated and buckled in. He then walked around to the driver's side and settled down inside.

Because Kelly hadn't decided to attend the event until the last minute, there'd been no time to purchase a new gown. Her closet held a variety of appropriate choices in evening apparel from formals to after-five attire in both dressy and casual-dressy, so she hadn't had to fret. As a doctor, Kelly was invited to many social events throughout the year. Her practice also held a formal black-and-white winter ball annually.

The dinner hour was seven o'clock but the cocktail reception was slated for six. The hardest part for her had been to call her parents to let them know she'd be in attendance, only after she'd taken care of the RSVP with the committee.

Even the strongest of women had an occasion to become weakened by emotional stress. Inside the ballroom of the Hyatt Regency Hotel, Kelly and Houston were seated by a greeter. The pretty young woman had shown the striking couple to a table very close to the reserved head table for the honored guests. The premier spot was close enough to hear and see everything happening onstage.

Several other reserved front-row tables were filled with the Charlestons' constituency. Kelly was relieved that she hadn't been seated at the head table even though she also felt a little slighted. It was hard for her to act pretentious and she wouldn't indulge in that kind of behavior this evening. Kelly vowed to keep it real. It allowed her to be comfortable right where she was. Still, she knew she'd be far from relaxed in the company of the award recipients. Tension already had her in its clenching grip.

Looking worried, Houston covered Kelly's hand with his. "Are you okay?"

Kelly nodded despite not feeling so hot. Her nerves were on edge and nothing she'd done so far had calmed the jagged edginess. "I'll be okay. Thanks for asking."

Houston eyed her closely. "Why don't I believe that?"

Her hackles rose and then fell, all in the same second. Taking out her frustration on Houston over her dilemma wasn't fair. He'd done nothing except offer to escort her to something she knew she should attend, yet clearly wasn't happy about.

"Hello, my darling Kelly," a sweet, slightly raspy voice cooed.

Kelly didn't need to look up to know the voice or to identify the soft, warm hand on her shoulder. "Mama Tilley," she cried happily, getting out of her seat to greet the older woman. "Papa Joseph, you're here, too. Why am I so surprised? You both look wonderful. Your new haircut has slashed away a few years, Mama Tilley. You're hot."

Mama Tilley laughed. "Thank you, dear child. I try to keep myself up."

Kelly hugged and kissed the two people who meant the world to her, the understanding souls who'd gotten her through some pretty rough preadolescent and teenage spots. These people loved her unconditionally and she loved them back with the same pureness and intensity. They had taken care of Kelly, living in the Charleston home as full-time caretakers until she'd gone off to college.

Papa Joseph took Kelly into his arms and squeezed her tightly. "How's my beautiful girl? Look at you! You're stunning." He then noticed Houston, immediately recognizing him as the power forward for his favorite team. "Houston Carrington, what an honor to see my favorite Cyclone. I couldn't have dreamed up meeting you this evening. It's a pleasure to be in your company. I'm Joseph Rose and this is my lovely wife, Tilley. We began taking care of Kelly when she was six. We're also very proud of her."

"Thank you for your kind remarks, sir. Kelly *is* a force to be reckoned with. There are a lot of things about her to be proud of." Houston got to his feet and extended his hand to Papa Joseph. "Mr. Rose, I'm just as pleased and honored to meet you and Mrs. Rose."

Houston then pulled out two chairs for the Roses to be seated. Once everyone was comfortably settled, he sat back down.

Kelly reached over and gently touched Mama Tilley's smooth, tawny-brown face. Inside her chest her heart danced over the kind remarks Houston had made to Papa Joseph. "I'm glad we're seated at the same table. I'm more comfortable now."

Mama Tilley nodded and smiled. "I'm sure your parents are responsible for the seating arrangements. I'm just so happy you're here, child. Wasn't sure you'd show up."

"I sometimes forget how well you know me. Because of the positive influences you've had on me, I couldn't stay away. It wouldn't have been right," Kelly remarked.

"Praise God," Papa Joseph commented. "You always did try to do what's right."

Houston looked on as Kelly interacted with the older couple. He could easily see her fondness for Mama Tilley and Papa Joseph. There was still a lot he didn't know about her, but something constantly urged him to stick around and find out all there was to know. It was risky. But then again, living life was one huge risk.

Chapter 6

Kelly and Tilley engaged in quiet conversation while Houston and Joseph hit it off exuberantly, talking about sports and the other Carrington sports heroes. By the look on the older man's handsome but weathered face, Kelly could tell he was in seventh heaven over his good fortune. Never in Joseph's wildest dreams had he thought he'd meet and spend time with one of the starting five for the Texas Cyclones.

"How's your health, Mama T?"

Tilley smiled. "Losing fifteen pounds has been a miracle cure for my blood pressure. My doctor has taken me off the meds controlling it. It feels good to be thinner."

"That's good news," Kelly gushed. "Glad your BP is under control."

"Me, too. Thank you." Tilley nudged Kelly, nodding toward Houston. "Are you two in a relationship?" she whispered. "If so, why don't I know about you and him?"

Kelly kissed Tilley's cheek. "We're building a friendship," Kelly said softly. "He was kind enough to offer himself as my escort for this evening. Wish there was more to tell you, but there isn't. No hot romance to speak about."

"Nothing wrong with friendships, but I think there's more to it. I saw the way he looks at you. That gorgeous devil has more than just friendship on his mind."

Kelly giggled. "You are so headed in the wrong direction. Houston isn't the committing type. He leads a carefree life, one that doesn't include exclusive dating."

Tilley gave a low harrumph. "Tell me that a couple of months from now. Maybe I'll believe it then. His lips are saying one thing, but his eyes say something else. It might only be lust, but he definitely has a thing for you."

Holding in her laughter, Kelly directed her attention toward the stage. "It looks like the program is about to begin."

Tilley reached up and patted Joseph's shoulder. "Tune it down," she whispered. "They're about to start."

Houston laughed inwardly at how quickly Joseph obeyed. He had instantly grown mum. Tilley apparently yielded clout. Had she lectured Kelly on how to handle men and how to gain the upper hand? He was willing to bet the next season on it.

The master of ceremonies, a tall, ruggedly handsome gentleman wearing traditional tux and tails, opened the festivities with an enthusiastic welcome. Had there been no microphone, his voice still would've boomed. He acknowledged distinguished visitors, then introduced Carolyn and Jared, and smiled at the honored couple.

Kelly was surprised to see her parents already seated since she hadn't seen them enter the room. But they had to have seen her, she thought. Yet the honorees hadn't stopped by to say hello to their only child or to Tilley and Joseph.

Why send invitations if they had no intentions of acknowledging them? Kelly burned internally, her stomach feeling like a raging fire pit.

Tilley sensed Kelly's despondency, felt her agony. She rubbed the back of the young woman's hand to try and soothe her rattled nerves. Tilley knew the girl she loved like a daughter was still much too sensitive for her own good. The look on Kelly's face revealed the pain she felt inside her heart. She'd always worn her heartache overtly.

The Charlestons loved Kelly very much, but Tilley knew they weren't the kind of parents who openly expressed their feelings. She suspected them of not knowing how to show love to their child despite deep feelings for her. Kelly had hung out with a few close girlfriends and a couple of cousins, but she was happier operating as a loner. That she spent a good bit of time alone saddened both Tilley and Joseph.

As though Houston felt whatever Kelly was feeling, he took hold of her hand. "It'll be all right. Hang on tight. I'm here for you," he whispered. "You're not alone."

Houston *was* there, lifting her spirit higher than it'd ever risen before. Kelly found deep comfort in his sincere remarks. She liked how her small hand didn't feel totally lost in his much larger one. The warmth of his tenderness felt intimate to her.

How did Houston know she felt alone? Kelly had to wonder.

His comment had been said with conviction, as if he knew it to be a fact. Her facial expressions often gave her away, but she hadn't known her inner turmoil was showing. Darkness no longer threatened to engulf her as she turned her attention back to the emcee, listening closely to everything said about her parents' stellar careers.

Kelly's vulnerable appearance concerned Houston. The melancholy look in her eyes was heartrending. He tilted his head until it rested against Kelly's, like it was the most natural thing to do. His fingers gently squeezing her hand ignited tranquility and security inside her. The slight tremors in her hand confirmed her vulnerable state for him.

Scared to move a muscle for fear of separation, Kelly just sat there, staring up at the stage, though she could no longer tune in to what was said. The slight but steady pressure of his long fingers generated enough heat to melt her insides, stirring up her heart in ways she'd never dreamed of.

The announcement that dinner was about to be served allowed Kelly to redirect her attention to something other than how good Houston made her feel.

Crisp salads and hot rolls were served before the main entrée of chicken cordon bleu, fluffed sweet potatoes and steamed fresh green beans. Ice water and tea were at each place setting, accompanied by small plates of lemon wedges.

After eating, Kelly worked hard to concentrate on the onstage activities when her mother and father's names were enthusiastically announced by the emcee, who resumed his duties at the podium. The gentleman gave a condensed but powerful bio on the successful surgeons before relating their extensive contributions to health services in the Houston communities.

"I now present to you Doctors Carolyn and Jared Charleston!"

Dressed in fashionable formal attire, the mid-fifties couple was striking. Carolyn had a slender figure and was slightly taller than Kelly's five foot seven. Salt-and-pepper in color, the short, layered haircut was a good style for her. Well over six feet tall, Jared was handsome and debonair. His wavy hair also had gray mixed in.

Carolyn and Jared held hands as they came onstage to give brief yet meaningful comments. The emcee shook Jared's hand

and warmly hugged Carolyn, then spoke words of encouragement and deep gratitude to each for their lifetime medical services.

Jared looked out over the capacity-filled ballroom. He then acknowledged the awards committee and several of his colleagues. "Thank you for bestowing such a prestigious honor on us," Jared Charleston said, his words ringing with deep sincerity. "We are so grateful to each of you. The countless roads we've traveled were not always paved, but ours has been an awesome journey, one that many of you made possible."

Carolyn took the microphone. "It is not every day you receive a lifetime achievement award from your constituents and the people you've served. We are honored and grateful that we've impacted others in such a positive way. The people of Houston, Texas, mean so much to us. We are glad to be of service. As long as there is breath in us, Jared and I will continue to find ways to serve the people and the communities we love so very much. We are blessed."

"Thanks to all of you all," Jared and Carolyn said simultaneously.

Once the loud applause died down, Jared pointed out into the audience. "We'd also like to thank our lovely daughter, Dr. Kelly Charleston, for sharing in this great celebration. Many of you have watched her grow up from a tiny tot to become an amazing young lady. We are so proud that she follows in our medical footsteps. We love her very much. Kelly, please stand and take a bow."

Stunned by her father's praise, Kelly had mixed emotions over his comments. On wobbly legs, she stood and bowed from the waist. Her heart was racing and her palms felt sweaty. Her dad referring to her as amazing tugged hard on her heartstrings. Hearing him telling everyone present how proud he was of her had her fighting back tears. If only he could tell her these things in private, rather than in front of an audience. It would've had a greater impact. However, she believed his remarks had truly come from his heart.

"Isn't she beautiful?" Carolyn asked. "Keep your eyes on her. She's also doing remarkable things in community service. Our Kelly is an orthopedic surgeon."

Although Kelly would've preferred the guillotine to enduring this sham of a family reunion, she smiled warmly. Her mother calling her beautiful had only occurred when she was a small child, but it made her feel good to hear it now. Her remarks about her involvement in the community touched her. Carolyn finally acknowledging her as an orthopedic surgeon caused her eyes to fill with tears.

Kelly's heart had begun to soften toward the two people she loved the most.

"Thank you, Mom and Dad. Congratulations on your dedication and service to the communities you love! There's no one more deserving of this prestigious award than you are!" She quickly reclaimed her seat and swiped away her tears.

Kelly had meant every word of what she'd said about her parents' professional accomplishments, but she wished she could say the same about their parenting roles.

Houston squeezed Kelly's fingers again. Knowing what a hard time she'd had in getting through her comments, he was proud of her. Her expressions had been somewhat revealing to him and her hands still trembled.

Carolyn and Jared spoke to several of their colleagues and other guests before making their way over to Kelly's table. The couple embraced Tilley and Joseph affectionately, fussing over the elderly couple they'd relied on so much in years past.

The Roses basked in the loving attention from their past employers.

Looking rather reserved, Carolyn stood back, watching as her husband greeted their only child. It disturbed her that Kelly didn't look like she was happy to be there.

Jared brought Kelly to her feet, hugging her tightly, kissing each of her temples. His smoky-gray eyes drank in his daughter's lovely appearance. "I'm glad you came, love. I can't tell you what it means to us to have you here."

Looking dazed, Kelly just stood there. Then suddenly she made direct eye contact with her father. "I'm glad I was *able* to attend, too. I'm very proud of you both."

Houston wished he had a magic wand to cast over Kelly. The clear unhappiness she felt over the situation with her parents came through in spades. The resentment she felt was palpable, and she was totally estranged from them. According to what she'd told him, she saw her mom and dad on rare occasions, and only if they initiated contact. She never called them to extend any sort of social invite.

Carolyn finally stepped forward, taking hold of her daughter's hand. "Hello, Kelly. I'm so happy to see you. Your presence means a lot to Dad and me."

Unable to connect with her mother's hazel gaze, Kelly looked down at the floor instead. She had to attempt to take control of the situation to try and alleviate the awkwardness. Forgiveness was crucial, but her heart still felt bruised.

Finally, Kelly embraced her mother, trying desperately to put away the hard feelings. "Hello, Mom. You look remarkable! I'm really proud of your accomplishments. As I said to Daddy, I'm glad I could make it."

Kelly was acutely aware that she held her mother far more accountable for the frequent absences in her youth than she did her father. Mothers were born nurturers, though many males now filled that role. As much as she wanted to continue blaming her parents for how unwanted she felt back then, it was time for her to grow up and shelve past issues and stinging hurts. Kelly knew it was easier said than done.

Everything was at a quiet standstill again. Then Jared spotted Houston.

Jared's eyes widened with disbelief. "I can't believe it," he said, taking a closer look. "Are my eyes deceiving me? Aren't you Houston Carrington?"

Extending his hand to Jared, Houston stood. "The one and only, sir. Congratulations on the achievement award!" Houston's smile encompassed both parents.

Jared looked back and forth between the younger couple. "Why haven't we met your young man before now?" Jared asked. "You, of all people, young lady, know what a fanatic I am when it comes to the Cyclones and the Carringtons. This is a nice surprise."

Embarrassed by her father's reaction, Kelly wished she could disappear into thin air. "Houston and I are friends. He offered to escort me here this evening and I accepted. I'm also under contract with the Cyclone organization as a team physician."

Jared was obviously astounded by Kelly's news. Disappointment also flared in his eyes. "Why aren't we aware of any of this, Kelly? Working with the Cyclone franchise is a huge accomplishment. When did all these wonderful blessings come your way?"

Kelly shuffled her feet. "I only recently signed the contract. I planned to tell you once I landed the job, but my schedule got crazy. You both know how it is not to have enough hours in the day. So many things have a way of coming up unexpectedly. Before you know it, the day is gone." Kelly's remarks were sharp and to the point.

Carolyn knew her daughter's remarks were aimed at them. Her reference to the lack of time had been clear. It seemed as if Kelly wasn't ever going to forgive past mistakes. "It looks like we're not the only ones to be congratulated." She hugged her daughter. "Congratulations." Carolyn turned to Houston. "So nice to meet you, Mr. Carrington. I've heard and read a lot of positive things about you and your family."

Houston smiled broadly. "It's a pleasure to meet you, too, ma'am. And please, feel free to call me Houston."

"We'll remember that," Carolyn responded. "I hope we'll get to spend some time with you and Kelly real soon. We'd love to have you two over one evening."

"Sounds like a good time to me," Houston replied. "Thanks for the invite."

Kelly shot Houston a killer glance. If she had her way, this was the only social engagement they'd ever indulge in. A quiet evening for four was out of the question.

Houston instantly analyzed the evil look Kelly had cast his way. She probably felt he had interfered in personal family matters, but that hadn't been the case. It would've been rude not to respond at all. He quickly dismissed the idea of discussing the matter with her later. If she didn't bring up the subject, neither would he. The atmosphere was already charged with enough TNT to blow the hotel to smithereens.

Kelly felt horrible about how she'd scolded Houston with a wicked glance. None of this was on him. He looked as if a bout of sadness had paid him an unexpected visit. In her desire to smooth things over, she leaned closer to him, smiling softly. "Are you having as good a time as me?"

Happy over her change in mood, though doubtful about her comment of having a good time, Houston smiled back. "I'm really enjoying myself."

"Why don't we all sit down and have a drink," Jared suggested. Once everyone was seated, Kelly quickly struck up a conversation, hoping the others would soon join in. She felt totally responsible for this awkward situation and she desperately wanted to defuse it. Houston seemed pleased by the change in her attitude. The nod of approval from Mama Tilley let her know she had done the right thing. Joseph's warm smile helped to boost Kelly's confidence and lift her spirit.

Houston loaded Jennifer Hudson's disc into a slot on the CD changer. She was one of Kelly's favorite female artists. As the R & B music floated into the car, he looked over at her. The smile she gave him let him know he'd pleased her.

His hand found his way to her thigh, where he rested it as he drove on. He liked touching her and loved it when she laid hands on him. Her fingers and hands were very expressive. Her touch spoke to him in a language he enjoyed. Interpreting the meaning was a pleasurable task.

Kelly felt as if the skin on her thigh was melting beneath the gown she wore. Houston's hands never failed to heat her through and through. One look, one touch, one kiss from him could send her into orbit. His look was sensuous, his touch fiery and his kiss incomparable. But he was either unable or unwilling to commit to anyone. She knew he cared about her, but she wanted to receive more than care. Kelly hoped for his unconditional love, but she doubted it would ever happen.

Just to be incorrigible, Kelly pressed in the number to the song Jennifer sang in *Dreamgirls,* the one originally recorded by Jennifer Holliday, "And I Am Telling You I'm Not Going." It was her favorite cut.

Ignoring Kelly's orbs boring into him like a hot poker, Houston kept his eyes on the winding road. Even though he knew the song by heart, he still listened to every word Jennifer sang. The plain-as-English lyrics went without saying. He clearly received the message Kelly sent. How could he not?

Houston applied gentle pressure to Kelly's thigh. "I've never been good at denying the truth, even to spare someone's feelings." He briefly looked into her eyes, wishing he was in a position to pull her in close to him. "You already know me as well as anyone outside my family circle. I've been open and honest with you from day one. We've discussed the person I am on the inside and out and why I'm that way."

Kelly nodded. "I'm aware of all that, Houston. You're saying it to say what?"

"Maybe I don't have the right to ask you this, but here goes." He reached over and traced her lips with his finger. "Can you give me a little time to figure this all out? I thought I'd already nailed down the lifestyle that best suited me—footloose and fancy free. That is, until you came into my life. I'm no longer sure what's what anymore. I love being in your company and I want to continue seeing you."

To say Kelly appeared stunned wasn't a strong enough depiction. She looked over at him, fighting off the urge to feel his forehead to try and gauge his temperature. "Is that really what you want me to do or is it just one of your fancy behind-the-back passes?"

Houston had to laugh at her basketball jargon. "I'm not the quarterback in the family, but Austin would call it a forward pass. I believe that description fits best. Are you open to catch the pass?"

Kelly hid her shock this time, yet she still wondered if he was ill. "I'll do my best not to cause a turnover."

"Thank you." Thinking he'd said enough for now, he took Kelly's hand and laid it upon his thigh. "I'll have you home in a few minutes."

Thinking of all the countless hours she'd spent alone, crying and wishing her parents loved her like she needed to be loved, Kelly made the decision to try to be more patient with Houston, no matter how much patience was required. She had to admit they'd been good for each other. Their friendship was growing, but Kelly couldn't ignore her desire for much more. Whether she'd get it or not was anyone's guess. Houston was always respectful to her and too darn sweet and charismatic for words. Frequent absences from him, should they occur, would hurt Kelly to her heart.

Was Houston Carrington worth her effort and energy?

Kelly was pretty sure he was all that and more. Perhaps Houston just didn't know what his own worth was to a woman. She didn't mind taking time to show him.

Houston placed his hand over Kelly's. "I know of a coffee shop where they play live jazz up until 2:00 a.m. Interested in stopping by for a cup of brew?"

"Clayton's Coffee House off the 45 South?"

Houston grinned. "We *do* frequent some of the same haunts. Is that a yes?"

"Most definitely."

The first sip of hot coffee warmed Kelly as it went down. "Clayton's makes great coffee. It's delicious and robust. I hear they create their own blends."

"It's true. My parents are longtime friends of Madge and Jerome Clayton. My brothers and I went to the same schools as their son and daughter. What's so interesting is that Michael and Michelle Clayton are twins."

Before Kelly could respond, a pen and paper was thrust into Houston's hand. "May I please have your autograph?" the young woman asked. "No one's going to believe I actually met you in the flesh, not without proof."

Houston smiled up at the lady. "Maybe the autograph will convince them."

"I'm sure it will," she enthused excitedly. Without giving Houston a clue, she bent her head and kissed him gently on the cheek. "Keep scoring all those points. You sure have scored enough with me. I don't miss a single televised game."

Houston noticed the line of adoring fans awaiting his attention as he lifted his head. Shrugging, he gave Kelly an amused look. He would never snub the people who supported him. He didn't care whether they paid big bucks to come see him run up and down the hardwood or if they only watched his performances on television.

Kelly looked as if she understood, but Houston wasn't really sure. Whatever she felt about it, he had to do this. He was sure she'd never leave a patient unattended.

For the next twenty minutes, Houston signed autographs and happily posed with those interested in a picture with him. Questions came from everywhere and he took time to answer the ones he could. "Will you come home with me tonight?" didn't get any kind of response. Houston was good at dodging certain bullets and keeping folks in line. He did have boundaries and he didn't mind enforcing them when fans got out of hand.

As the last autograph was penned, he turned to face Kelly. "You see how crazy it can get for athletes? I hope you weren't offended."

Kelly grinned. "Not in the least. You are in popular demand. It'd take a strong woman to compete with all the female adoration you get. The guys were thrilled to meet you, yet the ladies with the raging hormones were ready to take you home."

"You heard that, huh? I don't encourage that kind of behavior. For the most part, my fans are respectful. But I do have to admit this was mild to what it's usually like."

Kelly scowled. "If it gets worse than this, I feel for you, Austin and Dallas."

"Save the empathy. We handle things okay. I don't know of anyone who doesn't want to be shown appreciation for what they do. The Carrington triplets are no different."

Kelly nodded her understanding. "It makes sense. My patients also show their appreciation for me. I get more sweet gifts than you can imagine. Many are homemade in the form of cakes, pies, flower arrangements and knitted or crocheted items. I'm grateful for every loving gesture."

For the next several minutes, the couple sat in silence, savoring the taste of hot coffee. Kelly reflected back on the entire evening while Houston thought about where this relationship was headed. He was definitely navigating in uncharted waters.

What made Kelly different from any other woman he'd come into contact with? What did she possess that made him want to see her again and again?

Houston didn't know the answers but he was interested in digging as deep as he had to in an attempt to unearth them. This woman really challenged his way of thinking. He couldn't believe he'd suggested coming in and visiting for a while when they got back to her home. But he simply was not ready for this spectacular date to end.

Houston's heart had rejoiced when Kelly had welcomed his suggestion.

Back at her house for another nightcap. Kelly came back into her family room, carrying a metal tray laden with napkins, a plate of oatmeal-raisin cookies, two teacups, a carafe of hot tea and condiments. Houston rushed over and took the heavy tray from her hands, setting it down on the thick woven mat she'd placed on the marble table before heading into her kitchen.

Houston grinned as he sat back down. "That was quick. I missed you."

"Missed you, too. Sugar only, right?"

"Right. You fix mine and I'll fix yours. Two Splendas, right?"

Kelly laughed. "You got it." This was one of many things he did that got to her.

Houston and Kelly had only had one cup of coffee at Clayton's. When they'd arrived at her home, he'd asked if he could come in for a cup of tea. She had paid close attention to how he'd taken his hot drink.

The couple drank their tea while listening to an R & B CD featuring a variety of singing artists.

"The cookies look tempting, Kelly, but I ate too much dessert at the hotel." He slipped his arm around her. "Perhaps there's something else sweet I can taste, without the worry of gaining weight."

Kelly giggled. "And what's that?"

Squeezing Kelly's shoulders, Houston chuckled. "Let's play a little show…and promise not to tell."

Kelly desperately wanted Houston to taste every part of her. She didn't like self-imposed limitations, but she had to respect his or move on. They both had options. Going to bed after he left and wanting him like crazy had her reluctant to let him show her anything. If he ever did make love to her, she'd want to tell the world by hiring a pilot to write it boldly across the skies. She had already had an abundance of dreams of the two of them making wild, passionate love.

His mouth came down on hers and her train of thought instantly went off the tracks.

Houston's kisses were getting hotter and hotter by the second, his tongue sweetly entwining with hers. It was sizzling up in her family room and she was sure her ears produced steam. She'd never had anyone kiss her this passionately. These kind of mouth-numbing kisses only happened in her fantasies.

Kelly had never experienced anything as hot as his mouth devouring hers. Her lips already felt swollen. At this point, she didn't care if they swelled to bursting. She didn't even want to come up for air. This Carrington triplet, the last born, was killing her softly, doing his best to show her what he suggested they promise not to tell.

Houston's hands roving over her flesh felt as if they were incinerating Kelly's skin right through her dress. This man definitely made it hard to think clearly and nearly impossible to remain in control. She didn't have the strength or desire to resist him if he wanted all of her. If it was his desire to put her out of her misery, she wished he'd hurry up. Kelly's entire body felt like an inferno. This was the furthest he'd taken intimacy. *Was he just caught up in the heat of the moment?* This was a pleasant and hotly delicious surprise for Kelly, but she feared it'd end before long.

His breathing totally out of control, Houston held Kelly away from him, looking deeply into her sable-brown eyes. "Before this goes any further, before we do what we both seem to want desperately, you know who I am. You know my take on relationships. What I feel for you is deeper than I can adequately express, but commitment is still an issue for me. Can you accept me just as I am? I don't want any regrets for either of us."

Staring at Houston like he was a perfect stranger, Kelly forcefully pushed him away from her. Jumping up from the sofa, she put a good bit of distance between them. The desire to slug him hard on the jaw had her hands twitching.

How dare he set her body on fire, only to douse the flames with cold indecision?

"Houston, you'd better up and disappear before I do something regrettable. You romance me, seduce me, then you pull back and make your little speech. Don't you think it's unfair to do that to me? You've been fanning the flames of my desire since our first outing, but this time you've nearly taken it to full-blown foreplay. Please!"

Wishing he could vanish without walking out Kelly's front door, Houston ran agitated fingers through his hair. He could plainly see he'd hurt her. It hadn't been his intent. Her eyes also revealed deep anger. Kelly was the last person he wanted to harm.

Trembling with outrage, Kelly glared at Houston. To her, he seemed clueless about how badly he'd injured her feelings. "You know something, Houston. I won't give you permission to run in and out of my life. There'll be no series of dates, only to not hear from you for long periods. You can't come knocking on my door again after casting me aside at will. I won't accept disrespect from you or from any man."

Purely frustrated, Houston shook his head from side to side. "I'm sorry. I don't want to continuously mess up with you." He suddenly looked vulnerable, as if he might break down emotionally. "Have you ever been terrified of something you clearly don't understand? Has fear ever gotten a stranglehold on you, making it impossible for you to free yourself? Have you ever wanted someone so bad it hurts?"

Kelly was stunned by Houston's questions. She gave it a minute of thought, unable to keep from including thoughts of her parents. It was all too clear, all too real. She'd had numerous fears in her lifetime. However, she'd always identified them and tried to face each one head-on. Getting through medical school had been a constant, nerve-racking battle. Kelly had eventually conquered one of the biggest trepidations of all time—unmitigated fear of failure. But she still hadn't conquered the fear of being left alone.

"I've had plenty of fears, Houston. But what does it have to do with us?"

"Everything, Kelly." Feeling totally out of his depth, Houston clenched and unclenched his fists. Talking about his fears wasn't something he'd ever gotten deeply into—and never with a woman. His brothers knew he ran scared all the time and that commitment was his archenemy. Even as close as they were, he'd never let Austin and Dallas know how deep his fears ran.

Sighing with discontent, Houston rested his head against the sofa's back. "Would it help to know I've never involved myself with anyone like I have with you? Would you feel better if you knew I really care deeply for you, that I don't see you as someone I can play with, disrespect…and then just toss aside? I don't think of any woman that way. I have endless respect for females. I love spending time with you and I love how you make me feel inside and out. But this is brand-new for me, Kelly. I'm just plain scared. Scared of all a relationship entails. The openness, the vulnerability…and of falling in love only to have the road trip turn a loving relationship into constant arguments and distrust over the amount of time I'm away from home."

Houston's comments *did* help Kelly, tremendously. His showing his vulnerable side was a total surprise to her. Well, maybe not. His sensitivity was one of the reasons she'd fallen for him. Although he hadn't told her how much he cared for her, he had confessed to caring. The way he made her feel inside would keep her door open to him. The chief complaint about Houston was his failure to give her any future hope for them, yet she'd known that from the beginning. He had never handed out false hopes.

Kelly sat back down next to Houston, resting her head on his broad shoulder. "I appreciate what you said. Thanks for saying you respect me and that you care. It means a lot." She sighed hard. "We should call it a night. We're both pretty worked up. A good night's rest should help ease the fiery tension. Cool with you?"

"I can live with it." He took both her hands in his. "I'm really trying, Kelly. I need you to understand that. You're too important for me not to try and get this right."

Kelly didn't comment but his remarks deeply affected her. However, the meaning over Houston's interest in trying puzzled her.

What was he trying to get right? What had he meant by that?

She wouldn't think of asking him to define his statements. Until Houston actually said he wanted to work on having a romantic relationship with her, she shouldn't try to read anything into his comments. She wasn't looking for him to further explain his ideology. He'd already been quite clear about who he was and how he operated.

Kelly prayed for irrefutable action from one Houston Carrington, actions she could interpret to mean he desired her, only her, just the same as she did him.

Chapter 7

Desiring to look his very best, Houston set out to dress up like the million-dollar man he was. He wanted Kelly to be proud of him in front of her colleagues and staff when he surprised her by showing up to take her out to lunch.

Removing a lightweight tan suit and a chocolate-brown silk shirt from his closet, he matched it with a multicolored silk tie. After picking out a pair of brown Italian loafers from the built-in shoe rack in the walk-in closet, which held numerous other pairs of footwear in various styles, Houston set them beside the leather bench in front of his bed.

Houston suddenly looked worried. *When had it become so important for him to care about what Kelly thought of him and how she viewed him?* No one had any idea how often she came to mind and how much space she occupied inside his head. His brothers would be stunned to know he'd let someone get into his blood this way.

Something had to give. Or perhaps it was time for him to give in to his ever-growing feelings and his constant need for Kelly.

Disappointed that Kelly wasn't in her office, Houston rapidly made his way to the large eatery located only a couple of blocks from where she worked. Her receptionist had willingly volunteered to him her boss's whereabouts. Kelly's favorite diner specialized in down-home Southern cooked meals and was her boss's favorite place to take lunch.

Thinking about the all-too-familiar reactions from the staff at Kelly's office, Houston laughed. If he were an egotistical ham, he would've sucked up the schoolgirl giggling, the buzzing whispers and admiring glances. It didn't matter how many times the power forward frequented a place or walked down a street, the wild, vocal reactions from those who recognized him as a professional basketball player were always the same.

After straightening his tie, Houston smoothed a hand over his sable-brown curls. Strolling into the restaurant, he steeled himself for more of the same reactions like those of only minutes ago. The gestures were grand, but they also embarrassed him at times. Waving at folks who shouted out his name, he quickly made his way to the back of the diner. He was told Kelly had a favorite window booth in the rear.

As Houston neared the area where Kelly was seated, he stopped dead in his tracks. The receptionist hadn't told him Kelly was dining with someone, a striking male someone. He wished he had been informed, but there was a good possibility she hadn't known about it. Dr. Charleston was a very private person. Whether to present himself or just walk away was the question of the day. Kelly hadn't spotted him yet.

Never one to shy away from anyone or anything, Houston proceeded toward the leather booth, his strides long and confident. As he reached his destination, Kelly suddenly looked up. The expression on her face was easy enough for Houston to read. He hoped she wouldn't have to be rushed to the hospital for shock treatments.

Without faltering, Houston slid into the booth next to Kelly, kissing her gently on the mouth. "So this is where you're hiding out. Glad I found you." Houston quickly introduced himself to her dining partner, extending his hand at the same time. For someone totally foreign to jealousy, Houston had a hard time keeping it at bay.

"Lynton Washington, M.D.," the man said, taking hold of Houston's hand in a firm shake. "Nice to meet you. You look familiar. Have we met somewhere before?"

"I doubt it," Kelly interjected, looking a bit dazed. "Houston is a member of the Texas Cyclones, our pro basketball team. He's a superstar." She hadn't been able to keep out of her voice the pride she felt, but she saw how Houston wished she hadn't gone there.

Houston managed to smile at Kelly's remarks, but he didn't consider himself anything akin to a superstar. A superskilled basketball player was more like it. He could definitely agree with that assessment. It was the fans who possessed the superstar, celebrity mentality, raising the popularity of sports figures to staggering heights.

Acknowledgment flashed in Lynton's eyes. "Houston Carrington, of course! Nice to meet you." Lynton looked at Kelly. "You never told me he was a friend of yours. In fact, I've never heard you mention him, period."

Kelly thought she should ignore that sarcastic remark. "There are actually two more brothers who look just like Houston. Each of the Carringtons is a popular sports figure. Houston is a triplet. His brother Austin is the Texas Wranglers' quarterback and Dallas plays pro baseball for the Texas Hurricanes."

"I know," Lynton remarked. "I know all about the local heroes. What I didn't know is that you make friends with the players you treat professionally."

Houston's eyes narrowed. "Kelly and I are a little more than friends, Dr. Washington. We're actually very close."

Kelly felt like slugging Houston again. The boy was seriously perpetrating—and he damn well knew it. How dare he delineate territorial rights on her without even knowing what her relationship was to Lynton?

Houston Carrington was getting mighty nervy.

"Do you and Kelly have some sort of history?" Houston had asked the question without compunction. "I'm afraid she hasn't mentioned you, either."

Looking like she wanted to slide under the table and slither away, Kelly was mortified at both men's rude, sarcastic comments.

Lynton raised an eyebrow. "We have quite a history, a long one. We were in medical school at the same time, ran in the same crowds and loved the same extracurricular activities. We also had a pretty good personal relationship going for us...."

"I noticed you said *had*," Houston interrupted. "I take that to mean it's over between you two."

Lynton sat back in his seat, stroking his chin thoughtfully. "If you're as close to Kelly as you claim, you should know for sure," Lynton responded in a matter-of-fact tone. "At any rate, Kelly and I will always be close." Lynton got to his feet. "I was just leaving before you came in so please don't think I'm running off on your account. I have another business appointment to make. Nice to make your acquaintance, Mr. Carrington."

Lynton made eye contact with Kelly. "I'll think about your

generous offer and get back to you ASAP. Talk to you later on. Perhaps we can have dinner this evening."

Houston looked Lynton dead in the eye. "She's already booked for breakfast, lunch, dinner and in-between snacks for the next several weeks. After that, who knows? She may be married by then."

Lynton decided not to respond to Houston and Kelly was most grateful.

Glad the clash of the titans was over, Kelly sighed with relief. "I look forward to hearing from you later, Lynton. Have a great afternoon."

Bristling at Kelly's last remark, embers of anger smoldered in Houston's eyes.

Kelly rolled her eyes hard at him. "What the hell was that about, macho jock? You were incorrigible to Lynton, you know. What gives you the right to act rude to my friends? I'd never do anything like that to embarrass you."

Looking right at Kelly, Houston didn't so much as bat an eyelash. "Me, incorrigible?" He shrugged, feigning ignorance. "Not a chance. I merely spoke my mind. If your boy has a problem with it, I don't know what to tell him. He's just a little too smug for my liking."

Kelly gritted her teeth. "Try that again…and see what happens. You won't get away with it so easily the next time. Lynton is a very dear friend of mine. He just moved to Houston to start up a medical practice. Until he gets things up and running, I offered him a temporary job in my office. He relocated here from Memphis, where he practiced sports medicine."

"From what he was spouting off, you two are more than friends. How much more than friends is what I want to know. Wondering if I'm bothered by seeing you with him? Hell, yeah! I'm highly perturbed."

Surprised by Houston's outburst, yet loving it at the same time, Kelly began to sense she meant more to him than he'd revealed. He was suddenly doing a complete one-eighty. Maybe he didn't plan on being in and out of her life like a revolving door after all.

Kelly still wasn't going to get her hopes up. Houston was the only man she knew who could smash her desires and dreams to smithereens. Keeping him in the doghouse for a while might do the trick. He was way too hot and bothered by Lynton. He had no idea what he'd done by exposing himself to her. Houston wasn't as unaffected by her as she'd thought. Jealously was written all over his face—and in bold print. "Perturbed" was a totally inaccurate assessment. He was beside himself with jealousy and outrage.

Kelly rested her elbows on the table. "It's not like you to show up unexpectedly, so what brought you down here? Is something important going on I should know about?"

Houston shot Kelly an intolerant glance. "Maybe you should tell me. Are you dating the good doctor?"

Kelly sighed heavily. "Listen, you're making a mountain out of a molehill. There's nothing there but friendship. But why the heck do you care, Mr. Noncommittal? As far as things go, you and I *are* only friends, nothing more than that. I think you've made yourself perfectly clear on the issues, repeatedly."

Houston eyed Kelly with deep curiosity, moving closer to her, until he had her practically wedged into the corner of the booth. "What's this all about? We parted ways on a good note. As for me caring, I told you I cared a lot for you. Have you conveniently forgotten, Kelly-Kel? Am I on punishment now, or what? I've called you several times."

With Houston so close to her, Kelly found it hard to breathe. His manly cologne wreaked havoc on her senses, making her want to press her lips into his and kiss him without cessation. His firm, rigid thigh brushing against hers made her think of the most intimate part of his body.

Total insanity was not that far away for Kelly. She felt crazy with desire every time she was near Houston. Then he'd turn around and make her half-crazed with anger. "I planned to return your phone calls this evening. I've been superbusy. You're here right now, yet you haven't told me why."

Houston pressed his nose into her hair and inhaled the gentle scent. "You've never lied to me before so I accept your answer. But if you're so busy, how'd you find time to have lunch with an old beau? Can you answer that one for me?"

Kelly glared at Houston. "I can, but I won't." She blew out a shaky gust of breath. "You are really beside yourself over this, aren't you? You're the last person I'd expect to come off this way. Where've you been hiding the insecurities? This is so unlike you."

"You mean to tell me you aren't flattered as hell by it? Isn't this how some women want men to act? How can you flaunt another man in my face and expect me not to have any reactions to it?"

Kelly bumped Houston hard with her shoulder, nudging him

to move away. He was hitting all the wrong buttons, the ones he should really be careful of. "First of all, you're not exclusively my man. That's just another thing you've made perfectly clear to me. Secondly, you came in here to find me, not the other way around. To flaunt a man in your face, I'd have to bring him where you are. Sound practical?"

Houston moved closer to Kelly, gently grazing her lips with his. "I don't like the way this is going down. It isn't turning out in my favor. I didn't come here to fight. I'm sure it seems quite the contrary. I keep screwing up with you big-time, huh? How can I make it right between us?"

Kelly fought the urge to taste Houston's sweet, juicy lips with the tip of her tongue. Her inner thighs were already trembling something fierce. Just the thought of connecting with him in a compromising position made her hot and wet. Her mind momentarily wandered to the cushy chair in her bedroom, imagining him sitting there naked while she straddled him.

Please have mercy on me. As Kelly's thoughts nearly incinerated her steely resolve, she quickly snapped out of the dream world she'd escaped to. "You can start by telling me why you're here."

"Fair enough. It's about the cruise. Are you still going?"

Kelly looked perplexed. "I already gave you my answer. Nothing has changed. Why'd you think it had?"

Houston shrugged. "No return phone calls are my best guess. The balcony cabins are at a minimum so we have to get on with the bookings. I'll call Austin and let him know you're still aboard. If you don't want to bunk with Lanier, I'll pay the single-supplement for a separate cabin. I know how you women like your privacy."

Kelly shook her head. "I don't mind bunking with Lanier. If I did, I'd pay the extra fees myself. Rooming with her should be loads of fun. I like Lanier."

Houston wiggled his eyebrows suggestively. "What if the sleeping arrangements are just for appearances' sake? How would you feel if Dallas wanted Lanier to sleep in our cabin on one or more nights? If so, would you let me spend the night in yours?"

Deciding she couldn't go off the deep end here, Kelly shrugged. He was only baiting her. "Sure. Twin beds are separate and they're standard in most cabins. You'd have your bed and I'd have mine. I'd never deprive Dallas and Lanier a shot at being together all night."

At odds with Kelly's response, Houston looked deeply into her eyes. "What if I wanted to push the twin beds together? Would you go for it?"

Waving for the waiter, Kelly sucked her teeth. "It's time for me to get back to my office. I've heard enough of your bull for one day, Houston Carrington. Your alter ego is a real maniac. I'm glad I never met him before now."

The waiter arrived at the table with the bill. Kelly scanned the check then laid her credit card on the black lacquer tray. Though she waited to see what Houston would do, she already had a good idea a macho response was forthcoming.

Houston removed the credit card from the tray and replaced it with one of his own. Eyeing her intently, he threw up his hands. "You mean to tell me Dr. Lynton Washington stuck you with the tab. How rich is that?"

Kelly swatted Houston on the shoulder. "For your information, I invited him to lunch." She tried pushing him toward the end of the booth to get out, but it was like trying to move a bull out the ring. Houston was solidly built and had huge muscles—and then some. The man only possessed brute strength. But he was a gentle brute with her, tender and sweet.

Houston smiled devilishly. "In a hurry to go somewhere?"

Kelly refused to show her irritation. "Back to work. I have several patients to see this afternoon."

Houston nodded. "I'll let you go, but not without conditions. Please *do not* make plans for dinner with the good doctor. Don't encourage him. The man acts on his own instincts, without any prompting from you. Instead, I'd like to fix dinner at my place, around seven. Are we on?"

Kelly looked like she wanted to murder Houston in cold blood, only she wasn't sure how she'd manage to live without him. "Seven it is." She was so curious about this sudden change in Houston she was willing to do most anything to find out his agenda. The man sure knew how to stir up intrigue.

Had he had a sudden change of heart about commitment? Did seeing her with Lynton cause reality to check in on him or had he lost his mind altogether? She was definitely curious about his altered attitude toward her.

It then dawned on Kelly that Houston had come there without knowing about Lynton. The unreturned phone calls may've prompted the surprise visit, but he could've reached her at her office or home at some point. His jealousy was painfully obvious but it was also adorable. Kelly couldn't wait to find out what was next.

Houston stood first and then helped Kelly up. "I don't have the heart to make your patients wait. That's not cool. I'll walk you back and then see you at my place later on."

Kelly lifted his hand and kissed the back of it. "I *will* be there. Goodbye, Houston." She didn't respond to his remark of walking her back to the office.

Dissatisfied with Kelly's skimpy farewell, Houston waited until they got outside to take her into his arms and kiss her thoroughly, as if he had something to prove. "That's more like it. Mind if I walk you back to the office? I don't plan to go inside. I've stirred up enough drama with your staff for one day." He kissed her again, passionately.

Kelly looked at Houston, her eyes acknowledging his remarks in a positive way. Shaken down to the core from his earth-shattering kisses, she could barely speak. As she began walking toward her office, she did her best not to fall back into his arms and beg for more. Houston was the best kisser she'd ever known, making her wish they didn't have to end. Did ignoring his phone calls cause him to react this way? Kelly had no clue what prompted the changes in him, but she wasn't interested in making him jealous.

Downtown Houston streets bustled with folks heading to lunch and those returning to their offices from a number of popular eateries. The weather was overly warm and horribly humid, but native Houstonians were used to it.

The downtown skyline was breathtaking, especially at night, featuring some of the most unique and magnificent buildings ever designed. Numerous high-rises and posh condos had popped up all over the place in the last few years. Houston was one of the few places in the nation where real estate was relatively affordable, especially when compared to the realty markets in California and New York.

"I'm thinking of buying a downtown condo I fell in love with. Since real estate sales are depressed right now, making it a buyer's market, my Realtors, Melville Campbell and Jessica Holcomb-Pack, are keeping a lookout. They feel the condo prices may fall even more." Houston laughed. "Too much information, huh?"

Kelly laughed, too. "But seriously, you should take time to make up your mind about a major purchase."

Houston had considered buying the condominium for a while now. It was a recently built structure near the Toyota Center, where the Cyclones played. His home wasn't terribly far from downtown, but it'd be nice to have a nearby place to crash after the home games, especially if the guys partied hard after a win.

"As you know, the Cyclones are a fast-breaking team. We love to run up and down the hardwood. By the time the fourth-quarter buzzer sounds, I'm totally pumped. But right after my shower, I'm looking for a soft place to land...and as quickly as possible. The condo would afford me that luxury. Plus be a good investment property." His eyes scanned her lovely body.

Definitely a soft yet firm place to land.

Kelly hunched her shoulders. "I don't know how you guys do it, but your bodies are in amazing condition. I get tired just watching how hard you play the game. Doesn't Austin own a second home? I believe I read that somewhere."

"Austin and Dallas both own more than one residence. Dallas owns a town house on South Padre Island. He loves the peaceful little beach community, up until the spring break crowd arrives. Then there's the resort condo in Puerto Vallarta, Mexico. Both are investment properties. Austin owns a resort home in the Caribbean, although the upscale high-rise apartment in Manhattan is his favorite property. He spent a lot of leisure time there before he married. Ashleigh loves to go there to shop."

"How do the guys manage so many homes?"

"Property management companies lease out the places so there's no worry for them. The homes are fully furnished and completely stocked. The places can be rented for a weekend or an entire week. I only remember one time that the Caribbean property was leased out for a full month. For the most part, the mortgage payments are paid by the renters. Austin and Dallas block off the times they plan to be there."

"Not a bad deal," Kelly remarked. "I'd like to own a resort property someday, but I think I'd worry about people damaging it."

"Just require the renter to pay a higher security deposit, equal to what the home rents for monthly."

Upon reaching the front of Kelly's office building, the two

stood toe-to-toe, their eyes locked in a warm embrace. Her insides jiggled like jelly, making it feel like her stomach was full of Mexican jumping beans. No matter how many times she was around Houston, he affected her as if they had just met, producing the same jitters in her as their first passionate kiss had.

Houston bent his head and kissed her lightly on the lips. "Until this evening."

"How many times have we said that already?" She laughed. "Until this evening," she breathed on a soft sigh.

Stretched out on the black leather sofa in his state-of-the-art media room, utterly annoyed, yet worried beyond understanding, Houston glanced at the wall clock for the umpteenth time. Kelly hadn't shown up at seven o'clock. It was nearly eight. He hadn't reached her on her home or cell phones although he'd made several attempts. He saw no point in trying to contact her at her office since it was way past normal office hours.

Rising from the sofa, Houston sauntered into the formal dining room, where the table had been intimately set for two. China, silverware and crystal were laid out in fine fashion to reflect the romantic interlude he had in mind.

Angelica had even been called on to help out Houston with his dinner plans. After she had baked a peach cobbler, one of Kelly's favorite desserts, she had helped him prepare the meal and also arrange the crystal vase of beautiful pink and white roses.

The taper candles had burned down considerably, so Houston blew them out. Hoping the expensive tenderloin hadn't overcooked, he ran to the kitchen to take it out of the oven. Grateful that he'd turned off the gas earlier, he removed the roasting pan and placed it on the granite counter.

As his flesh made brief contact with the hot metal, Houston yelped.

After tending to his minor burn with ointment and a Band-Aid, he stuck a long-handled fork into the meat. When juices began to flow instantly, he knew he hadn't ruined the tenderloin. The rice, mixed with peas and mushrooms and sautéed green beans, only needed warming. Just about everything was ready. Houston hadn't planned to put Angelica's homemade yeast rolls into the oven until just before his guest arrived.

Worried sick about Kelly, Houston began to roam his seven-bedroom home. Each one of his magnificently decorated rooms mirrored his free spirit and engaging personality. The spacious living areas were light and airy and extremely warm and inviting. Houston didn't have too much in his home that he feared someone damaging. His decorator had created a worry-free environment. He had the type of place where his family, friends and their children would feel comfortable.

Since Houston's special trophy room was off-limits to most, he wasn't concerned about anything happening to his precious sports memorabilia. Only a very few ventured beyond the double doors where many of his priceless treasures were securely stored in showy glass-shelved enclosures.

Houston stopped abruptly. He always went after what he wanted on the court so why not in his personal life? He didn't think, just grabbed his keys from the kitchen and raced out to his car.

Houston hated showing up at Kelly's place unannounced, which he saw as different from the appearance he'd made at her job earlier. He couldn't let it become a habit. Instead of trying to contact Kelly again by phone, Houston had made the irrational decision to go to her home. Something wasn't quite right. He could feel it, had convinced himself that this unannounced visit was warranted. All he had to do was figure out why.

The on-duty security patrol had allowed Houston to pass through the wrought-iron gates without question. Kelly had requested security to put him on her guest list as an authorized visitor. Houston Carrington was not a threat to her posh community.

Before ringing Kelly's doorbell, Houston took a deep breath. More nervous than he'd ever been, he stood back to await an answer. It took several minutes for him to get a response. The person standing in front of him was not Kelly. Just a few inches shorter than Houston, Lynton Washington stood there, looking smug and overconfident. Pure devilment twinkled oddly in the eyes of Kelly's friend.

Lynton smiled in a false yet charming way. "Why, Mr. Carrington, good evening. Nice to see you again. Twice in one day, no less." Lynton extended his hand to Houston.

Houston totally ignored Lynton's outstretched hand. As he turned to walk away, Kelly appeared in the marble foyer. Dressed in a green satin robe, she looked beautiful and appeared completely surprised to see him.

That Lynton had dared to answer her door had Kelly seeing red. She had just come out of the bathroom and hadn't heard the bell. Still, that didn't give her friend the right to take liberties in her home. Perhaps the offer she'd made to him had been a mistake.

"Houston, please wait," Kelly called out to him. "Where are you going?"

Houston turned toward her, giving her a look that left no uncertainty about his deep disappointment. It was one thing not to return his phone calls, but to stand him up for a date with another man was downright unforgivable. He was too upset to even address what might be happening between Kelly and the good doctor.

As though he'd been stabbed with a sharp knife, Houston felt deeply wounded. The gut-wrenching pain was excruciating. He needed to get away from this situation in a hurry. He wasn't a violent man, but he'd like nothing better than to smash in Lynton's pretty face. The smug expression he wore was enough to get anyone's blood boiling.

With tears threatening, Kelly ran after Houston. She caught up to him just as he was about to get into his car. Her short strides had been no match for his extremely long ones. "Houston, come inside and talk to me. Don't do this. Please."

Houston's razor-sharp gaze nearly leveled Kelly. "Don't do what? Disregard your feelings like you've done mine? This is insane. If you're trying to make me jealous, you've succeeded. But you've also lost out on more than you can possibly imagine. I can't be involved with someone who has a need to test my emotions. You've picked the wrong guy to try this jealousy crap on. I'm not the one, lady."

Trying desperately to hold in her emotions, Kelly moved closer to Houston. "You've jumped to the wrong conclusions, Houston Carrington. I know how this may look, but your perception is totally off the mark. I can't believe you're acting this way. Didn't you get any of my phone calls? I phoned you several times."

Houston narrowed his eyes. "Saying what? That you preferred the good doctor's company over mine? Save your lies for someone who gives a damn, Kelly. If you dialed my number, maybe it rang at some other location."

Kelly's hands itched to slap Houston across the face. She wasn't the type to lash out in a physical manner, or she would've leveled severe corporal punishment against him by now. Houston was almost as arrogant as he was sweet and charming. Kelly sucked in a deep breath to try and calm her careening nerves.

Houston was hurt. That much was obvious to her. She'd be in pain, too, under the same set of circumstances. However, she'd at least let the other person be heard. "I'm sorry you feel that way, but I'm not a liar. I resent the charge. Maybe we can discuss this when you calm down. I'd eventually like to be heard."

Houston reared up like a bucking bronco. "Don't hold your breath, Kelly. Turning purple wouldn't become you." Houston got inside his car and started the engine.

Hoping he'd let the window down, Kelly tapped on it.

Houston finally let down the driver's-side window. "What do you want from me, Kelly? If you couldn't make dinner, you could've called. I waited and worried, thinking something might've happened to you. I guess it just didn't matter to you."

Kelly huffed in frustration. "Why won't you believe I called?"

"No calls came in to my house. And why do you care what I believe? Look at how you're dressed. It appears you were involved in a real cozy evening before I arrived."

"I am dressed for bed," she said, teeth clenched. "I'm tired from a long day at the office and a serious emergency at the hospital. I was in the bathroom when the doorbell rang. My next move was straight to bed."

Houston's eyes widened. "I can believe that," he answered, revving the engine.

Kelly watched in utter agony as his car sped backward and out of her driveway.

What had happened here? Why was he so suspicious? Would she ever see him again? All Kelly could do was wonder since he hadn't revealed his intent for the future.

Houston's behavior was way over the top. Her best guess told her he was wrestling with his feelings for her. That wasn't necessarily a bad thing, but an unfair assessment of her character wouldn't bring them closer. If he believed she'd use another man to make him play ball or get off the court, he'd probably run further away. If he actually thought her capable of such a thing, the game was already lost.

Kelly wasn't the kind of woman who used a man to make another one jealous. It hurt her to think for a measly second that Houston believed she was capable of doing so. As she turned to go back into the house, she looked back and saw the car disappearing beyond the wrought-iron gates. Refusing to cry, she stifled her emotions.

Chapter 8

Feeling more anguished than ever before, Houston wrung his hands together. With his head hung low, he walked away from his brother's front door, only to turn around and go right back. His emotions had taken a severe pounding. He was a mess and he needed someone to help him make sense of what had just occurred with Kelly.

The sound of the doorbell caused Dallas to frown, hoping he wouldn't get hung up with whoever was outside. Since he wasn't fully dressed, he was worried about being late for his movie date with Lanier. Perusing his game schedule and discussing the cruise plans with the agent at the travel agency had taken longer than he'd anticipated.

Dallas instantly knew his brother was in trouble. The tortured look on Houston's face was a dead giveaway. The siblings greeted each other with a warm, manly hug. "Come on in, man. What's up? You look upset."

Houston followed Dallas into the family room, where they took seats on matching leather recliners. Dallas offered his brother something to drink. Houston declined.

Immediately launching into what had happened with Kelly and him, Houston's eyes blazed with fury as he told Dallas the entire story. His anger over the situation came across to his brother in spades.

Houston's ranting over a woman surprised Dallas, yet he already knew his brother cared about Kelly. He now had a clear indication of how deep his feelings ran. Dallas was amused by Houston's foreign encounter, but he wouldn't let it show. It appeared to him that his brother could no longer deny what he felt for Dr. Kelly Charleston.

Houston had finally fallen off the deep end. Dallas was pretty sure of it.

Dallas slapped his hand down hard on his thigh. "Man, you should've seen this coming. What do you expect from Kelly under the present circumstances? She has no way of knowing if you plan to run in and out of her life at will. With all your so-called rules, the lady is probably worried sick about getting too involved with you."

Houston put his face into his hands. "Man, this is not cool. I don't like what's happening to me. I've never been jealous of another man or envious of any situation in my adult life. Kelly hanging out with Lynton has me insane. I guess it *is* my fault."

Dallas smirked. "*You guess?* Who else's fault could it be? You've been shadowboxing with this relationship from the start. *Are* you in love with Kelly?"

It was a query Houston really didn't know how to answer; he looked puzzled by it. What he felt for Kelly was deep—deeper than anything he'd ever felt before. If love made folks go as crazy as he felt, he wasn't sure he wanted any part of it.

Looking bewildered, Houston scratched his head. "Let me put it like this. I desperately want Kelly and I don't want anyone else to have her. I hate this Lynton guy being anywhere near her. I can barely stand the thought of her with another man. She occupies way more space in my head than I'm comfortable with. My heart is breaking over what went down between us this evening. I can't believe I'm terrified of losing her. Now please answer this question for me. Am I in love, Dallas?"

Feeling sorry for Houston, Dallas nodded in the affirmative. "Madly!"

Houston had to wonder if Dallas was right on the money. He couldn't admit the truth if he wasn't totally sure about his feelings. How could things change so drastically? Would he feel so scared of losing Kelly if Lynton hadn't come back into her life?

The honest answer was that Lynton really didn't have anything to do with what Houston felt or didn't feel for Kelly. He may've sped things up, but Houston didn't want to give him any credit. However, her friend *had* introduced him to the ugly green monster called jealously. Houston realized he had some serious decisions to make. His inability to commit was the core issue and he knew he had to deal with that first.

Dallas had just finished looking over his game schedule before Houston had arrived. "Man," he said, "I have a conflict with the dates for the birthday cruise. I don't know why I didn't see it when I first checked my calendar. A home game is slated at the very end of the cruise. I'd have to leave the ship early, just like we did on the Valentine's Day sailing." Dallas scanned the schedule again, shaking his head in dismay.

"It's a real bummer." Houston shrugged. "But we've already said if all of us can't make the trip, we'd just send Mom and Dad. We can do a family cruise later on."

Dallas suddenly smiled. "Since the home game is late evening, I can fly back to Houston before the ship leaves port. It's the only solution." Excited that he could possibly work things out, Dallas pumped his fist in triumph.

"I hope scheduling works out for you, man. Speaking of out, I'm out of here. I've got lots of thinking to do. Never dreamed I'd be in this position. Not ever. I'm still not sure I'm in love. Whatever it is it has turned my world topsy-turvy."

Dallas chuckled. "It's love, all right. You need to stop denying it. It is what it is."

Houston palmed both sides of his head. "Whatever, man!"

Listening to Kelly's messages, one right after the other, Houston cringed inwardly. The time of the incoming calls indicated she'd called while he'd been at the market with his mother earlier in the day. He hadn't heard the stutter dial on the house phone, which was the message indicator. He'd only used his cell phone.

The situation didn't explain to Houston why Kelly hadn't bothered to call his mobile number about the hospital emergency. Nor did it explain why Lynton was at her home when he'd arrived or why'd he'd opened the door. Houston still had a hard time with the way she was dressed. He considered a silk robe intimate apparel.

After listening to the last message, Houston hung up the phone. Silently, he vowed to get rid of the answering device and get one equipped with red flashing lights. Unless he actually picked up the phone to use it, he wouldn't know he had messages. He had to admit the internal message center hadn't been a bother until now.

The device had only caused him to make an absolute fool of himself with Kelly.

Houston knew for a fact he had to eat crow. Thinking about how horrible Kelly must've felt by his accusations, he wouldn't blame her if she demanded him to eat it raw. That was, if she agreed to see him again. Giving things time to cool off wasn't in his best interest. Now that he'd finally heard the evidence of her calls, he knew he had to immediately let her know how sorry he was and how deeply he regretted doubting her.

As Houston dialed Kelly's home number, his fingers trembled. When he didn't get an answer, he wasn't too surprised. But it hurt like hell. *Was she busy with the good doctor or just refusing to take his call?* The mental queries caused his stomach to tighten.

It was 9:20. *So much for a romantic evening.* Eating dinner alone wasn't appealing to him, but he rarely got upset enough to lose his appetite altogether. He thought of all the uneaten food. Houston was past hungry. Ravenous was more like it. Eager to chow down, he made a beeline for the kitchen.

Just to bring about a calmer mood within, Houston lit a few candles to dine by, after turning on a CD featuring serenity-inducing music. After fixing his plate, he sat down on a metal-backed stool at the granite breakfast bar. Piled high on a dinner plate was the delicious-smelling food he had warmed in the microwave.

While Houston consumed his meal, he thought about the things he had planned to discuss with Kelly over dinner. They really hadn't talked about what each expected from the other if they actually ended up dating exclusively. The topic had been pretty much taboo with him from day one. The way he'd been carrying on throughout the hours of this day, like a jealous lover, a totally directionless maniac, no one would ever guess that he didn't already think of Kelly as exclusively his.

Faced with a possible rival in Dr. Lynton Washington, Houston had wisely put himself on notice, just as Dallas had recommended. His brother had spoken to him about it in no uncertain terms. The Carrington men didn't pull punches with each other, no matter how painful the subject. Dallas had given Houston much food for thought.

Neither of Houston's brothers or his father lied to him when he went to them for advice. He'd only gone to Dallas because he hadn't been able to reach Austin. Dallas was aware that Austin was normally the first one they both sought out during troubling times. He had even mentioned it in a joking manner. Austin dealt fairly with his siblings.

Houston's mind turned back to Kelly, who was exactly what he had in mind for the woman he'd one day marry. She was loving, warm and outgoing—in other words, she possessed many qualities he found so endearing in his mother. Austin had married a mirror image of their mother and Dallas had found a lot of Angelica's characteristics in Lanier.

Could good fortune strike thrice among three brothers in the same family?

Kelly could easily fit in to the fast-paced lifestyle of a popular sports personality. She was classy, kind and even-tempered, somewhat laid-back, but not easily intimidated by anyone. Houston had seen what female fans did to the more timid spouses of athletes. Female groupies often ignored sports wives like they weren't even there, daring to boldly flaunt and throw themselves in the faces of their favorite superstar heroes.

The often out-of-control groupies were one of the things Houston didn't want a woman he loved to be faced with. Deciding not to marry until after he'd retired from the world of sports was in part due to the blatant behaviors of some females. The same madness occurred at home games, but it happened more frequently on the road.

Houston wanted his wife secure in the knowledge that he loved her, only her. He didn't want her to think he was off cavorting with any woman who offered up her body to him. Road games were especially hard on personal relationships. He'd seen the vast amount of unrestrained cheating and lying that went on in sports arenas and entertainment venues all over the country and around the world. Houston had no desire to be a part of those wild scenes as a single man, let alone as a married one.

After Houston gave a lot of thought to what marriage might be like for him, he concluded that he first had to commit to an exclusive relationship. Considering anything deeper than that only came after a relationship had grown into something beyond romance. *Could he and Kelly have that kind of special liaison?*

If the relationship didn't blossom, Houston was sure he'd be the one at fault.

Realizing how arrogant and unfair his thoughts were, Houston laughed nervously. Here he was thinking of possibly committing to an exclusive relationship, but he hadn't even considered that Kelly might see things differently. Maybe she didn't want that kind of closeness with him. He certainly hadn't bothered to ask her what she wanted.

Houston knew he'd been awfully busy telling Kelly what he didn't want.

A relationship involved the feelings of both parties. Discussing Kelly's take on the situation had to come before he ever attempted to make any sort of commitment to her. Houston finally realized he'd been presumptuous all along about a possible relationship with Kelly. That had to change immediately. He wasn't alone in this.

As Kelly had stated earlier, she'd like her voice to be heard. He quietly vowed to hear what her needs were, without commenting until after she was through. Until he and Kelly knew what level of interest they had in each other, there wasn't a fighting chance.

Ashleigh and Lanier were happy to see Kelly when she'd shown up. Lauren, one of the foster girls, had twisted her ankle at the park. They'd called on Kelly to see if she could check out the injury. Neither was sure if emergency treatment was necessary.

Kelly gently and carefully wrapped the swollen left ankle in an Ace bandage. "Lauren, you need to stay off this foot. Keep it elevated and rest it on a couple of pillows when you're seated or lying down." The young girl nodded and smiled.

Kelly turned to Ashleigh and Lanier. "I'll need to see our girl in the office tomorrow for an X-ray. I don't believe it's broken, but we need to be sure. I also want to fit you for a pair of crutches to get around on."

Ashleigh and Lanier were grateful for Kelly's help. It was very late in the evening and she had gotten out of her bed to come to Haven House to tend to Lauren's injury.

"We appreciate you," Ashleigh said. "What about a cup of coffee or tea?"

Kelly nodded. "Coffee might help keep me alert on the drive back home."

After Lauren hugged and thanked Kelly, Ashleigh helped her to her room.

"We just can't thank you enough. Lauren and her sister, Stephanie, are the only girls we haven't gotten medical cards for yet," Lanier explained to Kelly. "We hope they come soon, for this very reason. We never know when an emergency will arise."

"Don't worry. You can call on me for any medical emergency before you get the insurance coverage. If it's something out of my area of expertise, I have wonderful colleagues I can tap. There are a number of good physicians who'll help me out if I ask a favor. It's a pretty common practice among health-care professionals."

"Can't doing that open you up to malpractice suits?" Lanier inquired.

"I take the Hippocratic oath seriously. I'm here because medical help was needed."

Ashleigh came back to the table with coffee and two mugs. "And we'll never forget this act of kindness. It means a lot to us, Kelly."

Once Ashleigh served hot drinks to Lanier and their guest, she slowly maneuvered her pregnant body into a brown leather recliner. While sipping on her bottle of apple juice, she took one look at Lanier and frowned. "You look troubled, Lanier. Is there trouble with Dallas?"

Lanier curled her legs up under her to get comfortable. "Dallas is nothing short of my heaven. It's not about him." Lanier scowled. "I didn't want to bother you with this, Ash, especially with you expecting. But I'm concerned over a conversation Lauren and Stephanie had with me about their aunt."

Ashleigh looked concerned. "What was said?"

Lanier waved her hands about. "The girls overheard their aunt talking to her live-in boyfriend about taking them from here because she needs extra money. According to the girls, Sandra talked about petitioning the courts for legal guardianship. They *do not* want to live with her. Lauren and Stephanie made that point clear to me."

Ashleigh shook her head in dismay. "Sandra Gossett is Karen Liggin's sister, who is the deceased mother of Lauren and Stephanie," she explained to Kelly. "There's nothing we can do to stop her from trying to get custody. If the girls don't want to go, the courts should consider their feelings."

Lanier nodded. "The boyfriend is a convicted felon. That should heavily figure into the court's decision if her home is fit or not. The social worker shared the sensitive information with me when I called to ask if Sandra could take the girls. She told me Karen didn't want her sister to have her children under any circumstances. Stephanie and Lauren became wards of the state a month or so before their mother died."

Ashleigh sighed heavily. "We'll have to wait to see how it unfolds. I just hope whatever happens is favorable for the girls. Never worry about sharing anything troubling with me because I'm pregnant.

Everyone thinks I'm terribly fragile, especially Austin. I won't shatter into tiny fragments. I can promise you that."

Lanier smiled to show her appreciation of Ashleigh's reassurances. "Are you and the baby excited about the cruise? I am. I can hardly wait to sail."

Ashleigh massaged her stomach. "We're ecstatic. I'm glad you and Dallas worked out the details for you to go. Martha and Norma will do a great job. The girls love them. Besides, they're so motherly. You need to relax and chill out. Nothing will happen to our children under their loving care. I have a lot of confidence in both women, Lani."

Ashleigh looked over at Kelly. "Sorry about that. I hope you don't feel left out."

Kelly smiled with understanding. "Not at all. I'm a real good listener."

"I'm relieved. It wasn't our intent to be rude to you. Are you excited about the cruise?" Lanier asked Kelly.

Raising her brows, Kelly shrugged, setting down her coffee cup. "I was. I'd planned to go, thrilled by the invite, but a rather unexpected twist has occurred." She explained to Lanier and Kelly what had happened with Houston and her earlier.

Ashleigh's mouth fell agape. "Houston acted like that? That's hard to believe. He's always so cool, calm and collected. I hope you know what his behavior means."

Kelly shrugged. "I'm afraid I don't. What *does* it mean?"

"The boy is in love," Lanier responded before Ashleigh got the same words out her mouth. "There's no other explanation for his odd behavior. *Did* you call him?"

Kelly nodded. "Several times…and I also left numerous messages."

"When he hears them," Ashleigh said, "he'll probably feel like a heel."

"I don't want him to feel bad." Kelly sighed. "I want him to know I'm not a liar." Kelly drained her coffee mug. "I really need to get on home," she said, hastening to her feet. "Come to my office at noon tomorrow so you can get right in and out. We close for lunch. No other patients should be there, unless we fall behind schedule."

Lanier hugged Kelly and Ashleigh followed suit. The two friends escorted the doctor out to her car. Austin pulled up as Kelly got into her car.

* * *

His nude body still wet from his morning shower, Houston wrapped a large white towel around his waist. He then reached for the ringing phone. Hearing Kelly's voice made him smile and put fear in him, all at the same time. Walking into the bedroom, he sat down on the edge of the mattress. "Good morning to you, too. Nice greeting. You sound pretty chipper today."

Kelly couldn't stop staring at the flowers on her desk. Houston had had them sent to her office. The white, yellow and pink long-stemmed roses were arranged to spell out a special message: *I'm sorry.*

"You *are* an original, Houston. The roses are beautiful! Thank you so much."

Lying lay back on the bed, Houston dangled his long legs off the end of the mattress. "I *am* sorry, you know. I was horrible to you last evening. Is there anything else I can do to make up for it?"

"There is. I'd like for you to simply talk to me about what's happening between us. Our relationship is all over the map. I think we need clarity. Is it possible?"

"I agree. It's actually imperative. Does this evening work for you?"

"After six o'clock is fine. My last patient is at three-thirty, but I'll have paperwork to tend to. Can you come over to my place? Or do you want to meet elsewhere?"

"Your place is fine. I'll bring takeout. Any food suggestions?"

"Chinese or pizza is good. You decide."

"See you at six-thirty. Have a great day, Kelly."

"You, too, Houston."

Houston sat up to cradle the phone. As he lay back down, he thought about how sweet and innocent Kelly had sounded. She hadn't mentioned one word about his bad-boy tactics of the previous evening, but he had expected her to give him holy hell.

Had the shoe been on the other foot, Houston knew he would've acted sullen and withdrawn. Any conversation would've had to be pried out of him. Kelly had a forgiving nature, a great characteristic to possess. He was also pretty forgiving, but his other character flaws were numerous and glaring.

With so many things to do before the morning hours blew by, Houston jumped up and began to dress in haste. Always careful to look his best, his choices in attire included a pair of casual black slacks and a snowy-white, summer-weight V-neck sweater. A shiny pair of black Italian leather shoes complemented his relaxed look. No matter what style of dress he wore, the sexy power forward turned heads wherever he went.

Houston was having a hard time concentrating on the meeting with his brothers. His mind was on the early-morning call from Kelly and their date for later in the evening. Nearly finished with finalizing the details for the birthday cruise, the three brothers sat outdoors on Austin's patio. The four-day sailing itinerary would give them plenty of time to show Angelica how much she truly meant to them—and to also accommodate Ashleigh's traveling restrictions. Her obstetrician had approved the trip, but for no longer than five days.

The guys had also discussed the idea of purchasing their mother a complete formal ensemble and a pair of diamond earrings. Ashleigh and Lanier would help them select the clothing, shoes and jewelry. Both women had a keen eye for fashion.

Austin took a sip of his ice-cold lemonade. "Maybe we should just let Mom choose her diamonds, guys. She may not like what we select. What do you think?"

Dallas nodded. "Good point. We can give her a diamond gift card from one of the local, reputable jewelers. That way she can pick out anything she wants. Since I have back-to-back home games, I won't be able to shop with you guys. Think you knuckleheads can handle things without me?"

Houston feigned a punch aimed at Dallas's jaw. "I *know* we can. You always find a reason to disappear when it comes to shopping sprees. You won't be missed."

"Thanks for lifting my spirit, little bro," Dallas shot back sarcastically.

Austin laughed heartily. "Put a lid on it, guys. No matter who does it, the job gets done. Do we want to impose a spending limit for the jewels?"

Both Dallas and Houston shook their heads in the negative.

"If we choose the jewelry," Houston said, "a return policy will apply."

Austin nodded. "Good point. Split three ways, the sky is our limit! We'll discuss the final costs before purchasing the gift card or choosing the diamonds. Okay?"

Dallas and Houston agreed wholeheartedly to Austin's plan. For the next hour or so, the Carrington brothers talked sports. Austin and Houston planned to be in attendance for Dallas's upcoming home games.

Austin's off-season ran from January to August. If his team didn't make the playoffs, or if ousted before the Super Bowl, his downtime was longer. Houston's regular season ended in April. If they got into the NBA playoffs, the games ran until mid-June. Spring training began in March for Dallas. His season could run well into October, depending on how long his team lasted in winning a World Series spot.

Later that night Houston helped Kelly clean up her kitchen now that they'd finished eating the delectable Chinese takeout he'd brought along with him. The freshly cooked curried shrimp and mushroom chicken had been very tasty. The crisp, petite spring rolls were delicious. Houston had also brought along a steaming order of hot and sour soup.

While Houston thought about the topics he and Kelly might discuss, he rinsed off the glasses and silverware and put them in the dishwasher. After filling the dishwasher's soap dispenser, Houston turned on the power with a flick of an electric switch. Once Kelly hung up the dish towels to dry, she and her guest quickly escaped to the massive family room, where leather recliners and other comfortable furnishings were housed. A large plasma screen and state-of-the-art stereo equipment, featuring Bose speakers, made the room a great entertainment spot.

Since Kelly knew Houston planned to talk about their relationship, she didn't bother to turn on the television or stereo. She sat down on the sofa and he took one of the plush, oversize chairs facing her.

Appearing nervous, Kelly looked over at Houston, her eyes blinking abnormally. "Do you want to go first?"

Houston shrugged, desiring to get this conversation under way and over with as soon as possible. "Okay by me. I guess I first need to ask if you're interested in having an exclusive relationship. If so, what are your expectations?"

Kelly took a moment to ponder Houston's surprising questions. "Before I respond to your query about exclusivity, I'd like to know

KIMANI™
ROMANCE

An Important Message from the Publisher

Dear Reader,

Because you've chosen to read one of our fine novels, I'd like to say "thank you"! And, as a special way to say thank you, I'm offering to send you two more Kimani™ Romance novels and two surprise gifts – absolutely FREE! These books will keep it real with true-to-life African American characters that turn up the heat and sizzle with passion.

Please enjoy the free books and gifts with our compliments...

Glenda Howard

For Kimani Press

Peel off Seal and Place Inside...

EDITOR'S FREE GIFTS SEAL THANK YOU

THE EDITOR'S "THANK YOU" FREE GIFTS INCLUDE:

▶ Two Kimani™ Romance Novels

▶ Two exciting surprise gifts

YES! I have placed my Editor's "thank you" Free Gifts seal in the space provided at right. Please send me 2 FREE books, and my 2 FREE Mystery Gifts. I understand that I am under no obligation to purchase anything further, as explained on the back of this card.

PLACE FREE GIFTS SEAL HERE

168 XDL E4K4   **368 XDL E4K4**

FIRST NAME   LAST NAME

ADDRESS

APT.#   CITY

STATE/PROV.   ZIP/POSTAL CODE

Thank You!

The Reader Service — Here's How It Works:

Accepting your 2 free books and 2 free gifts places you under no obligation to buy anything. You may keep the books and gifts and return the shipping statement marked "cancel." If you do not cancel, about a month later we'll send you 4 additional books and bill you just $4.69 each in the U.S., or $5.24 each in Canada, plus 50¢ shipping and handling per book in the U.S. and 75¢ per book in Canada and applicable taxes if any.* You may cancel at any time, but if you choose to continue, every month we'll send you 4 more books, which you may either purchase at the discount price or return to us and cancel your subscription.

*Terms and prices subject to change without notice. Sales tax applicable in N.Y. Canadian residents will be charged applicable provincial taxes and GST. Offer not valid in Quebec. All orders subject to approval. Credit or debit balances in a customer's account(s) may be offset by any other outstanding balance owed by or to the customer. Offer available while quantities last. Books received may vary. Please allow 4 to 6 weeks for delivery.

If offer card is missing write to: The Reader Service, P.O. Box 1867, Buffalo, NY 14240-1867 or visit us at www.ReaderService.com

BUSINESS REPLY MAIL
FIRST-CLASS MAIL   PERMIT NO. 717   BUFFALO, NY

POSTAGE WILL BE PAID BY ADDRESSEE

THE READER SERVICE
PO BOX 1867
BUFFALO NY 14240-9952

NO POSTAGE
NECESSARY
IF MAILED
IN THE
UNITED STATES

how you define the term. And are you referring to *us* in this particular instance or just speaking in general terms?"

Houston wasn't surprised that Kelly wanted things spelled out for her in plain English. She liked to be well-informed on issues affecting her life. That she hadn't demanded clarity long before now was the real shocker. "A relationship involving just two people is how I define the word—sole, undivided. Of course I'm referring to us. Sorry I didn't make myself clearer."

"Thanks for clearing that up." Kelly wrung her hands together, praying she'd choose the right words. "We both lead busy lives, with very little time for ourselves, let alone nurturing a personal relationship. You're on the road a lot and I'm in my office or at the hospital all hours of the day and night. Under our present circumstances, I don't know if exclusive will work for either of us."

Houston looked as if a bomb had exploded right in his face. *Talk about presumptuous.* He had believed he was the only person not wanting an exclusive relationship, but it appeared he'd been dead wrong. Now that he was ready to make a commitment to date only Kelly, she didn't seem too interested.

At a loss for words, Houston stared at Kelly, his brain numbing. "For once in my life, I don't know what to say. I'm stumped. Your response isn't what I'd expected."

Looking perplexed, Kelly moved her head slightly back. "What did you expect?"

Houston hunched his shoulders. "I'm not sure, but it wasn't that." His expression turned somber. "I've been operating under the assumption that you wanted to make a commitment to our relationship. I thought you'd like nothing better than for us to date exclusively. How could I have been so wrong? Why do I suddenly feel stupid?"

Kelly got up from her seat and deposited herself on the floor at Houston's feet. After a few moments of silence, she looked up at him and placed her hand on his knee. "I don't know how to say this other than to just come out with it. I want us to see more of each other than we do, but not necessarily go exclusive. I know commitment doesn't work for you. It was made clear on our first date. Still, I had hopes of us growing close. I guess it's impossible, especially when you're fearful of personal relationships."

Houston really felt stupid yet less fearful. Kelly had intoxicated his mind. Coming up with something sensible was hard. His arrogance had left him with no easy way out. "I guess our communication hasn't been effective. After I shared my initial feelings on dating, I guess I expected you to accept it, regardless of how you felt. How close do you want us to get, Kelly? What exactly do you need from me?"

As though they needed warming, Kelly rubbed her hands together. "Establishing a great friendship with you was important in the beginning." *Even though my heart was already long gone on you.* "I'm not sure if I don't date other people due to the lack of time or if it's because I'm not interested. I can say I *am* exclusive with you, since I'm not seeing anyone else. It's not that I don't get daily offers, 'cause I get plenty."

"I'm sure you do. You're beautiful and I'm sure men are hotly pursuing you."

Kelly sighed hard. "Houston, I'm not trying to push you into something you obviously don't want. I'm not sure I can deal with long absences in a relationship. I've also thought about the cruise. Maybe it's not such a good idea for me to go. I won't lie about wanting more quality time with you, a lot more. I *am* already emotionally involved here. I should probably cut my losses before I get badly hurt."

Houston moved closer to Kelly and threaded his fingers through her hair. "Hey, slow down a bit, lady doctor. Neither of us will get hurt." He leaned forward until his chin rested on her shoulder. "We came together this evening to talk things through…and we're doing it. Don't turn and run the other way, Kelly-Kel, not when you're catching up to me. My feet *are* pretty tired," Houston joked. "I got a lot of blisters from running."

Kelly felt a warm rush deep inside her belly. Houston's boyish grin was heart-melting. Charm flowed from within him. Without a conscious effort on his part, he made her glow. He was a natural. The urge to kiss him nearly overpowered her. His lips looked inviting and hers were hungry for the sweet taste of him.

Kelly laughed softly. "Don't look at me like that, Houston. I'm not so strong."

His gaze grew intense. "Look at you how?"

She slowly lowered her lashes. "Like I'm the only woman that exists for you, like you could positively devour me in one huge gulp."

As Houston inhaled the flowery scent of her hair, his eyes softened. "Wow! That's some powerful eye contact. Would it scare you to know you're the only woman I see when I'm with you? And, when we're apart, you're the only one I want to be with?"

"Those are questions you should answer. Your fear has a distinctive odor. The question isn't if you're scared of me or not. It's more like *why* are you afraid of me?"

It wasn't Kelly Houston feared. The dread was in his deep feelings for her. His life was complex. It was hard enough dealing with his personal issues during basketball season, let alone taking on someone else's. Comings and goings would remain constant, as long as he was a professional athlete. Time wasn't always his to control.

Relationships involved deep emotions. Houston knew he'd have to be constantly mindful of his woman's emotional stability—and his own. Separations were hard on families and lovers alike, even for brief periods. How many times had he heard teammates on the cell phone telling loved ones not to cry, saying everything would be okay and they'd talk later, from the privacy of a hotel suite? *Countless times.*

Chapter 9

"Many unforeseen problems arise for professional sports couples, especially during away games," Houston told Kelly. "A road trip can sometimes cover a six-day span or even more. It's a long time to be away from someone you love. Personal troubles often show up on different fields of play, distracting players from their tasks."

Only one lover at a time. Houston had stayed committed to his motto, his one and only lover. Basketball was his leading lady. Then Kelly appeared out of nowhere.

Houston looked into her eyes. Taking hold of both her hands, he shook his head from side to side. "Just the thought of you not on the cruise disturbs me. More troublesome is not having you in my life. I don't want that to happen. If you're not interested in doing exclusive, please tell me what'll keep you around. I don't want to lose you, Kelly, or what it seems we're building together."

For starters, making love to me might keep me around. She could only wish.

Kelly was more interested in exclusive than Houston could imagine. Laughing inwardly, she puckered her mouth. Pressing her lips to his, she gave him a sweet kiss.

"I'd like more time with you. I don't want a relationship with far, few and in-betweens. We have fun together. Good times make it hard for me to wait until the next one. You men have the luxury of calling the shots. It occurs to me to ask you out, but I don't. It somehow doesn't seem right. I don't want to be seen as aggressive."

Touched by her sincere remarks, Houston tenderly framed Kelly's face with his hands, kissing her forehead. "I like aggressive," he joked, chuckling softly. "Spending more time together isn't such a tall order. It's not even an unreasonable request. I'd love more time with you. Nothing would give me greater pleasure."

Kelly's mind was hard at work trying to figure out what had

prompted the sudden changes in Houston. When the couple of episodes with the *good doctor* came to mind, she frowned. She didn't want Houston to spend more time with her simply because he felt threatened by her relationship with her dear friend Lynton.

Kelly didn't want Houston to feel jealous of anyone. Since she wanted clarity on why he had had such a sudden change of heart, she decided to ask. Wringing her hands nervously, she fastened her eyes on him. "You've certainly changed your position on things, drastically. Does Lynton have anything to do with it?"

"He does, inasmuch as it has to do with realization and revelation. Lynton helped me realize how much you mean to me. The personal transformations come from the changes you've caused in my heart. I had to acknowledge the alterations before I could act on them. Lynton also aided me in revelation. I want us to explore our relationship in depth, Kelly. I'm ready to take things to the next level. Are you?"

As Kelly fell into Houston's arms, she could hardly contain her joy. "I'm ready, Houston, definitely ready!" Sobering rather quickly, she tilted her head back slightly. "Now exactly what does that mean for us? What do you consider the next level?"

Houston laughed softly. "It wouldn't be like you not to thoroughly question it all. Even if you aren't interested in exclusive, I am. I'd like for you and me to hang out together as often as we can. Can we do just us?"

Kelly nodded eagerly. "I didn't say I wasn't interested in exclusive. What I said was I didn't know if it'd work with us. Sorry I wasn't clearer. I'm *not* opposed to your suggestion and I *am* willing to give it a try." Kelly giggled. "Isn't this the point where we should exchange class rings or utter some kind of vow?"

Smiling warmly, Houston removed his diamond NBA championship ring and placed it on Kelly's finger. "This beautiful baby will have to do until I can get you something dainty in gold or platinum."

Looking stunned, Kelly stared hard at the ring that was way too big for her slender finger. She quickly pulled it off. "I can't accept this, even as a temporary measure. I can wait." Kelly put the ring back on his finger and kissed it. "This is too precious to entrust to anyone, but thanks for making such a grand gesture."

"You're welcome. I understand not wanting the responsibility of safeguarding my championship ring. A kiss will have to do for now, a long, lingering one."

Kelly wrapped her arms around Houston's neck. "*That,* I can do."

The kiss was staggering, passionate beyond her wildest dreams.

Houston gently nudged her. "I need to know you'll still make the cruise."

"I'll be there. I promise not to back out."

Houston appeared pleased. "Good. I'm glad that's settled."

As the couple got into discussing the kinds of crazy things that happened to sports figures on road trips, Houston thought of his own wild experiences. Lifting Kelly's chin, he closely studied her lovely features. He then looked right into her eyes. "I promise to be faithful to you at home and on the road."

Kelly blushed. "You don't need to assure me of that. I trust you."

"I wanted to let you know where my head and heart are." Houston didn't want Kelly to imagine all sorts of wild scenarios when he was away from home. "Once I commit, I don't go back on my word. It's my bond. Houston Carrington has fully committed himself to Kelly Charleston."

Ecstatic by his remarks, Kelly smiled broadly. "My life as a doctor is extremely busy. I need someone in my life who understands my time isn't always my own. Last-minute and unavoidable situations pop up a lot." She then explained wanting a mate who didn't get upset because she was around superstar male athletes, and she needed someone who cared about her purpose in life. "Becoming a doctor was all I ever dreamed of."

"I know all about crazy schedules. I also understand how the unexpected comes up. I'm not the type of guy who has to know your every move. I admit I'll probably get worried if I don't hear from you for a long time. Unfortunately, you're familiar with that side of me. Sorry I made a mountain out of a molehill."

Kelly slid her hand down the side of his face. "I want to please you, Houston, but I can't forget to satisfy me. I tried to gratify my parents by following in their footsteps, but I fell short. That's not how it should be. I finally learned I had to be my own person, forge my own path and create my own successes. Mom and Dad were dead set against a career in sports medicine for me. I went with the desires of my heart instead of theirs. I guess orthopedic medicine wasn't as prestigious as becoming heart surgeons like them."

"You have a lot to be proud of. You're a brilliant doctor and I'm glad you took your own path. My brothers and I loved sports long before we were old enough to play peewee leagues. Dad tossed us footballs and baseballs and played basketball with us when we were tiny guys. I can't recall a time when we weren't active in sports."

"Like mine, your profession is in your blood. You should be proud, too. My busy schedule kept me from asking too much of others. There was a time I couldn't fit any social stuff into my life, period. I can assure you I'll trust you wholeheartedly. I'll also give you the royal boot if you trash my belief in you."

Houston wrapped up Kelly tightly in his arms. "I believe you'll do exactly that. But you won't have to. This is brand-new for me. I don't take on anything I don't plan to put forth my very best. I'll give our relationship all I can. But if it doesn't work for me, Kelly, I won't hesitate to tell you."

"Sounds fair to me. I'll do the same. Now I have something else to tell you."

Houston frowned. "Uh-oh! Got a feeling I'm not going to like it."

"You won't. I agreed to let Lynton stay with me until he locates a nice place. I promised to help him house-hunt, until he finds something. He promises not to take too long to sign a lease."

"You were so right. I hate the idea. But I think I can live with it. After I have a little talk with him, he'll probably rent a place a lot sooner than he originally planned."

"Houston, no, you can't do that. I can manage Lynton just fine."

"I hope so. I don't care for him one bit. He's arrogant and selfish."

"Hmm, sounds like somebody else I know, who can bring it on without any warning. I think you know him, too. You see him every time you look in the mirror."

"No way are you talking about me." He stroked his chin. "Well, maybe I'm a little cocky, but it's rare for that side of me to surface off the hardwood. I'm not selfish but I guess I can be somewhat arrogant. However, I prefer to think of it as confident."

"*Selfish* was the wrong word to use. You're definitely a very giving man. Please promise me you'll let me handle Lynton. He's a great guy once you get to know him. He has helped me on numerous occasions. I just want to give back to a friend in need."

Houston promised Kelly not to take Lynton to task. He knew she *was* a loyal friend. He easily recalled what she'd put up with from him already. "The one thing I won't do is become a controlling force in your life, not that you'd let me. I love your independence and the sultry sass in you. I won't tamper with either."

"I'm happy to hear it. This girl can't be controlled, but I am fairly easy to negotiate with."

Houston grinned. *"Negotiate.* Now that's a word I like to hear. Listening to what the other person has to say opens us up to all kinds of possibilities."

"I think so, too," Kelly said. "Entering into a discussion is much better than one person trying to have their own way all the time. Yet there are times when we have to refuse to negotiate. There are some decisions that only we can make for ourselves."

Houston felt they'd covered a lot of territory and had now arrived at a good understanding. It was time to put their plans into action. With that in mind, Houston kissed Kelly thoroughly. She shivered as his tongue found hers. Keeping his mouth locked onto hers, he stretched out on the sofa and brought her down on top of him. His hardened sex was hard to ignore, but he tried his best to do so for both their sakes.

As much as Houston wanted to make love to Kelly, he thought they needed to get used to the idea of being a couple. Lovemaking would hopefully come in time. He believed she'd eventually want to make love to him—and he definitely desired the same.

In the morning, seated at the kitchen table inside Haven House, Kelly, Ashleigh and Lanier were drinking hot tea. Kelly had stopped by before her office hours to check on Lauren and to drop off a few tubes of Biofreeze, an analgesic pain reliever in gel form. No fractures had been revealed on the teenager's X-rays from a week ago. The diagnosis was a bad sprain, just as Kelly had guessed. She had again recommended Lauren stay off the ankle and use the crutches.

The girls were in the game room watching television. It was raining cats and dog outside so the teenagers' usual trek to the park was canceled until the weather cleared. Plenty of indoor entertainment was provided for them.

As Lanier stirred low-cal sweetener into her teacup, Kelly couldn't help but notice how unhappy she looked. Her puffy and slightly red eyes indicated she'd been crying or that she hadn't slept well. Although Kelly was concerned she didn't feel she should pry into Lanier's private affairs.

Looking as if she were in another zone, Lanier stared into her tea. Sighing heavily, she dropped her spoon into the teacup. Tears brimming in her eyes, she looked over at Ashleigh and then Kelly. "I blew it with Dallas again. He isn't very happy with me. I haven't heard from him in two days. The *commitment* conversation came up again. He wants what I can't seem to give him. Help me here, ladies," Lanier wailed, sounding as if her heart was broken.

Ashleigh's eyes filled with sympathy. "I don't know how I can help you out on this one, Lanier. You have a great guy who loves you, yet you aren't able to accept it at face value. That really hurts him. I love you both and I know each side. I feel stuck in the middle. I can't champion either of you without showing prejudice."

Lanier pressed her fingers against her lips. "If only I could let go of the past, I'd have a future with Dallas. I know what I need to do, but I don't know how to accomplish it. The scar tissue inside my heart has hardened and is darn near impenetrable. People have disappointed me, letting me down in so many ways. How can I be sure Dallas won't eventually join the ranks? Yet I feel sure he loves me. What a twisted dilemma."

Kelly's heart went out to Lanier. This could easily be her, she knew. She had been in Dallas's shoes up until a few evenings ago. If Houston had seen the light, maybe Lanier would eventually see it, too. Because she still wasn't sure Houston could fully commit to her, she didn't feel comfortable sharing her good news prematurely.

"What about the cruise, Lanier? You *are* still going, aren't you?" Ashleigh asked.

Lanier hunched her shoulders. "Does Dallas still want me to go is the better question. I'm sure I'll find out sooner than later."

Ashleigh looked sympathetic. "I have a couple suggestions for you. They're not easy ones, but they might help. For one, I think it's time you try to reconnect with your parents, especially your mother. If you can mend fences with your family, you may be able to fully open up your heart to Dallas. Maybe closure is all you need."

Lanier's expression was strained. "I don't know. I'm not that generous of heart. Those people ruined my life. My anger still rages at them."

"They gave you life, Lanier," Ashleigh reminded her friend.

"Your mother wants to see you. Her letters have told you that repeatedly. Your parents were very sick at the time. To think they haven't recovered from their addictions is unfair. People do change. You've changed. I've changed. And for the better, I might add. Stop using your past pain to shield you from future happiness."

Lanier's tears flowed unchecked. "Maybe you're right, Ash. I'll give your recommendations a lot of thought. As far as not championing either Dallas or me, you've failed. You're more on Dallas's side than you may realize."

"I'm on the side of *love*. You two love each other. That's apparent to everyone who knows you guys. Stop fighting what you obviously feel for Dallas—stop fighting the inevitable. Take a page out of my book. Pump the brakes on your feet and stop running away from your destiny."

Lanier merely nodded her head, too emotionally upset to speak.

Deciding to leave Lanier alone with her thoughts, Ashleigh summoned Kelly to come into the office with her.

Ashleigh's cell phone rang the minute she dropped down on a chair at the desk. "Excuse me a minute, Kelly." The caller ID let her know that someone from the Department of Social Services was phoning.

Patricia Wright, Lauren and Stephanie's social worker, started right in on the reason for her call. She quickly informed Ashleigh that Sandra Gossett, the girls' aunt, had pulled her petition for sole custody of the girls. "Stephanie and Lauren are now free of the threat of being removed from Haven House."

"Thank you, Ms. Wright. This is wonderful news!"

"We'll be in touch. The biannual review for Haven House comes up at the end of the month."

"That's right, it does," Ashleigh said. "We'll be well-prepared. If we don't talk before then, I'll see you at our meeting. Have a nice day, Ms. Wright."

Kelly came over to the desk and rested her hands on Ashleigh's shoulders, squeezing gently. "I couldn't help overhearing your conversation. I'm glad you're not losing Stephanie and Lauren. They seem so happy living here. You guys have become a close-knit family."

"Thanks, Kelly, for the kind, encouraging words. I know the girls will be happy about the news. It's hard to keep from crying. I can't seem to forget the day I was removed from the Carrington home. It always haunts me in stressful situations."

Pushing her chair back from the desk, Ashleigh slowly got to her feet. She couldn't get to Lanier quickly enough, but she had to practice caution. She had a precious life to protect. Much to Ashleigh's pleasure, Lanier came into the office before she'd moved another inch.

"It's over," Ashleigh shouted with glee, dropping down onto the nearby sofa.

Ashleigh's breathing was coming a little too fast and erratic for Lanier's liking. "Calm down, Ash. What are you talking about?" Lanier sat down next to Ashleigh and took her hand. "Okay, what's going on that has you ready to blow a gasket?"

"Stephanie and Lauren, they're going to remain here at Haven House with us. The aunt withdrew her custody petition. The case is over, Lanier." Ashleigh went on to explain what she'd been told by the social worker, unable to hold back her tears.

"Oh my God," Lanier cried out, "I can't believe it. Thank God for His hand in this. Losing those girls would've been miserable for all of us. They love it here. Let's get them. We have to tell them now. Kelly, we are so happy this is settled."

Kelly smiled. "I can tell. I'm happy for you all. Glad I was present to hear the good news. Congratulations!"

Lanier buzzed the girls over the intercom and asked them to come into the office.

Laughing and crying at the same time, Lanier, Ashleigh and Kelly hugged.

Standing in the middle of his living room floor, Dallas's heart suddenly turned to mush. "This is a hand-written letter from Lanier postmarked three days ago," he told Houston, sounding emotional. "I know how hard writing this letter had to be for her. She is a prideful woman. No stranger to pain, she has spilled her heart out to me on paper, reiterating why she's so fearful of taking our relationship to the ultimate level. I'll read the last page."

Dallas cleared his throat. "'I love you, Dallas. Please make no mistake about that. Your patience has allowed us to get to where we are now. You haven't rushed me and I appreciate it. There are some things I need to do to help me move on with my life. I'm thinking of seeing my mother. If I do, I'll really need you. Please be there for me. I miss the strength of your comforting arms and the reassuring smiles and healing hugs you give me. Call me, please.'"

Dallas glanced over at Houston. "Can you believe this letter?"

"Sure I can. I just moved from the place where Lanier resides. Go ahead and call her, man. I'm hitting the kitchen. My stomach is growling."

Houston was seated at the breakfast bar, making a turkey sandwich, when Dallas finally entered the kitchen.

"Lanier agreed to come over. A candlelit dinner is just what we need." Before he reached the refrigerator, he looked out the picture window. His smile came brightly. "There are enough blooms on the rosebushes for a centerpiece. I'll cut the stems and arrange them in a vase, but first I need to scope out the fridge."

Laughing, Houston shook his head. "Boy, you're whipped. I've never seen you this nutty over a woman. Lanier has really put it on you. You're talking centerpieces!"

Dallas laughed. "That's not all I talk. I say and do anything that brings a smile to her lips. She's deserving of whatever I can do for her. Absence does make the heart grow fonder, but it can also make a brother go insane with longing."

"I'm beginning to know the feeling," Houston remarked, thinking of Kelly.

"Missing Lanier like crazy has been the downside of letting her come to terms with her true feelings," Dallas told Houston. "Although she didn't make any reference to marriage in her letter I won't let it put a damper on things. Tonight will be all about getting our relationship back on track. I've come to terms with a few important things myself. I'd rather Lanier be sure about marriage than for us to dive into it blindly."

Houston shrugged. "Marriage is a big step. You and Austin have come to terms with matrimony. I'm still not there. Figuring this all out is hard."

"Take your time, Houston. Kelly won't expect you to offer a marriage proposal any time soon." Dallas stroked his chin thoughtfully. "Firing up the hot tub has to be on the agenda, too. We might even take a swim in the pool. I can hardly wait to hold the lovely Lanier Watson in my arms."

Houston saluted his brother. "Let me get out of here so you can do your thing. Sounds like you're planning to put it down. Lanier's in for a sweet surprise. Hope you guys have a fantastic evening."

"Not so fast, little brother. You need to help me cook. Then you can split."

Houston bucked his eyes. "I don't recall volunteering a single service."

"You need an apron?" Dallas asked. "Mom keeps a couple in the utility drawer. If you want a manly one, Dad also has one or two in there." Dallas picked up the dish towel and threw it at Houston. "Don't just stand around here gawking. Get to work."

Knowing he'd gotten himself into a hopeless situation Houston walked over to the sink and washed his hands, wiping them off on a paper towel. "This'll cost you."

"It always does," Dallas countered. "You might just learn a thing or two from me. You're so scared of women getting the wrong idea you forget how to take good care of one. Let me show you how it's done, baby boy. You've witnessed Dad treating Mom like a queen your entire life. I'd think by now you'd be an expert at it."

Houston rinsed off the salad greens and put them in the spinner to dry. "That's it. I've never been involved with any female that way. I *don't* want women to get the wrong impression. I'm good for dinner, club hopping, dancing, bowling and a movie on occasion. I prefer meeting women at social functions over taking a date."

Vacations or cozy weekend getaways hadn't ever been a part of Houston's social scene. He was more comfortable with a group of women rather than singling out any one lady to spend time with.

Dallas looked concerned. "Then why commit to seeing only Kelly?"

"I'm different with Kelly. She has broken through the majority of my barriers. I still feel strange over the commitment I made several days ago, but I won't go back on my word. I mostly worry about what'll happen when I'm on the road again. I'm home for the summer so it'll be easy to see only Kelly. The long road trips are the rough part. You and Austin manage the road well. Austin is married now and you want to be. All this exclusive stuff is brand-new for me."

Dallas empathized with his brother, silently commending Houston for not lying to or cheating on women like many guys did. He had stuck to his guns, and he was still sensitive and considerate of others' feelings. Women practically threw themselves at the Carrington men, yet not one of them had misused or abused anyone. They had their pick of the finest ladies in every city. However, Houston had always seen things differently.

"The motto on the road for most guys is 'love 'em and leave 'em,' but not with you, Houston. Austin and I were concerned about your approach, until we realized it works for you and your female friends. Hanging out with groups of women is what you love to do—and the ladies don't seem to mind. No one can accuse you of breaking hearts intentionally. You're obviously a man who likes to have loads of group fun."

Smiling, Houston nodded. "I couldn't have explained it better. Glad you and Austin finally understand the method to my madness."

Kelly, Ashleigh and Lanier, excited and animated, were at the Galleria in Houston, a huge complex made up of fine department stores, fashion boutiques, first-class jewelers, shoe stores, specialty shops and numerous eateries. The Galleria was a favorite place for Houstonians to shop. The shopping choices were endless. An ice arena was also situated inside the development, located only yards from the food court.

Already worn-out from popping in and out of countless stores, the ladies made their way over to Chili's, which offered a great view of the ice rink. Austin and Houston were to meet the women at the restaurant for lunch. After eating, the ladies planned to help the men choose a few other special gifts for Angelica.

Ashleigh seemed extremely tired and it showed in her face, causing Kelly concern. "Are you okay, Ash? Are you up to more shopping?"

Ashleigh set her purse beside her chair. "I'm cool, Kelly, but the surface of the flooring has my feet on fire. I feel a little tired, but I'll be okay. Thanks for asking."

Kelly took a closer look at Ashleigh. "Are you sure about that? Your eyes say differently, Ash. But you've got a great doctor along with you. No matter what field of medicine physicians specialize in, we all rotate through the OB/GYN department. I *do* know how to deliver a baby."

Ashleigh grinned broadly. "That's good to know."

Lanier smiled. "I second that."

At that very moment, Austin walked up behind Ashleigh's chair and placed his hands over her eyes. "Guess who, beautiful." He'd made no attempt to disguise his voice.

Ashleigh sniffed the air, barely able to contain her joy. "I'd know that sexy scent anywhere. These are the same talented hands that tenderly massage my body on a regular basis. So I'd have to say it's my superstar husband behind me."

Austin leaned his head down and gave Ashleigh an upside-down kiss. "Make no mistake about it, sweetie. Your one and only!" Smiling, he nodded a greeting at Kelly and Lanier, taking a seat next to his wife. "Houston should be here any minute. Something in one of the stores caught his eye when we first got here. He went back for a second look. Have you all ordered yet?"

Lanier shook her head in the negative. "Not yet. The waitress is on her way over here now."

Just as Lanier finished her remarks, the waitress stepped up to the table.

"Welcome to Chili's. What can I get for you folks?" Her cheerfulness put everyone at ease. Then she took one look at Austin and gasped loudly. It was obvious she had recognized the hometown sports hero. "Oh, my goodness, it's really you, Austin Carrington. I can't believe you're seated at my table. Everyone in Houston loves you." She looked at Ashleigh. "If you two weren't holding hands, I wouldn't have known which triplet he was. I've seen you pictured with your husband in the paper."

Proud of her man, Ashleigh beamed, ecstatic that so many people loved him. It didn't disturb her when women showed a genuine, respectful liking toward Austin.

After a bit more gushing over the Wrangler quarterback, the waitress finally calmed down enough to take orders. Her hands visibly shook as she wrote on her pad.

Each of the women ordered some type of salad. Austin requested a hamburger with the works. Knowing the foods Houston liked, Kelly had chosen for him, causing the others to talk trash about it. Kelly shrugged off the teasing comments. No one knew about the commitment she and Houston had made. She was leaving it up to him.

Houston showed up just before the waitress left the table. Her excitement started all over again. Before leaving the area, she made a request for autographs.

Houston gave Austin a high five. "This just has to stop," he joked.

"You are too popular for words. I'll have to stop hanging out with you if this keeps up."

The ladies all laughed at Houston's antics. Austin wasn't a bit impressed.

Kelly covered Houston's hand with hers. "As if you don't receive the same type of treatment every time we're out. She had a fit over you, too. It must be nice to have it like that. By the way, I took the liberty of ordering for you."

Houston was pleased by Kelly's comments, pleased that she hadn't let the mushy stuff from female fans bother her. It was nice to have an understanding woman. He leaned over and kissed her softly on the lips. "What'd you order for me?"

Kelly smiled. "You'll have to wait and see. I think I did okay."

Amazed by their open affection, Austin closely observed the interaction between Houston and Kelly. If he didn't know better, he'd think their relationship had taken an unexpected turn. He'd never seen Houston looking happier. It appeared he'd had a change of heart. *Had his brother stopped running long enough to get himself captured?*

Houston opened the small bag he had set on the table. After taking out a small white box, he handed it to Kelly. "This is for you. I hope you like it."

Kelly's couldn't hide her surprise. "For me? Wow!" She quickly flipped open the top of the box. A huge smile came next. "Is this a symbol for the pact we made earlier?"

He grinned. "It is. What do you think of it?"

Kelly lifted from the cotton pad what looked like a fourteen-karat-gold map of some sort, threaded on a dainty gold chain. Wondering what the charm represented, she fingered it lightly. "It's a beautiful piece." She loved it, though she wasn't sure what it was.

The others were craning their necks to see what Kelly had received.

Houston cracked up. "You don't know what it is, do you?"

Kelly looked embarrassed. "Afraid not," she said in a small voice.

"It's part of a world globe." Reaching inside his shirt, he pulled out a box-link chain. An identical charm dangled at the end of Houston's gold necklace. "We both have a piece of the globe. When we're worlds apart, this will keep us connected. It'll serve as a reminder of our commitment. The two halves fit together to make a whole."

Everyone was highly curious now. Before anyone could ask what was really going on between Houston and Kelly, he graciously clued them in.

The others appeared genuinely happy for the couple, especially Austin, who'd feared Houston might mess around and let Kelly get away.

Austin affectionately pounded Houston on the back. "Congratulations! You guys look good together."

"Does this mean we'll hear wedding bells soon?" Lanier wanted to kick herself the same moment the words left her mouth. Pressure was the last thing the happy couple needed. "Sorry, guys. I shouldn't have said that. Please accept my apology. At any rate, I'm thrilled for you," Lanier voiced sincerely.

"Me, too," Ashleigh chimed in. "It's wonderful! We need to make a toast."

Right on cue, the waitress arrived with the beverage orders. Once she left the table, Austin wasted no time in proposing a heartfelt toast to Houston and Kelly's relationship. Then Kelly passed around her half of the golden globe for everyone to see.

Houston was impressed with the food items Kelly had chosen for him. "I see that you've been paying close attention to me."

Mozzarella cheese sticks was the appetizer Houston often ordered. A medium-well hamburger with a large order of French fries was just what he would've asked for, along with the garden salad. And a vanilla milk shake was his favorite drink to gulp down with hamburgers and fries. She'd even gotten the Ranch salad dressing right.

Houston leaned into Kelly and kissed the tip of her nose. "You did good, girl. I couldn't have done it any better. Thanks."

Kelly smiled. "You're welcome. Which one of you guys is going to pray?"

The group of five felt half-blinded by the sparkling diamond earrings they'd viewed at numerous jewelry stores. Even though a diamond card from Ben Bridge was settled on as one of the birthday gifts for Angelica, the guys had wanted the women's input on other items.

Austin had also gotten a feel for what won over Ashleigh. He planned on buying her diamond earrings as a gift when the baby came. They'd looked at dainty diamond studs created for infants. If the child was a girl, their daughter would have a pair, too.

After hitting several more stores, Kelly, Ashleigh and Lanier finally settled on the perfect formal dress for Angelica. The stunning, glittery dress in black and silver was both elegant and timeless. Ashleigh and Austin planned to pick out the evening shoes and matching bag at Angelica's favorite shoe boutique, but they'd save it for another day.

Houston simply looked on, fascinated with everyone's patience for nonstop shopping. A shopper he wasn't. He liked to wear fine designer clothing, but he also used a tailor to fashion a good bit of his attire. Browsing the Internet gave him an idea of what he wanted to purchase before he went into stores. It saved on time and also made the shopping experience somewhat easier.

The buying fever had gotten the best of Kelly and Lanier, who had both purchased formal dresses. With her and Dallas's issues resolved, Lanier felt comfortable in choosing an eggshell-white Dior for the formal night on the cruise. Kelly had selected a shocking red Ralph Lauren gown, with a low-cut back and front.

Dead tired, the group left the mall to return to their homes.

Chapter 10

Houston enjoyed seeing Kelly so excited while perusing the brochures Dallas had given him to share with her, as this was to be her first time out to sea. The cruise itinerary was featured, along with numerous onshore tours the cruise line offered.

After leafing through the pamphlet, Houston came up with a page he wanted to show Kelly. "These are the cabin floor plans." He pointed at a picture. "This is the type of cabin Dallas reserved. The balconies are right above the sea. Not too much can be seen at night, but the moon and stars will be vivid. We'll get to see a lot when the ship heads into port during daylight hours. I'm surprised you've never cruised before."

Kelly shrugged. "My parents cruised often, but they didn't take me along."

"Why not?"

"I never asked. They'd never dream of booking a cruise catering to kids and younger couples. Why sail on a big party boat when you want elegance, peace and quiet. They can be pretty stuffy and snobbish. But they're good with their patients, very loving, kind and sensitive. I used to think they cared more about strangers than me."

Houston frowned. "Have you spoken to them since the awards dinner?"

Kelly looked ashamed. "I haven't phoned them nor have they called me."

Although Houston wouldn't say it aloud he couldn't imagine not talking to his parents daily. They often spoke three and four times a day. There were also the family dinners everyone enjoyed. He understood everyone didn't have the family life he had, but he would've never guessed that Kelly had grown up feeling so alone.

"Who called who the last time you talked?" Houston queried, curious about the family communication habits.

"I only phone them when I'm returning their call. I get messages a few times a month." She grew quiet for a moment. "Lately, they've been calling more frequently. It's kind of strange. They've always been creatures of habit, predictable."

"Do you think they're calling more because they may want a deeper connection with their daughter? Have you given it any thought?"

"Why should I? They didn't say anything like that at the awards event."

Kelly's remarks had sounded so cold and detached, making Houston wonder if there was more to this family estrangement than what she'd said. He and his brothers fell out and had arguments like any other siblings, but it rarely lasted long. He couldn't recall a time they'd actually parted company upset with each other.

What were the real issues in Kelly's family? It had to be something pretty deep.

Since they planned to see a lot more of each other, Houston hoped she'd trust him enough to share whatever she hadn't been able to get over. There were clearly unsettled family issues in her past and present.

The doorbell brought Houston's thoughts to an abrupt end. He watched as Kelly took flight toward the foyer. The phone hadn't rung so he wondered who had dropped by unannounced. She'd been rather annoyed at him for that, so he'd probably get to see how she reacted to this visitor. Well, he thought, she could've already been expecting someone. Thinking he was giving the issue too much thought, he let it go, silently promising to stop analyzing every little thing Kelly did.

Lynton preceded Kelly into the family room. Houston's eyes went straight to the suitcases he carried in both hands. Doomsday had arrived and he was there to witness it. As Kelly excused herself to direct Lynton to the guest wing in her house, Houston's stomach knotted up. Kelly's friend moving into her home might mean that Lynton would become even more involved in her life.

Did Lynton have ulterior motives for moving in with Kelly?

Lynton had just relocated to Houston, he recalled her saying. He knew she'd offered him space at her office and had agreed to house-hunt with him, but he hadn't been pleased about him living there with her. He wasn't a bit keen on Lynton occupying space in Kelly's home, but she was a grown woman with the right to make her own decisions.

With plenty of housing for lease why was Lynton setting up shop here?

Houston had a pretty good idea what was on the man's mind, but he wasn't sure Kelly was aware of his agenda. Unless she brought it up to him again, he wasn't saying a thing about it. *Fat chance of that,* he thought. If he could keep his thoughts to himself for the rest of the evening, Houston knew it'd be a miracle.

Kelly came back into the family room and sat down next to Houston. "Please keep in mind his stay here is only temporary," she said, her tone soothing. "The house Lynton wants to lease in Green Tee Estates won't be available until August. We're only a little ways into June, but he'll move on the first of the month as opposed to the end. It won't be that bad. You'll see."

Houston rolled back his eyes. "That makes me feel a whole lot better," he said, unable to put a lid on the sarcasm. "Has he already signed a lease?"

"The owner promised to have the papers ready for signing within a week or so."

Houston looked skeptical. "It's the 'or so' that bothers me. We'll wait and see."

Once the deadline passed for signing the papers, Houston believed Lynton would have another bogus excuse as to why the lease wasn't signed. This man wasn't serious about leasing another place and he wasn't moving in with Kelly just to wait until the house was available. Houston was sure he wanted to make a personal move on her. Before the last thought cleared Houston's head, Lynton came into the room and plopped down on the sofa, on the other side of Kelly.

With another couch and several chairs in the room, Houston didn't understand why Lynton hadn't sat elsewhere. Then he mentally corrected himself. *He did understand.* If he intended to make a move on Kelly, then he'd want to be close to her, as often as possible. Houston had a big problem with that.

"Would you mind fixing me a cup of coffee?" Lynton asked Kelly. "Until I learn everything about the appliances, I don't want to mess with anything."

Houston got to his feet. "Since I'm familiar with everything, I'd be happy to show you how to use the coffeemaker." Houston wasn't remotely familiar with much of anything in Kelly's house, but it wouldn't take a rocket scientist to figure things out.

If looks could kill, Houston would've keeled over dead by the one Lynton had used to shoot him down. "Man, I'm not so sure I want another dude making me coffee. That seems kind of weird."

"Some of the best chefs in the world are men. Nothing weird about it. Do you want the coffee or not?" Houston appeared impatient. "If so, let's hit the kitchen."

Laughing inwardly, Kelly found humor in Houston's spunky attitude. He *was* a take-charge kind of man. She actually liked having him nip this situation in the bud. She didn't allow Lynton to move into her home to become his personal maid. It wasn't going to work like that. He knew how to make coffee and cook. If he didn't want to do the chores himself, he'd better find him a local restaurant to post up in.

Kelly's life was too hectic as it was. She had more than enough stuff to do. To take on a grown man's personal tasks just wasn't happening, not in this lifetime. Next he'd be asking her to do his laundry. She figured Lynton had been trying to goad Houston, as he'd already done before. Unfortunately for her friend, he had picked the wrong man to start something with. Houston wasn't having any of it, either. If it was a good sparring partner Lynton was after, he had found the right man. Houston Carrington kept his boxing gloves handy.

Kelly would love to be a fly on the kitchen wall. She knew full well fur would fly between these two macho male animals. Just the thought of them going at it tickled her. They wouldn't come to blows. These two were more into verbal fighting, with each of them trying to outwit the other. That didn't show a lot of maturity on either side, but these two men acted more like juvenile delinquents than highly intelligent adults as they walked into the kitchen.

Out in the kitchen, Houston plugged in the coffeemaker. He then retrieved the coffee container from the pantry. Rarely did he make his own coffee. He just didn't like to take the time and he wasn't all that good at it. It was easier for him to stop by a McDonald's, which he and Dallas were often teased about.

Lynton had seated himself at the table and that let Houston know he intended to let him to do all the work. "Man, come on over here so you can learn to operate this machine. It won't take long."

Houston went through the motions of showing Lynton where to insert the filter and how to measure out the coffee. He then took the water container over to the sink and filled it with enough liquid for four cups of coffee in case Kelly wanted a cup. Back at the counter, he poured the water into the appropriate tank and hit the red on button.

"Voilà! I told you it wasn't that hard. Now all you have to do is get you a cup and wait for the coffee to brew. Press the mug into this little silver bar and the coffee will flow like a stream. Think you got it down pat?"

Lynton glared openly at Houston. "Got it."

"Good! I'll show you how to use the toaster oven, microwave, blender and the washer and dryer whenever you're ready. They're as simple to use as the coffeemaker." Without uttering another word, Houston left the kitchen, proud of how he'd handled the good doctor. If Lynton hadn't gotten his pointed message, he should have.

Houston was still cracking up when he made it back to Kelly, who'd been praying for both guys to keep their cool. "I think your boy got it. Don't let him tell you otherwise. You are not his maid. Don't let him treat you like one."

"Interesting you should say that. The same thing passed through my mind. This girl is nobody's maid. What would I look like tending to his chores when my sweet housekeeper comes here to my house once a week to dust, vacuum, mop floors and clean bathrooms?"

Houston looked surprised. "That's all you have a housekeeper for?"

"Every three months she also thoroughly cleans the house from top to bottom. I do my own laundry and cooking, but she's offered to do both at no extra charge. I prefer to do my own clothes and cook. I normally wash the dishes as I use them."

"I guess they can't call you Dr. Diva, huh?"

Kelly grinned. "I'm no diva, Mr. Carrington. Not by a long shot."

With a coffee mug in hand, Lynton came back into the family room. Once he spotted the coasters, he removed one and set his cup down. Without asking if anyone minded, he picked up the remote and flicked on the wall-mounted plasma television set. "Let's see what's on. This is a great night for staying in and watching television."

Both Houston and Kelly looked astonished by the man's gall.

Houston knew that the bedrooms in the other wing in Kelly's house were fully furnished and fully equipped with the same electronic devices in her personal living spaces. Another huge master suite was in that part of the house, with a good-size alcove and a double-sided fireplace. A big office inside the suite was grandly furnished. Houston didn't know what rooms Kelly had assigned to Lynton, but he was willing to bet money she put him in the other suite.

Why had Lynton decided to invade Kelly's privacy? Houston had known the answer to his own question before he'd mentally posed it.

Lynton quickly found TNT and settled in like he was in his own home.

Houston figured this was a calculated move on Lynton's part since the NBA finals were on. No one needed to remind him that his team had been knocked out of the playoffs. He could either stay seated and suffer through the indignities or leave Kelly's home mad as hell. He wasn't about to do the latter and give Lynton satisfaction.

Kelly stood. Crooking her finger, she summoned Houston to follow her, with the intent of finishing their visit in her bedroom. Lynton wouldn't dare to follow. If he was that rude, Kelly would show him a side of her he'd wish he hadn't been introduced to.

Houston had only been in Kelly's master bedroom once. The first visit was brief, when she'd wanted to show him around her home. He noticed right away that a lot of the furniture had been rearranged.

The dark mahogany Cal King pier bed, covered in a beautiful brown-and-blue comforter set, was now on the opposite side of the room. The massive headboard unit with attached nightstands and recessed lighting took up a full wall. Two plush overstuffed comfort chairs in blue, complete with ottomans, were stationed on each side of a framed picture window. A round mahogany table furnished with a lovely bronze antique lamp was nestled between the chairs.

Silky wildflowers, large and small, looked as if they'd been hand-sewn onto the down comforter. Houston liked the blending of blue and brown. It appeared nice and subtly soft, lending the huge room a calming effect.

"I see you redecorated since I was last here. Did you do all of it yourself?"

"A few male colleagues rearranged the heavy furniture for me. It's difficult for me to change sheets on the pillow-top mattress, especially the fitted one. Keeping the heavy bedding lifted long enough to do hospital corners is a big challenge. Several other friends helped me put up the wall borders matching the comforter." Kelly pointed at the borders just below the crown molding. "Let's go into the retreat and have a seat. That's where the television is. The fireplace there can be viewed from both areas."

"Thanks. My weary bones could use some rest," Houston joked.

The couple stepped into the cozy alcove off the bedroom, where Houston sat down on the plush sofa. "I like the feel of this couch. My body sinks down into the cushions yet it's firm." He lightly bounced up and down to make his point.

"I can't tell you how many nights I fall asleep there. It's extremely comfortable. The chairs are pretty comfy, too." Kelly pointed at the built-in bar, equipped with an office-size refrigerator. "Can I get you a drink? I have wine, sodas and juice. There's also liquor and mixers in the upper cabinet and a blender stored in the lower ones."

Houston shook his head. "I'm fine. What about you?"

As if she was trying to decide, she glanced over at the bar. "I think I'll pass. Is there anything I can get you?"

Patting his knee, Houston grinned. "Does holding you on my lap apply?"

Kelly threw her head back and laughed. Then her house phone jangled, causing her to frown. "I have to get that. I'm on call this evening."

"Not a problem."

After picking up the receiver, Kelly put it to her ear. "Hello."

"This is Lynton...."

"What are you trying...?" She rapidly bit off her caustic remark.

"Just wanted you to know I'm going out for a while. It may be late when I get back. I'll use the entrance off the guest wing I'm staying in, but I need a security code."

Both wings of the house had separate entries but were maintained by the same alarm company in charge of all security surveillance.

The system was set up so she could reset the codes whenever she desired. The code Kelly gave Lynton was one of many.

"Feel free to come and go as you please. You don't have to phone me each time." Kelly hung up the phone. "Now where were we?"

"I think you were about to sit on my lap." He looked at her with a glimmer of hope in his ebony eyes.

Smiling sweetly, Kelly nodded. "Hmm, I think you're right."

As Kelly walked over to Houston and dropped down onto his lap, she tried not to predetermine the outcome of this evening. She didn't want to entertain the idea of him heating her up, only to have him leave her body cold and her heart lonely. Things had changed for them, but she had yet to find out how drastically. She wanted him, all of him, but she'd never take the lead.

Houston didn't know what Kelly expected from him, but it definitely wouldn't be more of the same song and dance he normally sold the ladies. No more backing away or down for him. He was hers to do with as she pleased. All the soul-searching he'd done had finally paid off. He was at peace. Houston couldn't have committed to Kelly if he hadn't been sure he could protect her fragile heart from breakage or irreparable damage.

Houston laughed inwardly at something that had suddenly come to mind. Over the years he'd seen these signs in a number of retail stores or gift shops. The ones that said "Break it, you own it!"

Kissing Kelly had been on Houston's mind since he'd first arrived. As he took possession of her sweet mouth, he closed his eyes, losing himself to paradise. His passionate kisses and tender caresses quickly put Kelly nearly out of her mind with need. He let go of her long enough to pull his sweater over his head. It was hot even though the air conditioner softly hummed on and off at timely intervals. The prickly heat he felt probably had more to do with his body temperature.

Kelly had a hard time sitting still on Houston's lap. His sex was hard as stone and every time she moved a muscle a part of her lower anatomy rubbed against it. The strong desire to see and touch what felt larger than life had her thinking all sorts of naughty-girl stuff. If it were Christmastime, she'd only get coal in her stocking. Santa would probably have it written on his list that she'd been naughty rather than nice. Saint Nick would give her a good scolding!

Houston had no idea how much of a bad, bad girl Kelly could

be. Under the right circumstances, she could positively give him something he could feel.

His next fiery kisses had Kelly fidgeting all around. She didn't think she'd ever be the aggressor, but she was ready to become just that. She slowly got up from Houston's lap. "Excuse me. I'll be right back."

"Is something wrong?"

"Very wrong! But I'm about to make it right." With that said, she slipped into the master bathroom and on into the walk-in closet housing a chest of drawers.

Kelly pulled open her intimate apparel drawer and rifled through her silk, satin and lacy night things, wondering what she should wear to blow Houston's mind. She had dozens of lacy teddies and other sheer sexy nightwear and lounging items. Victoria's Secret intimate apparel loungewear was where she loved to shop for luxurious unmentionables. The perfect silk set finally came into her view, a hot and sexy cinnamon-brown teddy. Houston would positively love her in it. There was no doubt in her mind.

As Houston looked at Kelly, the most beautiful woman he'd ever seen in a natural state of undress, he could hardly contain his desire. Perfectly rounded breasts summoned him. Nipples, invitingly erect, caused him to lick his lips in a provocative way. Kelly's smooth, sienna skin shimmered from the glittery, oil-based lotion she had just applied to her body.

For all the flirtatious moments between Houston and Kelly and all the constant verbal and physical foreplay, it was hardly believable that they hadn't actually made love. It looked to him as if that was about to change.

As she walked around the room in the nude, lighting candles, creating a romantic mood, she knew their commitment to each other was resolute. The last-minute change in what she'd wear for Houston was bolder and more sexy than she'd ever before dared. She'd known that wearing her birthday suit would go over big with the triplet she adored.

Touching Kelly all over her stunning body was Houston's first delectable order of the evening. He wanted to feel her skin sizzle beneath his fingertips and hands. Kissing her deeply, tenderly caressing her flesh, he further heightened the fire of their desires.

His tongue thirsted to mingle with hers, eager to make her wet down where her molten treasures burned for his attention.

Houston slowly walked the few steps to where Kelly stood in the nude from head to toe. Leaning against the doorjamb, she looked as if she couldn't wait to receive all he had to offer. Coming together with her in a union of fiery passion was something he'd dreamed about night after night, yet it was something he hadn't acted upon. The worthwhile wait was nearly over and Houston wanted desperately to be inside Kelly.

Possessing a body to completely come unglued for, Houston was rock-solid, muscles bulging and flexing everywhere. Kelly couldn't wait to oil down his body with baby oil. His organ had thickened and hardened considerably, yet she felt it hadn't reached its full potential. Her tender touch would tell the story. Making wild, passionate love to Houston was something Kelly had begun to dream about right after their first romantic kiss.

Houston brought Kelly into his arms, stroking her back tenderly. The throbbing between his legs was unbearable, his manhood straining against her nudity. Houston was so excited he thought his heart might come to a dead stop. Although he'd only begun to heat up her flesh premature release was threatening him something awful. That would never do on their first time. Kelly had Houston more lathered up than he'd ever been.

Completely unaware of Houston's concerns about early release, Kelly gently enclosed her hand around his manhood. The warmth and hardness of his sex had her desiring him like crazy. If he didn't take her within the next couple of minutes, she vowed to take him. So much her for not taking the lead, she thought. Her body was already an uncontrollable inferno and she needed the consuming flames doused.

Palming his firm buttocks, squeezing gently, Kelly pulled Houston in closer to her, grinding her hips against his. The heat was on, full blast.

Houston's tongue found Kelly's inner ear, as he manipulated a hardened nipple with gentle fingers. Her soft but deep moans of pleasure were encouraging, increasing his desire to cut to the chase. However, defining moments were never to be rushed. This was definitely a significant moment in taking their relationship to the next level.

As her fingernails lazed up and down his spine, the painful, maddening throbbing of his manhood had thrown him off stride. Houston moaned softly as his mouth crashed down over Kelly's, his tongue and breathing mingling with hers.

In one swift but gentle motion, Houston lifted up Kelly and carried her over to the bed. First, he pulled back the comforter and then laid her down. Once he positioned himself alongside her, his hands and mouth restarted the thrilling seduction of the woman he craved like crazy. She was already writhing about and squirming like crazy, but he wasn't quite ready to get on with the grand finale. The foreplay was too, too hot to stop now. He had a few more fiery moves to increase both their sexual desires.

Houston never wanted Kelly or himself to forget this night of pure passion, the very first night they'd come together in the sweltering heat of erotica, the tantalizing thrill of ecstasy gone wild.

Houston's lips grazed Kelly's earlobe. "Do you have any idea what you're doing to me?"

"If it's anything like what you do to me, we're in for one incredible journey. We may need to call the fire department before this night is over." Kelly thrust her head back, exposing her creamy throat to Houston, tempting him to explore it with his mouth.

Houston agreed with her comment as he gently stroked Kelly's throat with his fingertips. His hungry mouth then followed the tracks of his fingers, kissing and gently caressing her satiny flesh.

Kelly urged Houston to roll over onto his back. She then straddled him, smiling sensuously, her eyes telling him everything she thought he might want to hear. She needed him physically, emotionally and in the same way he desired her.

As Kelly looked away, Houston's eyes followed the direction of hers. It was then that he spotted the crystal glass half-filled with wine and small wedges of fresh citrus fruits. She had removed the items from the bar's refrigerator before she'd returned to the bedroom and had set the goblet on the nightstand.

Houston raised an eyebrow, his eyes questioning what he saw in the wineglass. "Wine, lemon, orange and lime slices? What's that all about?" He was highly curious about what she had in mind for the fruit—and it excited him even more.

Seducing Houston with the wily devilment shimmering in her eyes, Kelly smiled wickedly. "I'm into citrus. It livens up the wine. It's my theory that it greatly enhances the taste of bared flesh, though I've never tested it out. I love to suck on citrus slices, love the tartness and tangy kick on my tongue." She then reached over and removed from the glass one wedge of each fruit.

Houston couldn't help wondering what the heck was coming next, so he closely watched Kelly's every move, not wanting to miss out on a thing. Before he could take another breath, Kelly held the fruit high above his body and began squeezing the juice all over him. His gasp came loud, growing even louder when Kelly's tongue began to lave the drops of citrus from his bare flesh.

Completely surrendering his body to Kelly, Houston threw his hands back over his head. "Kelly, baby," he whispered hoarsely, "I'm all yours."

Turning over, she lay on her back and squeezed a mixture of juices over her flesh, inviting Houston to sample the different parts of her sweet body. She parted her legs, but only slightly, wanting to give him the opportunity to make them spread wider upon his command, through his desire and need. As though he'd read her mind, his knee gently nudged her thighs farther apart. The heel of one of his capable hands tenderly massaged the area above her femininity. Then his fingers gently parted her moist flower. Protecting them came first.

Kelly's entire body shuddered as his fingers gently probed inside her. His mouth tended to her nipples and all the other sensitive spots on her body, many of which she hadn't known existed. His body now hovered over hers, as he looked down into her eyes. His expression told her he was ready to take her over the rainbow.

With infinite tenderness, he united their bodies as one. It was astonishing to finally be inside her, filling her up until it felt like they were spilling over into each other. His hips ground into hers and she mindlessly matched his fervor. Up and down, in and around, he took her to heights she'd never imagined, let alone attained.

"Houston," she whispered, "I'm losing it here. You *are* driving me wild. Oh, yeah, stay right there. Oh, my goodness, it feels so good, so delicious. Please repeat what you just did. I'm fighting to hold on." She gasped. "I've never felt anything close to this. Take all of me, sweetheart. And I want all of you, too, nothing less."

Taking Kelly at her word, Houston eagerly and happily fulfilled her requests. His thrusts slowly sank into her treasure trove overflowing with moisture. The deeper he went, the deeper she wanted him to go inside her, arching up to meet his thrusts, screaming out her desires with wild abandon. Thrust after thrust ripened and readied her for the climactic ending. No, she thought, she didn't want it to end. She wanted Houston inside her all night. *Was asking him to spend the time with her taking things too far?*

Kelly did take Houston—all of him—and he took liberties with all of her. As he propelled her toward the precipice she was only too happy to leap from in order to arrive in paradise, Kelly went back and forth between wanting to and not wanting to climax, all at the same time. Her mind continued to waffle with every deep thrust.

The decision was out of Kelly's hands when nature finally took over. As her body shook like a mammoth earthquake, she felt herself floating higher and higher above the bed they lay upon. Aftershocks followed next, causing her body to jerk and tremble with delicious force. "Houston," she cried, tears streaming from her eyes, "I'm there. I arrived. I'm on top of the mountain looking down. Wow! The sensations coursing through me are amazing." Then she fell silent, peering up at the ceiling. As though she had fallen into a trance, her eyes grew hazy.

Houston turned up on his side and stared down at her, his eyes drinking her in. The telltale signs of fulfillment were there. Glazed, dilated eyes, a half smile playing at the corners of her mouth and the flush of her sienna skin were the normal signs of physical satisfaction. Laying flat on his back, he brought her into his arms, nesting her head onto his chest.

No one in the world but him knew how wonderful Kelly made him feel. Houston liked these untamed, uncontrolled feelings she elicited from him. For certain, he didn't want them to end. This wasn't just a physical attraction he had for Kelly. His whole mind, soul, body and spirit were involved in their romantic liaison.

When did all this wonder happen? Why had this amazing phenomenon occurred to someone who had opposed it for so long? This had been a lengthy, hard-fought battle, one that he'd obviously lost. The strangest thing was that he didn't mind losing because he just might end up with a win. To win Kelly's heart and capture her true spirit would be like hitting a major jackpot. It would make them both winners because he believed she had already won his heart.

Seconds later, hypnotized by the rise and fall of her full breasts, Houston noticed Kelly's even breathing. "She sleeps," he whispered.

The sienna stunner was knocked out cold. While he felt great satisfaction over his part in the accomplishment, he wished she were awake for an encore. Making love to her again was all he could think about.

Chapter 11

Houston turned off the radio and bedside lamp before settling down for the night. His thoughts turned to Kelly the minute his head hit the pillow. If he didn't know better, he might think he'd just awakened from a magnificent dream. However, what he and Kelly had experienced earlier in the evening had been very real. There were only a couple of things in his life that compared to what they'd shared, like the contract he'd signed with an official NBA team, winning a world championship his rookie year and earning the coveted MVP award his fourth season with the Cyclones.

Other than the fact Kelly hadn't asked him to spend the night, Houston wasn't sure why he hadn't asked for the privilege. The old rules he'd played by should no longer apply. As he took a moment to reflect, not being asked to stay *was* kind of strange.

Perhaps Kelly thought he should've requested the honor, not the other way around. At any rate, it hadn't happened—and it was too late to worry about it now. Considering the fact Lynton now lived there it may've been for the best. Maybe she didn't want him to have knowledge of her private business. It certainly made sense.

Houston's personal rules had been shattered—and all of them by him. Making love to a woman in her residence had been an absolute no-no before Kelly. Rendezvous points were always first-class hotels or motels, definitely not pay-by-the-hour kind. A relationship commitment between him and another woman hadn't occurred, either, not until now. Kelly had brought about so many unbelievable changes in him, good ones and questionable ones. For him to have remained celibate since their lunch date was an amazing feat in itself.

Houston had to admit that the wait had been very worthwhile. Kelly had caused him to stand up and take notice and to take inventory of his defects in character. She was good for him, so much so that he was eager to see what other changes she might bring about in him. The lady had made an impressive impact on his life.

The next several days had been challenging for Kelly. There were a lot of things she had to get done before leaving on the cruise with Houston. While taking care of some of the more personal stuff she had neglected, like answering numerous correspondences and writing out checks for the bills, she sat at the built-in maple desk in her kitchen. Waiting for the coffee to brew was also included in her things to do.

Dressed in all-white tennis gear, Lynton popped into the kitchen. "Morning, Kelly! How are you?"

Kelly looked up at her friend and smiled. "I'm fine. Thanks for asking. Looks like you're ready to hit the tennis court."

The residential complex Kelly resided in had a full range of amenities available to the home owners. Besides the park, pool, spa areas and tennis courts, there were also basketball courts, volleyball nets and walking, biking and jogging lanes. Kelly's favorite amenities were the fully equipped exercise room and the guest clubhouse. Residents were permitted to hold private parties and other special events in the clubhouse. A small refundable deposit to cover possible damages was required upon booking.

"Did you think to make enough coffee for me to have a cup or two?"

Thinking about how Houston had dealt with this same issue several nights ago, Kelly had to laugh. "There is probably enough for you to have some, but I didn't think about you when I made it. I'm not your maid."

Lynton feigned a shiver. "That was kind of cold, don't you think?"

Kelly heaved a sigh. "Who made your coffee before you moved in here?"

He shrugged. "I did."

Her thoughts turned to him trying to make Houston believe he didn't want to damage any of her appliances by improper use. "It should continue. I don't see why it has to change. You have full kitchen privileges."

"Thank you, I think. Why don't you take the day off and play tennis with me?"

Kelly laughed, wondering why a doctor asked such an asinine

question. "You've got to be joking. I have patients this afternoon and lots of charts to update and sign. By the way, have you talked to the owner of the Green Tee property you're leasing?"

"I've left several messages but no return phone call has come in yet. I'm sure I'll hear something this week. They assured me I landed the lease."

Getting up from the table, Kelly walked over to the cabinet and removed her personal mug. Before she could fill it with coffee, the phone rang. As Houston came to mind, she hoped it was him. With so many interesting topics to discuss, they had recently been talking on the phone for hours.

Just as Kelly reached for the receiver, Lynton all but snatched it from the wall mount. She stared at him in stunned belief as he greeted the caller like he had every right to. Had he seen Houston's information on the caller ID? Probably so, she surmised, knowing Lynton loved to goad Houston every chance he got. Both men were guilty of antagonism. She'd have to lay down some fast and hard rules. Lynton had to respect her and her home. Evicting him before he ever got the chance to feel settled into the lavish suite she'd graciously offered him rent-free was an option.

"Can you call Kelly back later? We're about to discuss a few important matters over coffee. You know how it is between folks with a long history."

Kelly's mouth fell open. Unable to believe her ears, she forcefully wrestled the phone from Lynton's grip. A machetelike glare in her eyes cut him down to size.

"Houston, Lynton is acting pretty foolish this morning. I'd never reject a call from you, no matter what," she said, her eyes trained on her houseguest. "What's up?" Total silence came from the other end. *Had he hung up?* She called out his name, but still no answer. As she was about to hang up, she heard his deep sigh. "Houston, are you there?"

"Not for long. I'm on my way over there to deal with that jerk living in your house. What *is* up with him? I plan to put him in his place. He needs to stop getting in my way. Stat."

Kelly wondered if he'd used the medical terminology because she was a doctor. Her eyes followed Lynton as he left the room. "Come on now. You can't resort to that kind of behavior. Ignore it and it'll go away. Ignore him and he'll hate it. He doesn't like to be disregarded."

"Ignore him like hell! I'm about to put my size thirteen and a half all up in his narrow behind. Your boy is tripping hard. He'd better come down from whatever he's high on. I'm not taking much more lip from him. I called to wish you a pleasant day and look what ended up happening. He purposely tried to ruin my good mood."

Kelly laughed to ease the tension. "I'm glad he failed. I'm happy you called to start my day out on a bright note. But can I call you back once I get settled in the car? As it is, I'll need to take my coffee with me. Lynton and I don't have a thing to discuss. I don't want to be late for my first appointment. I'm not a doctor who keeps her patients on ice while chatting with staff or handling personal phone calls. That's disrespectful."

"Call me on my cell. I'm heading out to Austin and Ashleigh's ranch. We're meeting about the cruise to get everything finalized. We're only a few days away from sailing. I can't wait to be out on the high seas with you."

"I've been thinking about it a lot, too. I'll call in a few minutes." She smiled as she hung up the phone, happy Houston had called. It *was* a great start to her day.

Kelly grabbed a foam cup and poured fresh coffee into it, dumping the old. During the conversation with Houston, Lynton had come back into the room. She'd made up her mind not to address his ignorance right now because of time restraints, but he would get a huge piece of her mind later on.

"Are you ignoring me, just like you told that arrogant son of a gun to do?"

"You know what? You need to leave well enough alone. I thought you were an adult, but it looks like some ground rules have to be set. For one, please don't answer my door or telephone unless I ask you to. Lynton, I love our friendship, but you have to respect me and my home. If you can't do that, please check in to a hotel until you can move to Green Tee."

Lynton looked shocked. "You're serious, aren't you? I was hoping we'd eventually get back to where we left off with each other."

"About that, Lynton, you know we've never been anything but close friends since med school. I resent you trying to make Houston believe we had a love affair. I didn't say anything to the contrary because I don't want to embarrass you. We can't pick back up on something we never had."

Lynton's laughter was sarcastic. "You either have a bad memory or you don't care to remember. We went out on our first date two days after we met."

Kelly looked a little surprised by the comment. "We went to the library together! And we did that to work on an assignment. So how do you qualify that as a date? Everything we did together had to do with school. When we attended parties and other social events, we went with our group of close friends."

"You just burst my bubble. I've been operating under the assumption that we had something special going on back then. I thought the timing was just bad for us."

Kelly felt a sudden rush of sympathy for Lynton. Walking over to him, she took his hand. "I'm sorry if you're lonely. I know relocating is hard. Been there, done that. But you can't use me to fill the void. That is what you're doing, isn't it?"

"I wouldn't do that to you." His expression grew serious. "I've always been hot for you. We were extremely close friends before you transferred back to Baylor. We've never been out of touch."

"And we never have to be. Before you moved to Houston, we *did* talk a lot. You're my friend." She kissed his cheek. "We'll always be friends, but I'm in love with Houston Carrington. My heart chose him instantly. Listen, I've got to run." Kelly grabbed her purse and briefcase and ran for the garage door. "Have a great day, Lynton."

"What if he doesn't love you?" Lynton shouted after her.

Feeling the dead weight of his heavy-handed comment, Kelly slowly turned to face him. "It won't change my feelings for him. I love him. As my friend, I hope you'll try to be happy for me. If not, I won't be subjected to your negativity."

In her car, Kelly leaned her head against the steering wheel. Lynton's barbed question had impacted her more than she'd let show. Loving someone was no guarantee to receiving love back. Houston hadn't said he loved her nor had she told him how deep her feelings were for him. They'd just committed to dating exclusively. No way would she ask him if he loved her. If he did or didn't, he'd tell her in his own time and in his own way.

What if Houston can't return my love? What will I do then?

"Continue to love him," she whispered emotionally. "I will always love Houston."

As Kelly picked up her cell to punch in Houston's code, the ring tone "Hot Like Me" sounded. She glanced at the caller ID and drew in a deep breath. "Good morning, Mom. How's it going?"

"We need to see you, Kelly. When can you come to the house?"

"I don't know. My office schedule is pretty full and I'm trying to tie up all loose ends before I go on a cruise." Her parents lived on the other side of town in Sugarland.

"A cruise? With Houston Carrington?" Carolyn asked.

"The entire Carrington family is traveling. The trip is a birthday gift from the triplets to their mother. I was invited by Houston to join them...and I accepted."

"I see," Carolyn said, sounding slightly miffed. "If you can manage to squeeze us in for a visit before you go away, as soon as you possibly can, we'd appreciate it. You're welcome to bring Houston along. I'll wait to hear back from you."

"Okay, Mom. I'll get back to you. Give my best to Dad." Without further comment, Kelly disconnected the line, immediately feeling empty inside.

As Kelly rewound in her head the conversation with her mother, the strain in Carolyn's voice echoed in her head. *Was something wrong with one of them?* She hoped not. Recalling her promise to get to back to Houston, she punched in his code.

"Hey, beautiful, you all settled down in your car?"

"I am, finally. What are your plans after the visit to the ranch?" she asked.

"I have a few errands to run, like picking up my dry cleaning and getting a new battery for my watch. Then I hope to have dinner with my lady later on. Are you free?"

"If I wasn't, I'd change my plans." Kelly smiled. "I can hardly wait to see you. Surprise is in every moment I spend with you."

"I know what you mean." He paused for a moment to gather his thoughts. "What are we going to do about Lynton? I'm not so sure I can handle much more from him."

"I know it's an awkward situation for you. I feel the same way. I'll try to pin him down to a move-out date. I won't let him continue to interfere in our private affairs."

"That's good to hear. Everyone has a breaking point...and I'm at mine."

"Don't worry, Houston. I'll handle it."

"I believe you will. Do you have a full patient-load today?"

"Unless someone cancels, I'm booked solid. I have hospital rounds to make. I also plan to visit the physical rehabilitation center. I like to check on my rehab patients. I get progress updates from the therapists, but it's more personal than that for me."

"That's because you're one of the best doctors in your field. Hope I never get injured, but I'd put my health-care needs in your hands in a heartbeat. I trust you as a doctor and as a woman. I trust you completely, Kelly." *I even trust my heart to you.*

"You've just made my day brighter than bright," she sang out.

Kelly then told Houston about the odd conversation she'd had with Carolyn.

"You sound concerned. It feels like you need some moral support. Besides that, you might want to do the visit before we leave town. Since we're getting together later, maybe we could stop by your parents' home before having dinner."

Kelly didn't have to think about Houston's remarks to know he was right. She was pleased that he'd offered to go with her, though she hadn't asked, nor had she mentioned her mother's offer for him to come. "Is five-thirty or so good for you?"

"It's fine by me. I'll pick you up at your office. It's closer to our destination."

"Great. I'll need to get back with my mother and see how she feels about the timing. I'll only call back if our plans need to change."

"I hope you know you don't need a specific reason to call me. I love hearing from you any time of the day or night."

Kelly blushed. "Thanks. Same goes here. See you later."

"Have a great day, Kelly-Kel."

Houston stood on the west bank of his brother's ranch, just a few yards from the grassy knoll, where Austin and Ashleigh were looking out over the lake, fully stretched out on a blanket. Even though the sun always rose and set in their eyes, the happy couple loved to watch sunrises and sunsets together. It was part of their normal routine, along with numerous other adventures they loved to indulge in.

As Houston started toward his family, he watched as Austin engaged Ashleigh in a lingering kiss. He was happy they made each other feel beautiful inside and out. Although Ashleigh had gained weight and her protruding belly kept them a distance apart, Austin still thought his wife was the sexiest, most beautiful woman on the continent.

Houston hurried across the lawn. "Morning, folks." He dropped down on the blanket. "It must be nice to never have to wonder where you stand with one another. You guys say and show your feelings in so many ways. Your love is a thing of pure beauty."

Austin was surprised to hear Houston sounding so sentimental. The tone he'd used had been soft and his heart had been in it. Maybe Kelly *was* getting through to him. Out of habit, Austin looked down at his watch, only to realize he hadn't put it on. "Is Dallas up at the house?"

"He wasn't here yet the last time we talked, but he wasn't too far from the ranch. That was about twenty minutes ago."

"The cook is scheduled today so Dallas probably has her fixing breakfast." Austin got to his knees and then slipped Ashleigh's slippers onto her feet. Being as gentle and cautious as possible, Austin helped his wife up from the ground.

Houston and Austin looked at each other and laughed. Seated at the kitchen table, Dallas was all smiles. The amount of food set out before him was astounding. Pancakes, sausage, eggs, fluffy biscuits, toast and apple butter were all within easy reach of his fork. Pitchers of cold milk and apple and cranberry juices were at his disposal.

Once Houston sat down, he picked up a plate and began to fill it with food. "Man, you had a head start. Looks like I'll have to play catch-up."

Dallas grinned. "You won't catch me, not on this round. This is my second plate."

"Didn't your mother teach you not to talk with your mouth full?" Houston asked Dallas in a playful tone. "I just happen to know that she did."

Figuring he'd have to referee his two carbon copies, Austin took a seat.

Houston shot a puzzled glanced at Austin. "How can you sit in front of all this delicious food and not eat? The aromas alone have to be killing you."

Shrugging, Austin grinned. "I'm waiting on Ash so we can eat together."

Ashleigh sauntered into the room. "I just heard my name. And here I appear."

Austin jumped up and pulled out the chair to the left of his. Knowing just what foods his wife liked, he fixed her plate before taking care of his own.

Houston felt like he was right in the middle of a love story every time he was with Ashleigh and Austin. There were so many people who envied what his brother and sister-in-law had. He'd never begrudged their love, nor had he ever desired the same kind of relationship they had. Even if he'd wanted what they had he wouldn't be jealous of them. All he desired for them was profound happiness, peace and utter contentment. Although he had been closely watching the love his brother and wife had for each other—not to mention his parents' relationship—he'd never fantasized about a "future in forever."

Leading the life of a loner was something he no longer saw in his future.

Kelly had grown on him unexpectedly and in magnificent ways. He'd come to realize that she wouldn't have been okay getting too emotionally involved with him without a commitment. Although he remained somewhat confused about the drastic changes in their relationship he also felt happy and at peace. The incredible times he'd shared with Kelly kept him smiling.

"I'm assuming everything for the cruise is finalized," Austin said to Dallas.

Getting up from his seat, Dallas nodded. "Hold up."

After retrieving the leather, shoulder-style briefcase he'd hung on the back of a bar stool, he reclaimed his seat. He then opened the briefcase and took out several stacks of paperwork. "I made everyone a copy of the itinerary." He handled stapled sets to Austin and Houston and kept one handy for referencing. "I'll hold on to Mom and Dad's paperwork until we get to the port. Giving it to them before then will spoil the surprise."

"Did we all get the type of cabins we asked for?" Austin inquired.

"Everyone has balcony suites. The travel agent said she'd get us a substantial group discount. And she did. With you and me sharing a suite," Dallas said to Houston, "we'll have plenty of extra room to move around in. There was about a hundred dollars more in the price of the balcony cabins after all discounts were applied. If you guys don't want to pay the extra money, I'll take care of it."

Both Houston and Austin reassured Dallas the monetary increase wasn't a problem. The family group then went over the cruise itinerary, adjourning the meeting a short time later. The guys decided to hang out and shoot a game or two of pool since they more than likely wouldn't see each other again until the cruise.

Kelly looked at the wall clock in her office. She had less than a half hour before Houston would arrive. She hadn't signed as many charts as she'd hoped to, but she decided to take them home and finish up there. Reading all the medical notes before she signed the charts was the only way for her. She would never put her John Hancock to anything she hadn't read and understood thoroughly.

After stacking the last ten or so charts into her briefcase, Kelly slipped out of her office and headed straight for the ladies' room. All other employees were gone for the day. She used the bathroom first then washed and dried her hands. A fair amount of sanitizer was used next. Just as she exited the lavatory, her cell rang. It was Houston.

"I'm in the parking garage, parked right next to your car. Are you all ready to go, or do you want me to come up to the office?"

Kelly's heart fluttered at the sound of his voice. "I'll be right down, sweetheart, as soon as I grab everything I need and then set the alarm. See you in a minute or two."

"I'll be eagerly waiting."

Carolyn and Jared Charleston lived in a gated community, inside a beautiful estate home, with a four-car detached garage. The home's European-style furnishings were exquisitely posh and the artwork alone was worth a small fortune. The magnificent backyard and bar-equipped patio area had been designed with lavish entertaining in mind.

Houston wasn't easily impressed by material wealth, yet the Charleston home was an overwhelmingly expensive architectural design. As the owners gave him a brief tour, he closely viewed the period pieces throughout the palatial estate. It wasn't the home Kelly had grown up in so he didn't try to imagine her roaming the lavish surroundings.

"Houston, I'd love to show you my private collection of sports memorabilia. Some of it dates way back to the era of segregated sports leagues. Interested in checking it out?" Jared asked.

"Most definitely," Houston enthused. "My family also owns an extensive sports collection. We all have trophy rooms in our homes. On display in our parents' home are the trophies and plaques from our sports activities long before we turned pro."

"That'll work out nicely," Carolyn interjected. "Kelly and I can have a mother-and-daughter chat while you men talk sports." She looped her arm through Kelly's. "We'll have tea in the main library." There was also a medical reference library on the premises.

As the two couples split up, smiling, Kelly waved farewell to Houston.

Carolyn and Kelly sat down in navy blue leather wingback chairs. A silver tray and antique tea service had been set on a large leather ottoman in the same color. Milk, sugar and artificial sweeteners were provided for use.

Kelly remained perfectly still while Carolyn poured tea into two fragile-looking, porcelain china cups. Covertly, she watched her mother's every move, surprised that Carolyn knew she liked milk in her tea. The acquired taste had occurred in college.

"Mom, are you and Dad okay health-wise?"

"Of course we are. Outside of old age catching up to us, we're in perfect health."

Carolyn served Kelly and then got comfortable in her chair. "How've things been for you since we last saw each other at the awards ceremony?"

Kelly turned her palms up and shrugged. "Fine. Things couldn't be better."

Carolyn's eyes narrowed a tad. "They couldn't be?"

Kelly knew all too well the particular tone of voice her mother had used. It normally indicated her annoyance with something. "Mom, I answered your question truthfully. What didn't you like about my response?"

"How is it that things are fine for you when you have very little to do with your family, your parents, no less? It's time we get things out in the open. You have been angry with us since you were old enough to know what the word meant. Why, Kelly, why are you always so angry with your father and me?"

"I'm not getting into this with you." Shaking her head from side to side, Kelly leaped to her feet. "Once I locate Houston, we'll let ourselves out."

"Sit back down, young lady, this very minute," Carolyn thundered.

Stunned by the loud command, surprised by the threatening tone, Kelly obeyed.

"We *are* getting into this. It's long overdue. We can't right what we don't know is a wrong. Until you share your grievances with us, we're forced to live in the dark."

Rapidly, Kelley's eyes blinked back the burning tears. "Oh, Mom, please don't try to make me believe you don't have a clue about my anger problems. You can't convince me that you have no idea."

"I recall an angry outburst from you when you were around sixteen—and a few more that followed later on. The crux of those situations, if I recall correctly, was about us being away so much. Is that still a sore spot for you, Kelly, after all these years?"

Kelly appeared reluctant to respond. She felt like crying but was fearful of showing how deeply emotional she was. Her anger had bubbled and festered for many years now, eventually turning her into a raging river of raw resentment. Referring to it as a "sore spot" was a gross understatement. And it also greatly lacked sensitivity.

"Simply put, I'm filled to the brim with resentment." She licked her lips. "I've felt discarded by you and Dad for as long back as I can recall. You weren't there for me when I needed you most. It wasn't either of you, *doctors, no less,* who taught me about my menstrual cycle. Neither of you were there when I got home from school toting straight-A report cards. I can sit here all night and name instances where I felt abandoned. But what good would it do? The wall around my heart has become impenetrable."

A curious glint suddenly appeared in Kelly's eyes. "Why are you asking me about this now? Why does it matter to you all of a sudden?"

Carolyn smiled gently. "It has always mattered. And I haven't asked before now because I feared your responses." Her eyes appeared filled with remorse. "Then we saw you with Houston Carrington. Dad and I saw the way you two looked at each other. We not only observed the strong chemistry between you, we felt it, as did Mama Tilley and Papa Joseph. How many young men have you brought around for us to meet?"

Kelly took a minute to think over the query. The answer surprised even her. "Other than you and Dad meeting my dates for high school proms, I can't remember there being any others."

"Exactly!"

Kelly shrugged. "And what does that mean?"

Carolyn folded her hands and placed them in her lap. "If our baby is falling in love, and we believe you are, we want to go through the total experience with you. The metamorphosis is astonishing, Kelly. We want to be around to see you open up your heart to all the possibilities true love imparts. Can you please forgive us and let us into your life? You'll only understand the sacrifices we've made once you have kids of your own."

Kelly was speechless. This conversation flew so far below or so high above her radar she never would've guessed the topic. It took her a few seconds more to find her voice. "This talk about love. Where is it coming from?"

"It's in your eyes, your smile and overflowing from your heart. It's everywhere."

Carolyn and Jared had only been in her and Houston's company for a couple of hours. How could they possibly know how she felt about him? Kelly wasn't buying into the idea of love oozing from within her, yet she *was* crazy in love with the man. "I think you and Dad are getting ahead of yourselves over this. We just started dating exclusively. Please don't say anything like this in front of Houston. I don't want to scare him off."

Carolyn laughed softly. "Don't worry. That man isn't going anywhere he won't find you. Houston loves you as much as you love him. His feelings are crystal clear."

"Mom, please stop talking like that. Houston and I are so brand-new."

"Okay, okay, I'll silence my observations." She got up and walked over to her daughter. Taking both her hands, she propelled Kelly to her feet, pulling her into her arms. "Dad and I love you so much and we need you in our lives. Please give us some serious consideration. We're not getting any younger, Kelly, and we'd love to spend quality time together as a family. We want to have a meaningful relationship with you."

As the normally stoic Carolyn began to cry softly, an emotionally shaken Kelly immediately reached out to comfort her. "It'll be okay, Mom. The three of us will get together and talk when I get back from the cruise. I promise to make it happen."

Carolyn looked relieved. "Thank you, darling. Let's go find our men."

* * *

While her mother went off to tend to something in another room, Kelly stood back for a couple of minutes and watched Houston interact with her father. Though they had talked at the awards gala, there hadn't been much of a one-on-one opportunity. She was fascinated by body language and enjoyed interpreting the movements of others.

Slipping up behind her daughter, Carolyn whispered something in her ear.

Kelly turned to face her mother. "We didn't expect you to prepare dinner. We made plans to go out to eat. I don't know if Houston planned on a long visit here."

"Let's ask him. I did my best to fix your favorites. I had to consult Mama Tilley, of course. She recommended roasted leg of lamb and sweet potatoes whipped with lots of butter and a squirt of maple syrup. I came up with the steamed broccoli all on my own."

Kelly was pleased by her mom's desire to pleasure her palate. "It's a sweet gesture. If Houston can't stay, I will, but I'll need a ride back to the office to get my car."

"Anything you need, Kelly, anything at all. Dad and I are here for you. Now let's get in there and test your man's willpower."

Carolyn stepped into the gaming room and immediately announced to the men dinner was ready. Then she leapt righed into a rundown of the menu.

Houston smiled broadly. "I didn't know dinner was included, but I wouldn't think of declining." He looked at Kelly. "Are you okay with it?"

Impressed that he wanted her to weigh in, Kelly smiled sweetly. "I'm fine with it. I've never been able to turn down any cut of lamb. I can do marvelous things with lamb shanks and Indian curry. Mama Tilley often slips me some of her hot trade secrets." The look of regret on Carolyn's face had Kelly wishing she hadn't added the last remark.

"I'll have to keep that in mind," said Houston, reaching for Kelly's hand.

Seated at the formal dining table, large enough to accommodate a party of twelve, Jared asked God's blessing on the food and on the skilled hands that had prepared it.

The thought of Carolyn moving about in the kitchen, let alone cooking, niggled at Kelly's funny bone. It was even more comic to imagine her wearing an apron. She hadn't ever seen her mother prepare a single meal. Sure, she'd set a bowl of cold cereal, juice and hot toast in front of her daughter, but nothing beyond that. Tilley had run the kitchen, preparing all the meals from breakfast to supper. There were many nights the parents hadn't come home for dinner. On those evenings, Tilley and Joseph dined with Kelly.

After Kelly's first bite of lamb, she closed her eyes to savor the delicious flavor. Carolyn could take pride in the tender, juicy leg of lamb. "The meat is divine." She took a forkful of sweet potatoes. "Mmm, they're perfect." Despite the manners she'd been taught, she propped an elbow on the table. "How long has Mama Tilley been gone?"

Everyone laughed at Kelly's comical remark.

"Mama Carolyn fixed every bit of this food, daughter. Like I said, I did call and get some tips from Mama Tilley." Carolyn's eyes softened. "It was important to me to do this just for you, Kelly. I'm glad I'm making good grades."

"You get an A on everything, Mom. Thanks for *wanting* to do this for me."

The visit with her parents couldn't have gone any better under the current circumstances, Kelly thought. Both Carolyn and Jared had been extremely attentive to their only child. It was as if they'd found a way to anticipate her every need.

Kelly had to admit that she'd loved being the center of their attention. It wasn't a place she'd found herself in very often. When two people were totally wrapped up in their professions and in each other, they ignored everyone and everything else around them. She couldn't count the times she'd been made to feel like an inanimate object by her mom and dad. This evening had been a completely different experience.

Kelly laid her head back on the leather headrest. Both she and Houston had been quiet for the past twenty minutes or more. Jazz with vocals played nonstop on the radio channel. She'd worked hard to stay awake for the last few miles to her office knowing she'd have to be alert to drive home.

Houston rested his hand on Kelly's thigh. "The exit to your office is coming up, but I'd like you to spend the night with me. I can drive you to work in the morning."

She looked down at her clothes, apparel she'd changed into at the office just before Houston had picked her up. "Sounds tempting, but I don't have office hours until late afternoon. I don't want to be without my car."

"You can take this one. I have an SUV and a Mercedes."

"A Mercedes, huh? Maybe I want to roll in it."

He laughed. "Any one of the cars you want. Please just say yes to my offer."

She gave him a sexy smile. "Yes!"

Chapter 12

There was something strange yet wonderful about Kelly spending the night in his home, in his bed. He was excited about it, as he turned back the comforter. It wasn't that he'd never spent an entire night with a woman, it just hadn't occurred in their homes.

Houston's mother, sister-in-law and Lanier stayed there overnight in guest rooms, when it was his turn to host holiday festivities. All holidays had once been spent at their parents' ranch. A few years back, the guys had decided to take on some of the workload, in view of their mom and dad growing older. Entertaining was a lot of work.

Houston sat down on the edge of the mattress. "Come here."

Walking across the room, Kelly took slow but deliberate strides, lightly swiveling her curvy hips. The tone of Houston's voice had been low and seductive and she didn't want to seem too eager. Dropping down on her knees, right in front of him, she looked up at him, pursing her lips in a sultrily pouting way. "You summoned?"

Grinning, he reached down and removed her jacket, carefully laying it aside on a nearby chair. Keeping his eyes trained on her lovely face, he slowly undid each button on her white silk blouse before completely separating it from her luscious body. Then he slipped over her head the lacy camisole.

The red-and-white candy-cane-striped bra was physically pleasing to Houston, making him wonder if her panties matched. If so, maybe they were edible ones that tasted like the peppermint candy he loved. The provocative pattern revved up his sexual desires.

Houston popped open the button on the waistband of her red trousers. After she stood, he unzipped them, thoroughly enjoying sliding the slacks down over her hips, thighs, legs and feet. The panties *did* match the bra.

Instead of stripping Kelly of her sexy underwear, Houston picked up his freshly laundered shirt and helped her into it. "Since you don't have a nightgown, my shirt will help keep you warm. The heat from my body will do the rest." Stretching out in the bed, he reached back and guided Kelly down beside him. "I can't get over how beautiful you are. I love being intimately close with you."

With her eyes glazed over, Kelly appeared dazed. She liked how he clarified things for her. "I'm all excited now. How will I ever get to sleep?" Sleep was the furthest thing from their lust-filled minds, she knew.

Houston grinned wickedly. "I can definitely help you out with that. Just lie still and let me work my magic, girl. I know how to relax every single muscle on your sexy body. Leave it all up to me."

Houston never failed to make Kelly blush like crazy. Knowing what a special treat she was in for, she smiled, allowing her body to go lax. She could hardly wait to receive the mind-blowing muscle relaxants he'd prescribe for her and then expertly administer. He had a tongue made of silk and glowing embers for fingers. His hands were nothing short of bonfires.

Ready to take his lovely sienna-wonder to dreamland, Houston lit a candle and then turned off the bedside lamp. His eyes closed as his hands reached out and began tenderly caressing her body, showering her entire anatomy with featherlike kisses. Beneath his hands was a live one, a beautiful, sexy woman. He was extremely proud to have the incomparable Kelly Charleston in his life.

Houston recalled how making love to Kelly the first time had nearly brought him to tears. How blessed were they to be starting out in a wonderful relationship? Would they ever be crazy in love and eventually love each other enough to marry someday? How quickly his thoughts about commitments and nuptials had changed. Houston knew his sudden transformation was remarkably unbelievable to many, especially to him. ˙

After Houston had taken his sweet time in removing the last article of her attire—the candy-cane-striped bikinis—he lay along-side her and brought her into his arms. As the foreplay heated up, Houston and Kelly laughed softly, nipping, nuzzling, kissing wildly and squeezing tenderly. All she could do was lie in wait for her fine hero to make hot, sizzling love to her.

"Stairway to Heaven," an oldie by the O'Jays, had Houston's mind filled to the brim with suggestive notions. Already halfway up the staircase to eternity, Houston kissed Kelly passionately, his tongue uniting hungrily with hers. While stroking her inner thighs, he unashamedly looked at her naked beauty, wishing he could forever capture her in this natural state of erotica. The glow of the candlelight made her appear angelic.

In Houston's opinion, Kelly had the perfect sienna-brown body, the magnificently formed lips of a black goddess, thick and pouting, and the delicate hands of an angel. She was having tons of fun letting him teach her all the pleasurable things each physical feature was designed for.

Instructing her in the art of sheer erotica had him feeling as if his teaching methods showcased some of his finest talents. To make things even more exciting for Kelly and him, Houston reached over to the nightstand and picked up a book. Reading by candlelight a few paragraphs from one of Zane's fire-breathing novels came next.

Not long into the readings, Houston and Kelly got even hotter and heavier into each other. She didn't wait for him to place his hands where she needed them most. Lifting his right hand, she directed it to the moist, fleshy spot burning for him like an out-of-control brush fire. "Touch me deep inside, Houston," she whispered in a throaty voice. "I want to feel hell's fire all through me. Take me to where I want to go, high up on that mountaintop we've claimed as our own. I want you to lie deep inside me and slowly ride the rolling waves of fiery ecstasy."

Houston didn't need a second invitation. Mounting her sweet body would always be his pleasure. Kelly was getting more vocal in her requests to him, he noted. The first time they'd made love she'd only given him an idea of what she wanted, yet he hadn't failed to give her exactly what he thought she desired.

"Girl," he whispered in her ear, "I'm going to take you there right now. Draw me in deeper. Fasten your legs around me tightly, sweetheart. I don't want you to fall off during the wild ride. We're going to take everything to an entirely different level."

With that said, Houston's fingers slowly worked their way deep inside Kelly, paving the way for his grand entry. The teasing and taunting from his hands and mouth had her writhing in delicious agony. Once his tongue took over completely, she simply got lost in a haze of mindlessness. Moans, soft screams and incoherent babbling were all Kelly was capable of.

In one sleek, majestic move, Houston was inside Kelly, riding her up and down the mountaintop, hard and fast, slow and tantalizing, over and over again. He rocked back and forth in unison with the movements of her riotous body, riding fast and furious the waves of their wild fervor.

In climbing the last few steps to the stairway to heaven, he had them flying even higher up than she'd requested. Taking her to the mountaintop wasn't high enough. As she loudly screamed out his name, twitching uncontrollably beneath his weight, he shuddered, whispering her name softly. The powerful release came the same exact time.

Houston rolled over and pulled Kelly into his arms. "Girl, you've got me whipped! What am I going to do with you?"

Kelly smiled devilishly. "Exactly what you just did. Encore, lover!"

Houston looked surprised to see Lynton half-naked when he stepped into Kelly's house for an evening of fun and relaxation. He hadn't seen her in a few days due to her busy schedule. She had also been on-call. Her friend had far too much nerve, especially when he was only a houseguest. Answering the door without a shirt on was rude and totally inappropriate. Houston thought back on the phone conversation he and Kelly had had several days ago about the problems he had with Lynton living there.

"Hey, Carrington, what's up? You don't look too happy. Is Dr. Kelly giving you a hard time? Better get used to it. She's good for that."

To avoid a verbal retort, Houston bit down on his lower lip. He didn't know what Lynton meant by his remarks and he didn't care to find out. The last thing he wanted was to get into a verbal confrontation or physical altercation with anyone. If he was to so much as raise his hand toward another human being, a lawsuit would be filed. Athletes and celebrities were prime targets for people to sue. It was a lucrative practice.

Instead of taking the latest bit of unsavory bait Lynton constantly dangled before him, Houston headed toward the hallway leading to Kelly's private suite.

"You'd better get out of this relationship while you can. Kelly's playing with your heart, just like she's done with mine," Lynton yelled after Houston. "Do you really think we live here together in a platonic way? If you believe that, you're dumber than you look.

Kelly wants her cake while she eats it. She loves keeping a string of men on hold."

Turning quickly on his heels, Houston came at Lynton, fists balled tight.

"What's going on in here?" Kelly asked, having heard Lynton's loud ranting and raving. When she saw Houston in the room, it was all too easy to figure out.

Kelly's voice made Houston stop dead in his tracks. Silently, he thanked God for intervening. She hadn't arrived at that precise moment by accident. He believed that with everything in him. In saving him, she had also spared Lynton a serious beatdown.

Kelly rushed over to Houston and took his hand. "Let's go to my room. I'm glad you're here." She cut her eyes sharply at Lynton, giving him a hotter-than-angry look.

Houston hated asking himself inwardly what *was* going on with Kelly and Lynton. He didn't believe she was this cheating demon her friend had painted her as. But why would he say those vile things? He has his answer in the next instant.

Jealous people were deadly and desperate. Desperate folks lived out their desperation through ill accusations, near tangible threats and nasty deeds.

Once she was in her master bedroom, Kelly threw herself across the bed. "I'm sorry about this situation. Lynton living here is no longer working. I know that, but I still haven't gotten up the nerve to tell him he has to leave."

Houston shook his head. "It hasn't worked from day one." As much as he wanted to, he refrained from telling her what Lynton had said about her. He already had an idea how she might feel about it. The ugly remarks would hurt her. "If you hadn't come into the room when you did, the good doctor might have a busted face and a broken nose. I don't like him, Kelly. I can't tell you what to do about your friends, but his constant presence in our life is starting to affect our relationship."

Looking perplexed, Kelly sat up straight. "What are you saying, Houston? Better yet, what aren't you saying? I knew he was getting to you, but not like this."

"How in the world could you not know how bad it's gotten? He's rude as hell to me every time I come here. The only way to miss his bad attitude, you'd have to be blind. Even then, your other senses would be heightened to the point you'd feel his exploding animosity. I'm tired of the interference, sick of the tension."

She pursed her lips. "What do you suggest?"

"It's not up to me to recommend anything. You said you'd handle it. What do *you* want to do about it? What do *you* feel needs to be done? He's not living at my house."

Kelly rolled her eyes. "Don't be a smart-butt. I know where he's living. I invited him to stay here out of his need and not out of any desire on my part."

Houston threw up his hands. "I can't advise you. All I can do is let you know how it's affecting me and our relationship." He turned toward the door. "I should go now. I can't stop thinking about beating him to a pulp."

Kelly winced. "What would it solve?"

"Nothing. But it sure would help relieve all this tension."

"If you leave, you're letting him win. Is that what you want, Houston?"

Houston hurried across the room. Dropping down on the bed, he reached up and pulled Kelly on top of him. "Being with you, spending time together, making love to you is what I want. Having Lynton here restricts us. We should be able to walk around the house, nude if we want, raiding the refrigerator together after a bout of passionate lovemaking. With him in the house, everything we do feels guarded. He probably spies on us. Wondering if he's peering through the keyhole is not a comfortable feeling."

Kelly laughed. "Thinking like that is a bit eccentric, isn't it?"

He rolled Kelly off him, giving her a stern look. "I wouldn't make light of my feelings if I were you. I don't toy with yours. This situation isn't funny to me. Lynton says the relationship between you two is not platonic. What do you say to that?" The hurt in her eyes struck his heart. He'd done exactly what he hadn't wanted to do, what he'd tried so desperately to refrain from. His simply spoken question had floored her.

Kelly appeared genuinely horrified. "He said that?"

"Would I lie to you?"

The honesty of his statement was visible in his eyes. "Never. If anything, you're too honest. I don't know why Lynton says these things, other than to make you jealous. He's definitely envious of you. I will keep my promise about getting a move-out date, but not until after we get back from the cruise. His place won't be ready before then."

"He can go to a hotel. The man's a doctor. He's not destitute. If he can't afford a hotel stay, I'll pick up the tab. It's time for you to have him move on."

"Are you telling me what to do in my own home, Houston?"

His jaw muscles clenched. "It wasn't my intent, but I guess that's what I did. Do whatever you want about Lynton and I'll do what's best for me. In the interest of keeping me out of jail for assault and battery, I won't come back as long as he's here."

Kelly looked dumbstruck. "Are you saying we won't see each other again?"

"What I said is I won't come here. You're welcome at my place anytime. When a man knows he's being tempted, especially into committing an illegal act, he won't let himself be controlled. Lynton wants me to hit him so he can sue me. It's not happening. Staying away from here while he's present is what's best for me."

Kelly sucked her teeth. "I think you're acting unreasonable, but it's your call."

"Damn right it is." With that said, Houston walked out. If Kelly didn't understand him or what was happening to them, only God could help her get it.

Unable to believe what had just occurred, Kelly stared at the door Houston had nearly slammed off its hinges. She buried her face into a pillow, muffling her moans. This wasn't the wonderful evening she had planned with him. As she thought about the cruise, tears came to her eyes. The sailing was only a few days away. He hadn't said anything about it, but she couldn't help wondering if he still wanted her along.

After giving more thought to the situation she and Houston were in, she knew what part of the situation she could blame him for. As for her part in it, she had been rebelling against what others wanted for her ever since she was old enough to make decisions. Her parents hadn't been able to force her into a career in cardiology and Houston had failed at making her choose between him and Lynton.

No, she thought, Houston hadn't been asking her to choose. He only wanted to rid them of the tense confrontations Lynton created in their lives. She owed Houston an apology. Before she did that, she'd have to act on the very issue threatening to separate them forever. Houston wouldn't believe she was serious if she didn't give Lynton a notice to move. However, she knew she couldn't do it without feeling guilty.

If she was on or off the cruise was all up to Houston. She wasn't backing out of the deal. One way or the other, he had very little time to let her know exactly what he wanted. This was Houston's call.

Why was this birthday cruise such a flip-flop issue with them?

Kelly got up off the bed and ran into the bathroom. After giving her hair a few brisk strokes with the brush, she refreshed her lip gloss and rushed out. She went downstairs to take care of business.

From the doorway of the living room, Kelly quietly watched Lynton. As he put on the shirt he'd just picked up off the sofa, she wondered about it. *Had he taken it off just to greet her guest?* He'd only answered the door because she'd yelled out to ask him to do so. She'd had no idea he was shirtless, but he had known Houston was expected.

Feeling he was being watched, Lynton looked up and saw Kelly. "Hey, what's up with you? Has 'the man' already broken your heart? You look so unhappy."

Kelly came into the room and sat in a chair facing the sofa. "Maybe you should tell me what's up. Why do you continue to harass Houston?"

"I guess he's been bellyaching to you again. We hassle each other and he normally starts it. Can't your big man handle his business without involving you?"

"If he handled it the way he wants to, you might lose that smirk you constantly wear around here. Houston doesn't come to my home to hassle you. He comes to see me. That seems to be a big problem for you. Why's that?"

Lynton pushed his hand through his hair. "You know how I feel about you, Kelly. It is how I've always felt. Why do you keep ignoring what's between us?"

Kelly raised an eyebrow. "What's between us is friendship— nothing more."

"Whatever! I can't believe you're willing to give up true love for a passing fancy. Houston Carrington is a playboy. His team is out of the playoffs so you're probably nothing more than this summer's fling. What'll you do when the new season starts and he's back on the prowl again in cities all across the country? Can you trust he'll be true to only you? Do you believe he can resist having a woman in every sports venue he visits?"

Kelly's heart began to pound fast and her hands began to tremble. The look on Lynton's face seemed to suggest he enjoyed taunting her. This wasn't the same man she had come to know over many, many years. "Why *are* you doing this?"

"All is fair in love in war. I'm in a battle with Houston over your heart. I don't give up or back down easily. I'm relentless when I want something. And I want you."

"Even when you know there's no chance in hell to get what you're after?"

He raised a brow. "As long as we're both breathing, there's a chance. Kelly, I can give you what Houston can't. You need a stable man in your life, someone who'll be there for you both day and night. What you don't need is some guy who spends half his time out of town. You'll quickly become a basketball widow. Is that what you want?"

Kelly got to her feet. "I'm in love with Houston. Do you want a woman who's in love with another man? I can't love you the way you want. I love you as a friend."

Lynton shrugged. "If I believed you were in love with Houston, I'd back off instantly. I don't think you love him. You're gone on the idea of being with a superstar. You're into the hype and the mad attention you get when you're with him. It won't last."

"That's your opinion, one I'm not buying into. I had planned to wait until I got back from the cruise to ask you to move out, but you need to do it now, tonight. I want you gone. If you can't get all your stuff out right away, come back for it while I'm at work. I won't change the security code until everything of yours is gone, but it'll be changed before I go on vacation." With that said, Kelly calmly left the room.

Houston scrolled through his cell-phone contacts until he reached Kelly's number. He had left her home on a bad note. It was getting to him way more than Lynton ever could. She shouldn't have to get hurt because two men were rivals for her heart. If he didn't believe he'd already won her love and affection, he'd move on. Lynton was not the man for Kelly. Her friend acted like a spoiled little boy who had to have his way. "Well, he's not getting his way with her or with me." Houston cursed under his breath.

Instead of pressing the code to Kelly's number, Houston closed the flip phone. Important matters like this had to be handled in person. Turning around and going back to her house was his next thought. The stress of dealing with Lynton again made him falter. Making sure Kelly was okay overruled any bad feelings he had about her friend.

Picking up the cell, Houston scrolled the numbers again. This time he pushed Talk. As the phone rang and rang, disappointment hit him hard. Then her voice mail came on.

Unable to believe Kelly was standing at his front door, Houston brought her into his arms and kissed her deeply. Security hadn't rung him. It was unusual, but he didn't care how she'd gotten through the gates. They were back together.

Kelly looked slightly ashamed. "I'm sorry about how things went down. I felt I was being told what to do and I rebelled against it. A lot of the rebellion stems from my parents wanting me to go into their field of medicine. That's not what I wanted. Nor did I want to make Lynton move without anywhere to go, but I saw the necessity in it."

Houston kissed her gently on the lips. "All that matters is you being here with me. I tried calling you to say I was coming back, but I got your voice mail."

"I don't even have my cell phone with me. That's how much of a hurry I was in to get to you and apologize. I am sorry."

"I owe you an apology, too. I'm sorry I lost it at your place. I usually can keep a level head, but Lynton has a way of goading me in the worst way."

"It's over with now. We're back on the same page. I told Lynton he had to move out. I insisted he move out right away and I made it clear his things had to be gone before we left on the cruise. I hated it to end up like this but it did."

Houston easily empathized with Kelly. He could plainly see how much it hurt her to evict her longtime friend. But he didn't see Lynton as being true blue to her. People who cared about each other didn't cause the kind of aggravation he'd visited upon her.

"Are you hungry, Kelly? I was about to order dinner from one of my favorite local restaurants. They deliver."

Kelly nodded. "I could use a good meal. I'm pretty hungry. But

I wouldn't have been able to eat a thing if our differences weren't settled."

"They *are* settled and we're going to dine on a feast," Houston assured her.

Happy, full and contented, Kelly pushed back from the table. The Greek meals Houston had ordered for their dining pleasure had been superb. "You really outdid yourself on the food orders. Now what I need is a soft spot to lie down and relax."

Houston got up and walked around the table. He extended his hand to Kelly. "I have the perfect place." Once she was on her feet, his arm circled her waist. "Follow me."

Houston escorted Kelly to his bedroom, where he pulled from a lower dresser drawer a brand-new navy swimsuit and cover-up. "Will a dip in the hot tub relax you?"

She picked up the sexy spandex. "It's beautiful. I love the color." Standing on tiptoes, Kelly gave Houston a blistering kiss. "I can think of other ways for you to help me relax, but we'll start with a good soaking. Want to help me change clothes?"

Houston's grin was huge. "My pleasure."

Keeping gentle eyes trained on her, Houston slowly pulled Kelly's top over her head. Turning her around, he undid the hooks on her bra, allowing it to slip off her arms. His hands tenderly fondled her full, rounded breasts, massaging her nipples between two fingers. She squirmed beneath his exhilarating touch.

His mouth took possession of her right breast, suckling it passionately, hungrily. If this activity kept up, Houston saw a dip in the hot tub flying right out the window. The bed was calling out their names. His manhood was already hard as a rock and his body soared at temperatures hotter than the heated spa.

Even though Houston's mind wandered a bit, he still took his sweet time in disrobing Kelly. He enjoyed removing her jeans and then the itty-bitty bikinis. Now that she was totally nude, his hand went on a wild touch-and-feel spree. His heart trembling, he helped her into the swimsuit. The thigh-high cuts were a big turn-on for him and he couldn't wait to remove it later. His mouth sought out hers again. "You're beautiful, you know. Let me change in the bathroom so we can head out to the pool area. I'll be right back, sweetheart."

Kelly stretched her eyes. "Excuse me! I don't think so. You're not robbing me of the pleasure you just indulged yourself in. Boy, you'd better get over here and let me unwrap you like a Christmas package."

Houston cracked up. "It's summer, but I'd love to have you strip me bare. Are you aware we might not make it out to the pool? I'm already on fire for you. I don't know how much more tempting foreplay I can take. I want to be inside you."

Kelly smiled wickedly. "Let's see if you've really reached breaking point."

After drawing closer to Houston, she caressed his mouth with her own, heating him up more and more with wet and wild kisses. She then took her own sweet time in opening all the buttons on his shirt, removing it a lot slower than he'd removed her top. His nipples were already taut—and she wasted no time laving each one, nipping wildly yet gently with her teeth. Houston's muscles rippled as she torched a bonfire. Remaining in control of her desires was getting harder and harder. The bed looked so inviting.

Kelly spread out her hands across his chest, massaging his pectorals, loving the feel of his hard muscles. Her agile fingers then went to work on unbuckling his belt. Smiling up at him, she lazed his zipper down. While inching his pants off his waist and down his rock-solid thighs, she moaned at the satiny feel of his bare flesh. Massaging his nudity was definitely one of her favorite pleasures.

Once Houston was fully disrobed, Kelly couldn't resist caressing his manhood, stroking him up and down with sweet tenderness. Engaging him in a lingering kiss was nearly her undoing. If they were going to the hot tub, she knew they'd better get on with it. There were a few erotic moves that could be executed in the water. The thought of it thrilled her silly. "Let's get it on, Houston. The hot tub awaits us."

The backyard of Houston's estate home was very private, where prying eyes could not invade his privacy. The Olympic pool was crystal clear, the lighting soft and subdued. The finest in decking surrounded the pool and hot tub, extending outward as part of a very large patio. The French doors in his master bedroom led out onto a balcony overlooking the property. Panoramic views from several second-floor windows gave him an excellent view of his estate.

The swirling water was hot and steamy when Houston and Kelly stepped into the hot tub. The jets were forceful, kicking strongly. As she settled down on the curved seating, placing her back against one of the jets, she pulled him close to her, wrapping her legs around his waist. Since he hadn't put on swimming trunks, she felt the fullness of his manhood pressing against her flesh. All she could do was purr like a kitten.

As Houston bent his head, Kelly tilted her face upward to meet his kiss. His hands entwined in her hair as the kiss deepened. Once Houston seated himself on the bench, he lifted Kelly and positioned her on his lap.

Smiling lazily, Houston lowered the straps on Kelly's swimsuit. As he sprinkled her bare shoulders with butter-soft kisses, he locked his eyes with hers. "I don't know why we covered your natural beauty with a bathing suit in the first place, but it has to go." With that said, he began to peel away the spandex.

Kissing every inch of her naked flesh had Houston desperately wanting to be deep inside her. Her hands stroking him so fervently and her tongue teasing his nipples had him crazy with longing. As he raised his body, keeping her lodged tightly against him, he turned on the floor jets. He then made his way to the center of the hot tub, where it was deepest. The uprising of streaming water stimulated them even more.

As Houston's fingers entered the opening of Kelly's luscious treasure, her body began to tremble hard. His digits felt so gentle, massaging her inner core, causing her to bite down on her lower lip. As well as delighting in his ladylove's body language, he also loved to see the passionate arousal alight in her eyes. The magical look in her orbs always mesmerized him, making him smile. Fully satisfying her body in every way possible was his main purpose in life at this moment.

The hot tub temperature had grown rather intense, threatening to dry out Kelly's natural moisture. With the heat nearly too hot for them to withstand, Houston lifted her out of the water and carried her over to a padded chaise lounge. After he lowered himself onto the chaise, he slowly guided Kelly down over his manhood, thrusting upward gently until he'd entered her with tender care. Out of her mind with her physical need for him, she threw her head back, allowing him to pleasure her starving body.

As Kelly moved wildly over Houston, his hands held on tightly to her hard-thrusting hips. Feeling zoned out, she worked her man into a state of wild frenzy. When her gyrations came harder and faster, he quickly picked up on the shift in rhythm, moving in perfect tune to the harmony of her sweetly singing body. As climaxes roared through Houston and Kelly like a powerful force of nature, panting cries of passion rent the air.

Still locked tightly onto Houston's hard flesh, Kelly moved forward until she could rest her head on his chest. His arms instantly tightened around her like a band of steel, massaging her back, cooing sweet nothings in her ear. He wasn't alarmed when he felt the wetness of her tears on his chest. Kelly had also cried the first time they'd made love, showing him she was completely satisfied. Her emotional release was a good thing.

Houston stretched out his arm until his hand came into contact with one of the oversize beach towels he'd laid out on a matching lounger. He covered Kelly's body with the soft linen. "It's getting kind of cool out here. Are you uncomfortable, sweetheart?"

Kelly lifted her head slightly to make eye contact with Houston. "No. I'm actually very comfortable, but a shower and a nap will work wonders for this satiated body."

"Hmm, I thought I'd already worked wonders for you. Am I wrong?"

"You did more than that, Mr. Carrington. That's why I'm so sleepy. The shower will invigorate me, perhaps enough for an encore. It just might keep me here all night."

Houston grinned broadly. "Say no more, sweetheart. I've got the picture." He'd love to have yet another all-nighter with her.

Although Kelly had voiced her desire to shower and nap, she continued to lie in the safety of Houston's strong arms, basking in the sweet peace. She was so happy they'd cleared up their earlier misunderstanding. Talking things through had brought them closer. She had feared it was over for them, and she didn't know what she would've done if he had ended their affair. Being in love with Houston made her vulnerable—and she was highly aware of it every waking moment.

As Kelly tearfully told Houston about the conversation she'd had with her mother earlier in the day, his emotions nearly erupted, too, his heart reaching out to hers.

"The conversation between this daughter and her mother went very well, leaving me feeling optimistic. Hearing my mother say how much she loved me was like a healing balm to my spirit. She said things I've never heard her say before. My father loves me, too, and he wants us to grow closer. It was shocking to hear her admit that she and my father hadn't intended to make me feel unloved, unsafe and insecure. They'd thought they were securing my future. She said she honestly didn't know how left out I felt."

Houston was really understanding with Kelly throughout the explanation of her emotionally trying ordeal with her parents. He listened closely to all that she said. "It seems you felt like no one had ever been committed to you, not even your parents. Now I have a better understanding of why I've been somewhat cagey about commitment. Because I feel deeply for you, I promise to use extreme care with your heart."

Houston's passionate kiss left Kelly without any doubt to his sincerity.

He gently nudged her. "We'd better go back inside. Don't want you to catch cold." After Kelly got to her feet, Houston tightened the towel around her nude body.

Looking up at Houston, she smiled. "I'm ravenous again. What about you?"

He chuckled. "I'll warm the leftovers while you shower."

Kelly frowned. "I was hoping we'd shower together. Not interested?"

Directing Kelly's hand down to his manhood, Houston laughed heartily. "Is that enough of an answer for you?"

"Say no more. I feel you, Houston, every hardened inch of you."

Chapter 13

Angelica and Beaumont had no clue where Austin and Ashleigh were taking them, not until they reached the Port of Galveston. Even then the elder Carringtons didn't know the final destination. With suitcases packed and stored in the back of Austin's SUV, Angelica and Beaumont knew a trip was involved, but the idea of a cruise hadn't crossed their minds. A few days on Galveston Island was their best guess. The other sons were following behind in their vehicles with neither parent aware of their presence.

Angelica's eyes were bright and questioning as the SUV came to a smooth halt.

Austin got out and quickly ran around the car and opened the rear door for his mother. Beaumont slid out right behind Angelica. Austin then took her by the hand, waiting for Dallas and Houston to join them. "Have you guessed your surprise yet, Mom?" Austin queried, smiling broadly.

Tears welling in her eyes, Angelica couldn't suppress her excitement. "Oh, Austin, I never dreamed I'd get a cruise for my birthday. This is wonderful! I'm happy, but also a little sad. We've never spent any special day or holiday away from you boys."

Just as Dallas, Houston and their traveling companions walked up, Austin brought his mother into his arms and gave her a warm hug. The other brothers followed Austin's lead in showing their mother how much they cared for her.

"Mom, Dad, we won't let you spend it away from us this year, either," Austin said. "We're off to Cozumel for a few days. Kelly and Lanier are joining us."

The joyous expression on their mother's face expressed her feelings. The triplets couldn't be any happier with her response. They laughed heartily as she jumped up and down for a few seconds and ran around in circles for a couple more. Angelica flew into her husband's arms. Beaumont was as surprised as his wife by the extremely generous gift his sons had also kept a secret from him. Both parents beamed.

Tears spilling from her eyes, Angelica hugged each of her boys again. "Sons, you've really outdone yourselves. Every year your gifts are spectacular, but this one is tops. Thank you, Austin, Dallas and Houston. Thank you so much," she cried happily.

Angelica tightly hugged her daughter-in-law before embracing Lanier and Kelly. For a couple of seconds, a pained expression crossed her face. She then looked over at Austin with questioning eyes. "Passports. We don't have them."

Ashleigh opened her straw satchel and removed the elder Carringtons' passports. "I'm afraid we got hold of them under false pretenses. When Austin asked for a copy of his birth certificate, he took the documents from your firebox instead. It was the only way we could register everyone online and also keep the secret. Sorry for the deception."

Angelica smiled endearingly, her tears resurfacing. "In this case, you're all forgiven. Okay, Carrington crew, we have a birthday celebration to attend."

Now that the cat was out of the bag and everyone felt great about how well the surprise had been received, the group stored the luggage in the parking-lot van, which would be given to porters at dockside.

Because the family group had arrived at the terminal early, they had already reached the head of the line. Once the check-in process was complete, the party of eight headed to their respective cabins. After everyone got unpacked and settled in, they planned to meet on the uppermost deck to throw a thrilling bon voyage celebration.

Houston and Kelly were all smiles as they checked out the balcony suite he and Dallas would occupy. "This is an exact replica of the one I'll share with Lanier."

Extremely pleased with the lavish accommodations, Houston pulled Kelly to him and kissed her passionately. "I'm surprised my bags have already been delivered. Do you mind helping me unpack my things and put them away?"

Both were eager to freshen up and then reunite with their traveling companions.

Several minutes later, as the couple headed for the exit door, Houston redirected Kelly out to the balcony, where he kissed her breathless. This moment was so surreal for him. "I can't help recalling the Valentine's Day/football reunion cruise my brothers and I took together. We had a ball reacquainting with old friends and making lots of new ones. Austin was reunited with Ashleigh, whom he'd been searching for long and hard. Dallas met and fell in love with Lanier on the same cruise. I won't be surprised if the precious memories we make on this cruise exceed all my expectations."

Houston ran his fingers through Kelly's silky hair. "If we were traveling alone, we'd have our own celebration right here, right now." His mouth sought out hers yet again. "I want to make love to you badly. Are you as excited as me?"

Kelly kissed her lover's eyelids. "I'm past excited. I'm burning red-hot for you. We've already made plans to meet your family, but we'll quietly slip away after the ship sets sail. Everyone knows we're in the honeymoon phase of our relationship."

Houston grinned. "This cruise will be sheer bliss for us. How'd I get so lucky?"

Kelly grazed her lips across Houston's, her fingers entwining in his hair at the nape. "Blessed is more like it. I never stopped hoping for a romantic relationship with you. Our initial conversation about dating exclusively often tumbles through my head."

Houston smoothed his thumb across her cheekbone. "I think about it a lot, too. My cool-as-a-cucumber demeanor was an act. I was squeamishly nervous over it."

Kelly smiled gently. "Ashleigh told me about the vow Austin had made to her fourteen years ago. She'd held on to his promise with all her might, even when she didn't think it'd occur. His vow became their reality. I hope our dreams come true, too."

"'I will always take care of you' was the vow Austin made to Ashleigh back then, when she was our foster sister. I promise to be here for you, Kelly, come hell or high water." Houston wrapped her up in his arms, kissing her again and again. Having her in his arms and far away from Lynton had Houston feeling pretty good.

Would forever become their reality? Were they each other's forever fantasy? Both Houston and Kelly wondered the very same thing.

* * *

Boasting a New York theme, the cruise ship *Ecstasy* slowly pulled away from the dock. Peals of laughter and gleeful shouting rang out loud and clear. Numerous bon voyages were happily voiced. Champagne corks popped and confetti and colorful streamers flew all about the deck. The four-day celebration at sea was now under way.

For all the uproar, Houston felt this odd sense of sereneness surrounding him. A vehicle of such magnitude slowly making its way out to the open sea was a magnificent vision. He certainly felt at peace. This was only his second cruise and the first one with a female companion. He was sure it wouldn't be the last one for her and him.

Watching the wondrous expressions on Kelly's face was sheer pleasure for him. She appeared utterly fascinated by the celebratory atmosphere. He could see the awe in her eyes and hear it in her audible gasps.

Standing at the railing of a floating hotel, heading out for the unknown, Kelly watched the port give way to the fathomless distance. The deep seas held many mysteries, those that mortal man would never conquer or fully understand.

Houston moved behind Kelly, entrapping her between the strength of his massive arms and the railing. There were so many things he wanted to say to her, but there wasn't enough time to say it all right now. Serenity engulfed him, making him want to keep the silence sacred during these precious moments.

As Houston looked all around him, he saw that his family was also caught up in the moment. Seeing his mother and father looking so happy did his heart a world of good. Angelica deserved only the best and their father deserved no less. Dallas and Lanier looked as if they'd already found a slice of heaven's pie. Ashleigh and Austin floated on cloud nine every moment of every day so the angelic expressions on their faces were nothing new.

Houston leaned down and kissed the top of Kelly's head. "How're you feeling?"

Tilting her head back slightly, Kelly looked up at him. "Wonderful! There's such peace surrounding me. Do you feel as serene as I do?"

"You bet, sweetheart." Houston had to laugh. That Kelly and he were on the same page was a good thing. "In observing my family, it seems the serenity bug has bitten us all. Do you think we can get any closer to heaven than this?"

Kelly thought of the times they'd made love. She smiled brightly, the memory of their passion warming her up on the inside. "I think we've already flown higher than that, Houston. I'm eager and open for an opportunity for us to soar far beyond heaven."

His fiery gaze connected with hers. "That makes two of us."

Houston would've been surprised by Kelly's comments a few weeks ago. His sophisticated lady had shown him a totally different side of her during their hot and heavy rendezvous. She had completely satisfied his emotional and physical desires, surpassing anything he could've imagined. Wet, wild and willing was not an understatment.

The uninhibited tigress in Kelly had sprung free. However, he didn't see her as overly aggressive. Their softer, tender moments made him feel as if he was her black knight and she was the damsel only he could rescue from distress. Houston didn't know exactly when a trade-off of cabins would occur, but he hoped it would happen.

During the cruise ship's safety session, the Carrington group followed to the letter the crew members' instructions on how to use the life preservers, rafts and boats. Everyone listened intently to the important things they'd need to do in an emergency.

Opting to discover on their own the ship's numerous amenities, the group decided to tour the floating hotel from the lowest deck and then work their way back up to the top. With Austin and Ashleigh leading the way, the couples filed into the glass elevator capsule located dead center of the ship.

The *Ecstasy* shone brightly with miles of neon lighting, mirrors, glass, brass and chrome. According to the descriptive pictures in the brochures, at night the ship dazzled like millions of white diamonds. The Gothic-type decor of the leisure areas exuded mystery.

While happily chattering away, the eight individuals explored the main dining rooms, the Wind Star and Wind Song, moving on to the Blue Sapphire Theater, where they'd eventually watch a Las Vegas–style revue. City Lights Boulevard was home to a promenade of bars and lounges. Karaoke was held nightly in the Starlight Lounge.

Besides informal lunch and formal dinner settings, food was available from the all-night pizzeria, the New York deli and via room service. A sushi bar was offered and a full-service buffet was also available to satisfy the hungriest of appetites. The Rolls-Royce Café served imported teas, coffee, cakes, cookies, pies and other bakery treats.

The Crystal Palace Casino, only open when the vessel was out to sea, was grand and colorful. Bells and whistles sounded off as the couples swept through the gambling facility. The well-stocked Explorers Club Library was a great place to relax and read.

The gym was equipped with the latest state-of-the-art workout equipment, wet and dry saunas and large hot tubs. Massages could be scheduled by appointment. Both a beauty salon and barbershop were on board. The gift shop held loads of souvenirs, postcards and an array of other touristy memorabilia.

Houston and Kelly purposely fell a little behind the others. Their need to be alone was overwhelming, yet they remained mindful that the cruise was a family affair. He rather regretted the time he'd wasted trying to keep Kelly at a safe distance. So sure that there wasn't a *Miss Right* for him, he hadn't allowed himself to give in to her sweet, lovable disposition and charming ways. It'd hurt her to know what lengths he would've taken to keep from getting in too deep with her. Those plans were gone with the wind.

Houston gently squeezed Kelly's fingers. "You look as if you're doing a little reflecting. What *are* you thinking?"

Kelly chuckled. "About how hard you tried to keep yourself from falling for me. So much wasted time and energy. I knew I couldn't resist you but I still tried. I have to give it to you. You seemed determined to immunize your heart against me."

Houston brought Kelly's hand up to his mouth and kissed the back of it. "It didn't last very long. I kept finding excuses why I needed to see you again. You're a real challenge for me. I knew why I wanted to keep a great woman like you at a distance. Even when I desired to give in to my feelings for you, I still fought it. I craved you like crazy. Deep in my gut I knew you were someone special, way beyond the average."

Kelly's eyes, soft and moist, stared at her handsome lover. "That was then. This is now, Houston. We both gave in to giving romance a try. We've come a long way."

"*I've* come a long way, Kelly. You knew what you wanted from the beginning. I had to be convinced. I'm glad I saw the light. This trip will be great for us. I feel that strongly. Each of us will sail back into Galveston a changed person. I expect a few miracles to occur out here on the high seas."

"I like the sound of that." By the look on Houston's face, Kelly believed him. "Having you in my life *is* a miracle," she whispered softly.

God had blessed her in so many ways. To live a righteous life was at the top of her goals. Having all her fears about Houston erased by the end of the cruise would indeed be miraculous. "I want desperately to give you what you need…and then some." Kelly knew they were worthy of each other's love. Only time would settle it all.

Seated on the balcony in Houston and Dallas's suite, sipping on cool drinks, Kelly and Lanier chatted away about the latest in fashion trends and recently released music CDs and DVDs. They were clad in sexy swimwear, with their bodies well oiled for soaking up the sunshine. The guys had gone out for a brief jog around the upper deck. The women had been invited along, but they'd declined. Austin and Ashleigh were busy entertaining Beaumont and Angelica, but the entire group planned to meet up later.

Lanier took a sip of her drink. "Are you having a good time so far?"

Kelly nodded. "Super time! What about you?"

Lanier smiled. "Things are wonderful. The Carringtons are great folks to hang out with. I just love Mr. and Mrs. C. They're marvelous people."

"I think so, too." Looking thoughtful, Kelly tapped the glass tabletop with the tips of her fingernails. "If you don't mind, I'd like to ask you a couple of personal questions."

Lanier nodded. "What's on your mind?"

"How's your relationship with Dallas and do you see marriage in your future?"

Lanier pursed her lips. "We have a good relationship, but Dallas is not totally happy with the way things stand. He hasn't actually asked me to marry him, but he talks about wanting to. He's been patiently waiting on me to fully commit. Houston and I are a lot alike when it comes down to making commitments. I hope I can follow in your man's redirected footsteps real soon. Dallas won't wait on me forever."

Kelly laughed nervously. "Houston *has* made some major changes, but I can't help wondering how long they'll last. We've only been aboard the ship a few hours, but I already see how hard it is for him to resist communicating with his adoring female fans. Being cordial and friendly is a part of who he is. He doesn't have to protect me from the results of his popularity. I actually enjoy it. Should I let him know I don't mind all the female attention he gets? I don't want him to change any part of himself to please me."

"Houston and Dallas are simply friendly and flirtatious by nature. Austin is different in that regard. He's not a flirt by any stretch of the imagination, yet he receives the same female adoration. Ashleigh handles it so well. Not only is she self-assured now, her husband doesn't give her any reasons to feel insecure. Houston will know you don't mind him talking to women by your attitude and nonreaction. Silence *can* be golden."

Kelly shrugged. "I don't see talking and flirting as the same thing, Lanier. I don't mind Houston talking to other females, but I'm not keen on the flirting part. He has never openly flirted with any woman in front of me. Does Dallas flirt with women when he's with you?"

Lanier laughed. "The first night I met him I observed him closely. I quickly dubbed him as a man with a serious 'roving eye.' Those beautiful ebony orbs seemed to be everywhere, all at once. Then he fixed his seductive gaze on me. The rest is history, even though I tried my best to resist him. He doesn't flirt with women around me, but he's very open and friendly to his fans. The triplets will sign autographs without blinking an eye, no matter what they're doing. I love that about them. As successful as they are, the guys stay humble. In fact, all the Carringtons are humble."

"I see and feel their humility." Kelly nervously rubbed her hands up and down her thighs. "We both mentioned having difficulty with our own families, but we've never expounded on it. Where do you stand with your parents?"

Lanier massaged the nape of her neck with a jittery hand. "Do you know the story of how I ended up in foster care?"

Kelly shook her head in the negative. "No one has given me any specific details. Your friends don't gossip about your private business."

Lanier agreed with a nod. "Ashleigh and Dallas are very protective of me." A glazed look settled in her eyes. Family was a hard subject for Lanier to tackle.

Sorry she'd opened up this particular can of worms, Kelly hoped Lanier wouldn't hold it against her. The atmosphere had changed. The room was now charged with enough tension to blow the big ship right out of the water. Knowing she couldn't do a thing about it, Kelly reached for Lanier's hand, squeezing it in a reassuring manner.

Lanier frowned. "I hold my father, Joseph Watson, way more responsible for my disastrous life than I do my mother, Barbara. She was also one of his victims." The strain in her voice was easy to recognize. Embracing past issues was never easy for Lanier.

Although Kelly had earlier wished she hadn't started this she now saw a greater good in it. Lanier was purging. "Why do you see your mother as a victim?"

Lanier's eyes blazed with inner fury. "Mom was too weak-willed. She couldn't stand up to Dad. Our lives were a nightmare, one I thought I'd never wake up from. Every time I discuss my past it sets me back twenty years or more. I hurt like a wounded animal whenever I'm transported back to my childhood." She lowered her eyelids. "Yet it also helps me get rid of the toxic waste. I'm not sure I'll ever be poison-free."

Kelly was relieved that Lanier saw the benefits in discussing her painful past. This young woman was still hurting terribly, yet it seemed to Kelly she'd made some progress. It made her shudder to think of what Lanier might've been like before she'd gotten rid of some of the built-up waste.

"How does Dallas feel about your situation?" Kelly inquired.

As Lanier laced her fingers together, stretching them back, an anguished expression crossed her face. "He thinks I'm out of touch with reality. It bothers him no end that I refuse to communicate with my family. Mom has written me several letters, but I haven't responded to a single one. Dallas believes I'll never get on with my life if I don't come to terms with Joseph and Barbara, amicably or otherwise. 'Lanier, why is it easier for you to run away from everything than to stand your ground and face it down?' That's one of the questions he frequently poses to me."

Kelly was back to feeling horrible for Lanier, who looked as if death had just paid her a surprise visit. In her desire to show support, she reached over and hugged Lanier. "I wasn't a foster child, but there were times when it felt like it. My parents were gone a lot because of their professions. Try selling that to a young heart yearning to spend lots of fun time with Mommy and Daddy. I stuffed many of the things I wanted to tell them."

"They may not have been there, but I'm sure you didn't grow up with alcoholic parents who ended up fighting every time they took a drink. My father viewed his family as property, like it gave him the right to do to us anything he wanted to."

Kelly deeply felt Lanier's pain. She feared the possibility of her turning into a keg of TNT. When she would blow was anyone's guess. "I'm so sorry, Lanier."

Fighting off tears, Lanier's mouth turned down at the corners. "We were less than human to him, Kelly. His father raised him the same way. It's been like that in generations of Watson men. I don't know if my mother started drinking to deal with the stress and abuse, or what, but she eventually became a drunk just like him. There was hardly ever a pleasant moment in our house, whether he was home or not."

Kelly's eyes sympathized with the plight of Lanier's painful past.

Lanier flinched as she looked directly at Kelly. "I was shuffled into one abusive foster home after another, handed over to the kind of people I won't ever forget or forgive. Can Dallas be content having my parents as in-laws? There's nothing sophisticated about them. They're unpolished and my father is downright crude. I'm not ashamed of them for that. I'm mortified by the indecent and inhumane treatment they're capable of doling out as alcohol rules them. You get what I'm saying?"

"Every word of it. I'm nowhere near where you are emotionally, but I harbor ill feelings toward my parents." Kelly told Lanier about the recent dinner she'd had with her family. "What I'm starting to realize and accept is that people can change. How long has it been since you last saw your mom and dad?"

"Obviously not long enough. My parents are mean-spirited people. I don't want them treating my children the horrible way they did me. If they come back into my life now, they become a part of my future. At this stage, I'm not up for that. Dallas is a part of Texas royalty. How will he deal with commoners inside his families' palatial homes? These two very different lifestyles and outlooks will clash, possibly violently."

Kelly heard Lanier's last statements loud and clear, though they rang somewhat untrue for her. Did Lanier somehow think she was beneath Dallas? If so, there was nothing further from the truth. The fact they came from different economic and social backgrounds didn't figure one iota into his love for Lanier. He was crazy about her.

Money didn't make Dallas. He made money.

None of the triplets' lives seemed to be guided by the size of their bank accounts. From what Kelly had seen so far, they were down-to-earth, good old Texas boys who treated everyone equally. Kelly had gotten the same impressions of their parents.

"Dallas's status in life is not an issue where his love for you is concerned. This is all about you, Lanier. If you can't rid yourself of the past, you might not have a future. What your parents are or aren't won't affect your relationship. And for sure, they'll never physically hurt you again. Dallas can promise you at least that much. He needs you to put your trust in him. God is waiting on you to trust Him, too. He can't remove the obstacles in your life if you won't let go of them. I'm trying hard to practice forgiveness."

Kelly was aware she'd said a whole lot, perhaps too much, but she felt it had to be said. Even she herself had benefited from her comments. Unlike Lanier, she had to come to terms with her parents. The recent dinner was just the beginning of trying to build what she felt they'd never had before. Family unity meant everything to Kelly. After being around the Carringtons, her desire for family unity had grown powerful.

Kelly leaped up and brought Lanier into her arms, catching her just before she fell to her knees. Lanier had finally given way to her burgeoning emotions, her tears falling like torrential rains. Guiding Lanier back inside the cabin, Kelly got her to sit on the sofa. She then sat down right beside her and took hold of her hand.

As Lanier buried her face against Kelly's shoulder, Kelly tenderly stroked her hair. "Friend, you're going to be all right. Let out all the brewing storms. It'll be okay. The love you share with Dallas is stronger than any force you'll ever have to contend with."

Kelly hoped her comments would sink into Lanier's brain and help her regain some semblance of peace. She couldn't feel the pain for her, but Kelly knew what a heart in turmoil felt like. Letting go of the past was a surefire way for both women to secure their own futures…as well as a future with the men they loved. Kelly knew that Lanier wanted a lifelong relationship with Dallas more than she could courageously express.

Kelly wondered how Houston viewed what was happening with Dallas and Lanier since he had reacted a lot like Lanier. This talk had definitely helped Kelly clarify her own personal issues. Healing her family ties had to become one of her top priorities.

The guys reentering the cabin abruptly ended Lanier and Kelly's conversation.

Kelly patted Lanier's hand reassuringly. "We'll talk again later."

Kelly saw the look of concern on Dallas's face. He was worried about Lanier, but it didn't seem as if he planned to voice his apprehension. At least, not right now.

For someone who'd been out jogging, Kelly noticed that neither Dallas nor Houston looked as if they'd broken so much as a sweat. The cool, unassuming look on Houston's face instantly aroused Kelly's curiosity. When he reached for her hand, pulling her up from the chair, she suddenly felt calm. Houston had a way of making her feel safe and secure, even at the height of her insecurities.

Houston kissed Kelly on the lips, causing passion to stir within her. "Dallas and I have a huge surprise for you ladies. We'd like you to come with us."

Kelly looked puzzled. "What kind of surprise, Houston? I don't like surprises."

Houston brought Kelly closer to him. "I didn't know that, but I think you'll like this one. Let's go and see what it is."

The women donned knitted cover-ups before reluctantly following their black knights out of the safety of the cabin. Both looked as if they were heading out to meet up with a blind date. Neither woman could make heads or tails out of what the guys were up to. Kelly and Lanier were equally as curious about this so-called surprise but neither knew what had prompted the guys. There wasn't a single clue to be had.

One look at the line of beautiful women flitting about a private lounge further aroused Kelly's and Lanier's curiosity. Nothing about this scene gave them any idea what was happening. Exchanging bewildered glances, the women shrugged.

Two stunning ladies came over to Kelly and Lanier and escorted them to front-row tables, where they took seats. Male waiters showed up, carrying tall, tropical drinks. Seconds later, upbeat music filtered into the room.

A marvelous-looking brunette stepped onstage and picked up the microphone. "Welcome, Kelly and Lanier. We're here to give you your very own private fashion show, featuring the latest in beach and day wear, evening attire and lingerie. Houston and Dallas want you ladies to pick out your favorites. Sit back, relax and enjoy the show."

Kelly and Lanier couldn't believe what they'd just heard, but they definitely appeared pleased. Lanier lifted her hand to give Kelly a high five and then she blew Dallas a kiss. The guys came over to the table, kissed their ladies and quickly departed.

Kelly saw this surprise as an extraordinary one, wishing the guys had stayed.

Kelly and Lanier thought the private fashion show was the sweetest, kindest gesture anyone had ever showered on them. Ready for the festivities to begin, the ladies couldn't help giggling and acting silly over their good fortune.

Lanier smiled beautifully when the first model came out. The joy she felt lit up her eyes. Her heart was thrilled. "Although I just bought some new clothes, my wardrobe is far from adequate. The majority of my money goes into Haven House. I own very little in the way of social attire, especially for a woman dating a rich superstar."

Kelly's smile was sympathetic. "You always look nice to me. I love your style." She paused for a moment. "Has Dallas said anything negative about your clothing?"

"Never! He's doesn't go overboard with material stuff, but he does wear the best. If you think he's doing this to upgrade my wardrobe, don't. He's okay with the way I am. This is just another way for him to say he loves me. I'm willing to bet this was his idea and Houston joined in because he thought it was a great one."

Kelly leaned over and hugged Lanier. "I'd be foolish to take that bet." Kelly's mouth fell open. "Oh, my goodness, look at that sexy red-and-white-polka-dot sundress and matching bandanna. They have an excellent chance of leaving here with me."

Chapter 14

Now that Kelly was alone with Houston in his cabin, after they'd walked the decks in silent awe for over thirty minutes, she wished every second of the their time wasn't designated to one event or another for the entire cruise. Dallas hadn't mentioned swapping cabins so they had to wait it out. Lanier had to return there to change clothes.

Houston took Kelly's hand and guided her over to the sofa. "I didn't know you disliked surprises, but you handled the fashion show pretty well. I'm happy you enjoyed everything. I love the items you chose, especially the sexy, backless after-five pants set. You look amazing in basic black. I also love the hot red lace teddy and the white silk camisole set. I think I would've chosen many of the same items for you."

Kelly smiled. "My favorite is the floor-length sequined gown in ivory jersey. It clings to and outlines my figure beautifully. It's so feminine and delicately sexy!"

Houston smiled back at Kelly. "Anything you put on screams out sexy, babe. I can't wait to see you in all the purchases."

Kelly grinned. "I can't wear it all before the cruise is over, but I'll style as many items as I can." Kelly suddenly looked pensive. "Have you ever talked to Dallas about the situation between Lanier and her parents?"

"Countless times. Parental problems are foreign to us so it's hard to relate. Dallas hopes she can one day forgive her parents, but he's not sure she'll get there. Lanier is out of sorts with her mom and dad. And that's probably not a strong enough assertion."

"I know what you mean. Deep down inside is where the excruciating pain lives. Up until the night we had dinner with Mom and Dad, I still saw them as uncaring, only thinking of their needs and desires. That has changed. I no longer believe I was a mistake.

I see now that my parents sacrificed a lot just to provide me with a bright future."

Houston appeared relieved. "I never got any other impression of them. I'm sure they worked those hard, long hours to make sure your future was secure. Professional athletes who are parents are gone from home for long periods of time, too, but they don't like it. Their kids' futures are the reason they deal with heavy road schedules and such. I'm glad you have a better understanding of your parents' frequent absences."

Kelly sighed hard. "I am, too." Looking a bit remorseful, she laid her hand on Houston's thigh. "I was the rich kid who thought I had everything *but* quality time with my parents. I can't go back and change how I felt, but I'm glad I finally see some light."

He lazed a finger down her chin. "If you work hard at it, I bet the pain will lessen. I enjoyed the time we spent with your mom and dad. They're really cool people."

"I hate wearing false faces, the same painted-on ones I wore whenever I saw them. I actually felt guilty about taking this cruise without asking them along. I somehow managed to override the guilt. Coming here with you was a way of exercising my independence despite the fact I rarely see them. I'm rebellious by nature."

Houston raised an eyebrow. "Is that the reason you're on the trip?"

Kelly heard the hurt in Houston's voice. *This was one sensitive man.* He seemed to take every little thing personally. She understood him and his reasons for constantly guarding his heart. "Of course not, Houston. I'm here because I love spending time with you. Take it or leave it, I love you." Throwing her arms around his neck, she kissed him passionately. She didn't regret her confession in the least.

Much to Houston's surprise, hearing Kelly voicing her love for him hadn't scared him like he'd imagined. He felt deeply for her, too. But was it true love? If they were in love, where would it eventually take them? Was he cheating her by not being sure about his feelings? Perhaps it was too soon to make the call. *Patience,* he thought. *Be patient.*

Houston held Kelly slightly away from him. "Does the mind-blowing kiss mean you're over the surprise I sprung on you?"

Kelly chuckled at Houston's not-so-clever diversionary tactics. He clearly wasn't ready to discuss her confession. The man was too devilishly predictable, yet utterly unpredictable at the very same time. "I admit I didn't like the idea of a surprise, but I was curious. After finding out what you'd done, I definitely wasn't mad at you."

Houston met her watery gaze. "What's on your mind? You suddenly seem troubled again. You look like you're about to cry."

Hating the bitter taste in her mouth, Kelly swallowed hard. "Watching Lanier earlier was like seeing a mirror image of me. I've been that distraught before. Hearing her awful story made me realize my relationship with my parents wasn't nearly as bad. They may've been absent a lot, but heavy drinking, fighting and cursing didn't occur. Mom and Dad have always been in love with each other, which is how it should be. I guess you don't always see how bad things aren't until you see or hear worse situations."

Houston gently stroked Kelly's face with his forefinger. "Comparisons *can* make you see things clearer. We were blessed to grow up in a loving home. Mom was never far away from us. She volunteered at the elementary and middle schools we attended. By the time we went to high school, she felt we'd be okay. I can't imagine Mom and Dad not being there for us and I can't envision them fighting. I've never heard them call each other out of their names, yet I'm sure they've had their share of differences."

Tears fell from Kelly's eyes. "Poor Lanier saw a lot of bad stuff. I hope she'll be okay. As for me, I'm happy to be here with you, regardless of everything else."

"That's good news. Now we can get on with our agenda." Houston guided Kelly over to the bed, where he stretched out and pulled her down next to him. Rolling up on his side, he looked down into her eyes. "I want us to make love right after dinner, while everyone else enjoys the stage show. I'll make sure Dallas knows we want to be alone."

As Kelly pulled Houston's head down, aligning her lips with his, she blushed. "I don't know if I can wait that long, but it looks like I'll have to."

Flattered by her remarks, Houston grinned. "In that case, let me give you a little something to tide you over. What's your pleasure, fair lady?"

The responsive kiss Kelly gave Houston matched the passion in her eyes. "We probably should wait. Lanier has to come back here to change clothes for dinner. I wouldn't want her to walk in on our intimate moments."

Houston chuckled. "Thank God we're not exhibitionists. But that won't stop me from kissing you silly. Come closer to me, woman. My lips want to make love to yours."

They both laughed at the naughty-boy expression on his handsome face.

Beautifully dressed in after-five evening wear, the four women looked elegant and stunning. Although no one had discussed wardrobe choices, three of the four women wore navy blue dresses. Ashleigh was dressed in a white crepe tea-length dress.

The early dinner sitting had been selected throughout the cruise. The large group would dine first and then attend the Las Vegas–style stage shows afterward. The Carrington party was large enough to occupy a full table, which was by the window.

The first course of the four-course meal was about to be served, along with the finest in wine and champagne. Kelly had chosen a fruity Muscato, as opposed to one of the drier wines. Houston decided to try what his lady had ordered, though he wondered if it might be a little too sugary for his taste.

Kelly leaned into Houston. "I like how willing you are to try many of the things I favor. That's a big plus." She inhaled his scent. "I see you're wearing my favorite cologne. It does wonderful things to my senses," she whispered softly.

Flirtatious devilment twinkling in his eyes, he grinned. "Like what?"

"It makes we want to strip you down to nothing but your sexy Dolce & Gabbana designer cologne." She threw her head back and laughed. "That's an erotic thought."

"I'd love it. Keep it in mind, Kelly. We have the cabin to ourselves tonight."

Her eyes widened. "You made good on your promise! Is it for the entire night?"

"Every delicious moment is ours. Once we leave the group at the end of the evening, we won't see everyone until breakfast tomorrow morning."

Kelly couldn't help giggling. The thought of spending an entire night with Houston on the high seas had her body vibrating with physical hunger and desire.

Conversation was light and airy as the happy folks wined and dined by candlelight, enjoying the soft piped-in music. Angelica's birthday dinner was scheduled for the last evening of the cruise, which was the actual day of her birth.

Deciding to join the rest of the party for a little dancing before going to the cabin, Houston and Kelly had followed the others into one of the popular nightclubs, where the couple danced a sultry salsa to a popular Latin song. She used the upbeat rhythm as a way to work off the dinner calories. He loved watching her twist, turn and seductively gyrate her sexy body. He was barely able to wait for her to give him his own private dance later on. The kisses and wild flirting was a clear clue as to what was on their minds.

A few songs later, as the other members stood around and watched, they clapped enthusiastically as Beaumont and Angelica showcased their lively dance skills. The couple had been dancing together for many years. They also waltzed to the same tunes in their private affairs. They were very much in love and in harmony with each other.

Kelly couldn't help noticing how proud the guys were of their mom and dad. The triplets beamed over how much love existed between their parents. As she thought back on some of the events she'd attended with her own parents, she smiled. Jared and Carolyn's marriage was also in sync. Kelly knew she had to stop feeling like an outsider with her own family. It was up to her to change the nature of their relationships.

Before slipping off to take a leisurely stroll around the deck, Houston and Kelly stayed with the group and danced for a couple of hours more. Their journey would ultimately end up in the brothers' cabin. Lanier and Dallas planned to spend the night in the suite the two women had been assigned.

Moonlight streamed in through the suite's sliding glass door. Lying nude in bed, holding each other closely, Houston and Kelly eagerly claimed some serious "us time." His desire to romance her all night long was finally being fulfilled.

Slowly, Houston's eyes roved Kelly's beautiful body. "I had a good time at dinner and in the dance club. The romantic stroll was nice, too. What about you?"

Kelly smiled softly. "Everything has been fabulous." She reached up and tenderly caressed his face with the back of her hand. "Everyone appears to be having a great time. Does your family take many vacations together?"

"We all try to get away once or twice a year. Because our off-seasons occur at different times, we have to grab opportunities when we can all make it." He lowered his head and took possession of her mouth, gently caressing her soft, silky flesh.

As Kelly straddled Houston, she moaned softly. "In the words of Marvin Gaye, 'Let's get it on.' I want to be kissed by a Carrington."

Houston raised an eyebrow. "Any Carrington?"

Her fingertips caressed his face while her tongue sought out his. She kissed him passionately, causing him to moan with pleasure. Pulling her head back slightly, she stared into his eyes. "You're the one and only Carrington for me and yours is the only Carrington kiss I crave."

The next night, the time continued to pass by with the speed of light, but the Carrington group had already crammed in enough excitement to leave the ship quite satisfied if it came to an abrupt end. Leaving the older couple to their own devices, after dining at the midnight buffet, the three younger couples climbed up to the top deck to indulge in a little dancing and lots of romancing. The stars were out in full force. A brightly lit crescent moon hung low in the sky. Soft music could be heard strumming the air as it soulfully drifted from the disco club.

Houston whirled Kelly into his arms, holding her close to him. While swinging her around and around to the beat of the melodic music, he saw joy and peace in her eyes. She was so relaxed. He was proud of her and proud to be seen with this incredible beauty.

Even as Kelly settled comfortably in Houston's arms, she couldn't help wondering what her parents were doing at the moment. She wasn't eager for the cruise to end, but she was anxious to start making things right with her mom and dad. Why she thought of them at this moment was kind of puzzling, but maybe it had to do with seeing how wonderfully the Carrington family interacted. They were an incredibly close family. Kelly desperately wanted what they had for Carolyn, Jared and herself.

As the music continued to fill the atmosphere with stimulating melodies, Houston led Kelly outside and over to a table in a quiet corner of the upper deck. After he pulled out two chairs, they sat down. Taking a black velvet box from his pants pocket, he closed her hand around it. "This is for you. I hope you like it."

Kelly's fingers and face suddenly felt frozen. Whatever was inside the box had her mind wandering all over the map. A bad case of nerves clawed at her heartstrings and she struggled to get a tight grip on her emotions. Kelly felt sure the gift wasn't an engagement ring, especially since Houston hadn't even confessed to loving her. If it was a ring, she mused, she knew she could never turn down a marriage proposal from him. Kelly loved Houston like crazy, loved him with every fiber of her being.

Kelly loved Houston, but was she prepared to take the big plunge?

Taking the box from Kelly's trembling hand, Houston flipped it open. "It's only a promise ring, a promise to never hurt or humiliate you. This hand-crafted perfection symbolizes my promise to be faithful to you, to cherish only you whether we're together at home or miles apart." He slid the tiny diamond ring on her left hand. "If we decide to marry, you can select a much bigger rock. I might be able to afford a couple of carats."

They both laughed at his joking remark.

Kelly didn't try to hold back her tears. To show Houston how much she loved the gift, she kissed him until he gulped for air. Laughing, she held up her hand, wiggling her fingers. "This is beautiful! Thank you for the sweet promises."

Kelly really believed they belonged together, for better or worse, but they had such a long way to go before deciding on eternity. She had to think in more sensible terms rather than going off the deep end. It was too easy for her to lose it over him.

A diamond promise ring wasn't what she had expected, but the very idea of it thrilled her no end. Houston was remarkable. Although he hadn't made an affirmation of love to her she believed he cared deeply. Kelly silently promised in her heart to accept Houston's proposal of marriage if he ever asked. If he didn't propose, perhaps she would just ask him to marry her. She had a lot of work to do on herself, as well as handling her family affairs. She felt confident she was ready for both.

God willing, maybe Houston and I will end up together forever.

* * *

Kelly giggled loudly while listening to one of Houston's corny basketball jokes.

She inhaled deeply of his scent as he held her in his arms from behind. She still had a hard time believing all the changes in him, but she knew he was for real. His philosophy on marriage and commitment while on the road made perfect sense. Maybe he hadn't poured his heart out because he didn't love her, yet Kelly felt that he wanted to.

"Staring into the starlit sky is pretty tranquil," Houston whispered. "You never did tell me what you wished on the star for down at the lake, after your first Carrington dinner night. Tell me. Did your wish come true?"

Kelly tilted her head back and looked up into Houston's eyes. "It finally came true. My wish was for you to make love to me when we got back to my place."

Houston frowned slightly. "I'm glad I didn't know. I was way out of my league then. I had started something I wasn't sure I could finish, not in the absence of commitment. It's history now." He brought her around to face him. "I know I didn't say anything when you told me you loved me—and I'm sorry about that. I guess I wasn't ready to face my true feelings head-on. I love you, too, Kelly. I wouldn't confess to loving you if I didn't mean it. I'm opting to take your love rather than leaving it behind."

Kelly felt like crying. This was a beautiful moment, one to be savored. Hearing Houston confess his love for her was too surreal. "I'm nearly speechless," she stammered, genuinely bewildered. "Knowing you love me back has me ecstatic. Welcome into my heart, Houston." Crying softly, she flung herself in his open arms.

The Carrington family and their special guests had added some personal touches to the celebration despite the fact the travel agent had made special arrangements for Angelica's birthday. This was the last night of the cruise.

The younger women had earlier decorated the assigned table with the colorful party favors Ashleigh had packed away in her suitcase. A colorful, glittery Happy Birthday banner, balloons and sparkling streamers were all in place.

Angelica proudly wore the magnificent black-and-silver gown

the younger women had chosen for her. When she was told that Ashleigh, Lanier and Kelly had picked it out, she mentioned how close their taste ran in fashion. Although she was the only matriarch of the group there wasn't anything old-fashioned about her. At fifty-seven years of age, she was as stylish and upbeat as the younger women.

Beaumont couldn't keep his eyes off his strikingly beautiful wife.

Angelica's wrist, neck and ears dripped with brilliant diamonds. Lanier and Kelly's fine jewelry sparkled as much as the more expensive jewels. The men were dressed in stylish black tuxedos, crisp white shirts and complementary accessories.

One of the most beautiful women aboard the *Ecstasy,* Ashleigh shone brightly. The autumn-brown sequined dress sensuously hugged each of her full curves. Her eyes sparkled like flecks of gold and her cheeks were flushed with the healthy color of impending motherhood. Her large, copper ringlets had been left loose to run rampant. The low-heeled dress shoes she had on were safe and comfortable yet also stylish.

Ashleigh also wore the diamond teardrop earrings. Her husband had given them to her earlier. Poor Austin hadn't been able to wait until the baby was born to present her the gift. It had always been hard for him to keep surprises under wraps.

Since everyone's meals had been served, Beaumont asked for a humbling blessing over the food and for the hands that prepared it. "This is a beautiful day that the Lord has made. Let us be happy and rejoice in it. I also want to wish my lovely bride and the mother of my sons, Angelica, an extremely happy, happy birthday."

More happy birthdays and cheers rang out from the others present.

Once the meals were consumed, Austin passed out the birthday gifts.

Angelica read the card before opening the first gift. A fourteen-carat-gold heart pendant engraved with *Happy Birthday* and the date of her birth made Angelica smile, bringing tears to her eyes. "Thanks, Lanier and Kelly. The gold heart is as beautiful as both of your hearts and spirits." She blew kisses to the two women.

Next Angelica unveiled a beautiful set of handmade Mexican jewelry and a colorful silk shawl. She loved Mexican goods and artifacts. Ashleigh and Austin had purchased the authentic gifts during the shore excursion they'd taken with Angelica and Beaumont. Smiling beautifully, she thanked her son and devoted daughter-in-law.

As Angelica picked up the gift from her three sons, they came over and stood behind her chair. Each triplet bent over and hugged their mother. After kissing each of her rose-blushed cheeks, the brothers wished her a happy birthday…and many, many more. "We love you, Mom," they said in unison.

Tears cascaded from Angelica's eyes as she lovingly fingered the brilliant four-carat diamond earrings, two carats per stud. "These jewels are exquisite, sons," she cried happily. After removing the earrings she had on, Angelica replaced them with the new diamonds, holding back her hair so everyone could get a good look. "Are these precious gems beautiful or what? In fact, they're just too beautiful for words."

Austin, Dallas and Houston had come to the conclusion that the diamond gift card wasn't personal enough for their mom, so they'd gone back to the jewelry store and made the purchase two days later.

Ashleigh got up and embraced her mother-in-law with a warm hug, wiping away Angelica's tears. "It is okay to cry happy tears, Mom," she soothed. "Happy birthday!" Ashleigh then reached for Beaumont's hand, squeezing it gently. "I love you both."

Fighting back his tears, Beaumont squeezed her hand back. "We love you, too. Thanks for being so kind at heart and gracious, my dear. You're a beautiful young woman and a loving wife and a national treasure to our son, Austin. You're going to be a wonderful mother." Beaumont looked at Kelly and then Lanier. "You ladies are beautiful and gracious, too. We're happy you're sharing in Angelica's birthday celebration."

Nodding and smiling at the kind acknowledgment, Kelly thought of her parents again. The Carringtons had taught her that family was everything. It was now time for her to reclaim hers. After putting her arms around Angelica, Kelly tearfully wished the Carrington matriarch a delightful birthday.

Ashleigh smiled through the blur of her tears. "I wish my mother and father were still alive for me to celebrate their birthdays. On Father's and Mother's Day and other special holidays I ache painfully for them, although I've never met either one. You two are the closest

I've ever come to having a mother and father. I love you so much. Lanier and Kelly, you're so blessed, so fortunate to have your parents alive and well. There isn't anything I wouldn't give to have what you two possess, but my once foster parents now in-laws make me feel like a natural daughter versus an in-law."

As Ashleigh started back to her seat, a sudden rush of dizziness caused her to become slightly disoriented. In looking over at her husband, she had the oddest expression on her face. Glancing down at her feet, she saw water pooling there. "Oh, no," she screamed, laughing and crying at the same time. "Austin, my water just broke! I may be in labor."

Looking quite stunned, Austin was out of his seat in a flash, rushing to his wife's side, gathering her into his arms. "Are you in pain, Ash? Oh, God, this isn't happening right now. It can't be. It's too early."

Austin gave his mother a bewildered look. As Angelica made her way over to where Ashleigh was, she saw the anxious looks on her kids' faces. Her feet sprouted wings. The others all sprang into action to see what they could do to help out. No one had expected Ashleigh to go into labor. The baby wasn't due for another month, but the unexpected always had a way of happening.

"Dallas, Houston, help Austin get Ashleigh down to the infirmary," Angelica calmly ordered. "Thank God we're headed home. Our baby may be born on the ship. Kelly, we need you over here, too. Thank God we have a doctor in the family."

Houston heard that remark, loud and clear, but he didn't so much as bat an eyelash. His mother considered everyone as family, because that was how the Creator intended it. However, Houston didn't think his mother was too far off the mark. Time would tell all, he thought. He watched as Kelly zipped into action, eager to do her part.

Concern written all over his face, Beaumont, right along with his sons, rushed over to help carry their precious Ashleigh to the infirmary. The flurry of activity had caused a crowd of gawking onlookers to amass. Austin thought it was the last thing his wife needed in her delicate condition.

Ashleigh's contractions hadn't yet begun when the Carrington men lifted her with ease, extremely careful not to hurt her. A sudden sharp pain caused her to scream out, causing the guys to pick up speed but remain cautious and careful.

Austin smoothed back Ashleigh's dampened hair. "It'll be okay, Ash. I'm right here, sweetheart."

Ashleigh reached for Austin's hand. "Don't leave me. I need you. I'm so scared."

Austin kissed her forehead. "I'll never leave you. Don't worry. Hold on."

Then another contraction hit Ashleigh hard and she snatched her hand away from Austin's. Casting him an angry look, she groaned loudly, gritting her teeth.

All the way to the infirmary, Ashleigh repeatedly took hold of Austin's hand, only to snatch it away again when another stretch of unbearable pain came upon her. As a few mild expletives flew from her mouth, he became an off-and-on target for her rage and then her affection. Angelica assured her son that Ashleigh was reacting normally.

Inside the ship's infirmary, a doctor and nurse took charge, directing the guys over to where they wanted them to lay down Ashleigh. Everyone but Austin, Angelica and Kelly were shooed from the room. Once Kelly identified herself as a licensed physician, she was asked by the ship's doctor, Dr. Mark Carson, if she'd like to stay on to offer medical support. Helping Ashleigh bring her child into the world was a high honor.

"I'd like nothing better than to help deliver Ashleigh's baby."

The newborn might turn out to be my niece or nephew. Kelly smiled at the very idea of it. *Uncle Houston and Auntie Kelly.* She suppressed a tickling giggle.

For the next several hours, Ashleigh screamed her head off and yelped mild expletives, yet she refused to be medicated. Austin was often hailed as her beloved husband. When the pain was too much for her to take, he became her archenemy, her wild sway of emotions erupting like a bobbing yoyo. Through it all, Ashleigh bore down and inhaled and exhaled as she was instructed by Austin and the ship's nurse.

Angelica continued to assure her son that Ashleigh's reactions were common. "A display of anger and affection often occurs in deliveries. She doesn't hate you, son."

Austin knew his wife didn't hate him, yet her loathing seemed real at times.

* * *

Kelly quickly familiarized herself with the location of the emergency medical equipment inside the infirmary. She listened in as the nurse busied herself by making arrangements for Ashleigh and the baby to be airlifted to a hospital once the emergency birth took place. Ashleigh was already fully dilated. The baby would be labeled a citizen born abroad. Austin would have to make plans for them to fly home after his new family was released from the hospital.

The *Ecstasy* would sail into home port without Austin, Ashleigh and the baby.

"One last push. A big one," Kelly instructed Ashleigh. "We're almost there."

"I can't," she cried out. "It hurts. Don't make me do this. Drugs, now! Please!"

The doctor swapped places with Kelly to allow her to assist the newborn into the world. Unable to believe she'd actually be a part of this incredible delivery, Kelly looked totally bewildered as she sent up a quiet, heartfelt supplication.

Minutes later, eyes wide with pride and incredulity, Kelly scooped up into her sterile, gloved hands the chubbiest newborn she'd ever seen, the first delivery she'd ever helped in. Austin and Ashleigh had a new family addition, a beautiful son.

Kelly instructed Austin on cutting the umbilical cord.

Once the necessary suctioning and other precautionary measures were administered to the infant, he was handed over to the nurse for her to weigh and measure. This newborn may've come prematurely, but he appeared healthy.

Just as Kelly's emotions gave way, she handed the baby to Ashleigh.

The infirmary curtains were pulled back so all the smiling faces pressed against the glass could get their first peek of the new Carrington addition. Ecstatic over their nephew, Houston and Dallas gave the thumbs-up to Austin and Ashleigh.

Lanier was jumping up and down in celebration, crying her heart out, only calming down long enough to blow Ashleigh a few kisses.

Kelly's eyes were wide with wonder as she looked at Houston from behind the glass. Smiling and crying at the same time, she jabbed at her chest. "I delivered him," she mouthed, her tears rolling. "I assisted in bringing this tiny miracle into the world."

"I love you," he mouthed back. The smile he gave her caused her heart to rejoice.

Houston's mind suddenly swapped out Ashleigh's image for one of Kelly. Looking down with adoration and love for her newborn, it was Kelly lying there on the bed, bathed in sweat, tears running from her eyes. Kelly had just given birth to a Carrington son, his son.

No matter how hard Houston tried to shake the vivid visions, he couldn't get them out of his head. A son, he thought, unable to fathom such a wondrous miracle occurring for him. Nothing close to this phenomenal event happened for a man who had run from commitment his entire adult life. With Kelly, it seemed as if all things were imaginable.

As Angelica looked on through the blur of her tears, Kelly saw that she couldn't have been happier or prouder. Her only grandchild was born on her birthday. What a magnificent birthday present! Seeing her firstborn with his firstborn was a sight for sore eyes. Austin had led the way out of the birth canal and he'd been a born leader ever since.

The look on Beaumont's face showed he shared in his wife's sentiments. He had a hard time believing this miracle of miracles was happening, but it was. His daughter had brought their first grandchild into the world. The baby had been born at sea, no less.

Tears streamed from Austin's eyes as he was handed his firstborn son. Looking down upon his beautiful wife, Austin kissed the baby's forehead then presented him back to Ashleigh, who was sobbing uncontrollably.

Austin first kissed her tears away and then he kissed her mouth passionately. "Happy Mother's Day, Mommy. We'll now have to celebrate this special occasion twice a year and also on the baby's and Mom's birthdays. I love you. Austin Roderick Beaumont Carrington loves you, too."

Ashleigh couldn't believe her eyes. The baby looked just like his daddy. What she and Austin had created from their love was indescribable. Her lips caressed the head of their beautiful baby boy. She now had a family of her own, one that nobody could ever take away. Ashleigh's life was complete.

Ashleigh tilted her head up for another kiss from Austin. "Happy

Father's Day on your son's and mother's birthday, Daddy. We've got a lot of celebrating to do now and when this day rolls around again. I love you so much. Austin Roderick Beaumont Carrington loves you, too."

Houston turned his back so no one could see his tears falling. He wasn't embarrassed to cry but he didn't want his brothers to jokingly punk him later. He'd never seen anything like he'd just witnessed and it wasn't something he could ever take lightly.

Ashleigh, whom Houston loved and adored, had given his brother Austin his first child. There was overwhelming power in that labor of love. One of the most beautiful women in the world, inside and out, was now a brand-new parent, a mother to Austin's son. She had also given Angelica and Beaumont a grandson and Dallas and him a nephew. Houston could tell that Dallas was also extremely happy for the new parents.

The group enthusiastically waved to Austin and his family as the helicopter lifted from the ship's launching pad. Watching after the life-flight chopper, they stood stock-still. Beaumont, with his arms around his wife, hugging her tightly, moved Kelly to tears.

Houston's arms were open to Kelly as she turned into him, seeking solace. She had cleaned up and he could still smell the sterile soap on her. His lady looked as exhausted and spent to him as Ashleigh had looked. It was as though she had gone through labor herself. He was proud of the way she'd jumped in to help his sister-in-law, not that he would've expected any less from Kelly.

Houston kissed each of her eyelids. "Are you okay, Kelly-Kel?"

She looked up into his face. "I'm fine now. I don't remember my heart ever beating this fierce." She suddenly giggled. "Well, there have been a few times," she confessed. "All of them have been when I'm with you, lying beneath you or beside you."

Houston grinned. "Then I don't guess your heart can stand any more excitement tonight. I can wait until we get back home."

Kelly's eyes glistened with moisture. "I can't. Do we have the cabin to ourselves?"

Houston kissed the top of her head. "Just in case you were up to it, Dallas and I talked it over. Lanier doesn't mind in the least. So we're all happy. We haven't spent one night without each other. Recall me saying for appearances' sake?"

"Couldn't forget it," she said, winking her right eye.

Houston and Kelly left for the cabin after bidding everyone a good night. The ship would dock in Galveston early in the morning, and the couple wanted to watch it sail into port.

Minutes after Kelly and Houston reached the cabin, he popped the cork on a bottle of champagne he'd put on ice before the dinner hour. Although the ice was melted, the champagne bottle was still cold on the touch. He filled a flute for her and himself.

Guiding Kelly over to the bed, he sat down and pulled her onto his lap. He then touched his glass to hers. "To us, Kelly. I'd love to be the only Carrington you ever kiss."

"To us, Houston." Not only was he the only Carrington she wanted to kiss, he was the only man, period, with whom she wanted to share her lips.

After both took a sip of champagne, Kelly slipped into the bathroom to change into the lingerie Houston had purchased for her. He'd told her he loved her in black and white, so she chose the lacy white set to wear for their last night on the high seas.

Just as she stepped back into the room, she struck a sultry pose, nibbling at her fingertips. "How do you like me now, Urban Cowboy?"

Houston appeared to be at a loss for words. Her heart was beating fast—fierce as she said earlier. Crooking his finger at her, he grinned wickedly. "Look like we're about to indulge in another game of show and not tell. Come to me, baby. I need you."

Wasting no time getting to her lover, Kelly slid into bed beside Houston. "I guess we have to get right into the art of showing so we'll have something not to tell." With that said, she covered her man like a second skin. "Let the skin games begin!"

Chapter 15

Kelly and Houston had stopped by her parents' home after leaving the port and sunset was near by the time they reached her place. Surprised to see several rooms inside her house lit up, Kelly looked over at Houston and shrugged. A slight frown clouded her facial features as she tried to figure out what was occurring inside her home. "The lighting fixtures are on a timer. I only activated the downstairs entryway light and one in the back interior hallway."

Houston noticed how concerned and unsettled Kelly appeared. "Has the timer ever come on without being set?"

Looking worried, she shook her head in the negative. "Not to my knowledge. Maybe it has a short that caused it to go haywire."

Houston turned off the car engine. "I think we should call the police to go inside and check everything out before we do anything else. Although I can't imagine a burglar lighting up a place while robbing it stranger things have happened."

"No, please don't call the police. They'll think I'm stupid if everything is fine."

Houston didn't agree with her assessment and he couldn't follow her wishes in good conscience. "The police need to check it out." Without waiting for her response, he picked up the cell phone and dialed 911. The operator came on the line. He gave her the details of the emergency situation, disconnecting minutes later. "Give me your keys. Stay put. I'm going to check around the perimeter and the backyard. I might need the alarm code."

Kelly had already removed her keys from her purse so she handed them over. She pointed at a red button on a miniature remote device. "It'll silently disarm the alarm system. Inserting two, two, twenty-two will also turn it off."

"Got it. Lock the doors after I get out." Leaning across the console, he kissed her gently. "I'll be right back." *Hopefully.*

Houston was somewhat apprehensive but he didn't want Kelly to know. Alarming her further wouldn't serve any purpose.

While making his way around to the back of the house, Houston was startled when sensor lighting flooded the entire area for a couple of minutes. He regrouped under the cover of darkness then slowly edged up to the back entryway, hoping no one had seen the lights. Cautiously, he peered inside the French doors.

The family room television was on. Someone had to be inside, Houston thought. Kelly hadn't left the TV on. He knew that for a fact because he'd gone inside to carry her bags out for the cruise and had walked around with her while she secured the house. Calling the police had been the best course of action. As he thought about the security guards at the gate, he wished they had called them also. They would've come right away.

Houston went back around to the front where the car was parked in the driveway. He tapped on the window for Kelly to let it down.

Kelly had to end up opening the door since the engine was off. "Are you okay? What's happening?"

"The family room television is on. I know it was off when we left. Does anyone else have a key to your house?"

She shook her head in the negative. "Lynton gave me his keys after he picked up the last of his belongings."

A lightbulb came on in Houston's head. Nothing could've stopped her friend from having keys made before he returned them. He prayed that wasn't the case. If Lynton was inside her house, after she'd asked him to leave, he knew it was on.

Houston silently thanked God when he saw the police cruiser pulling up with two officers inside. They were the only deterrents he could count on to keep him from doing Lynton in. As much as he hated it, his gut had him feeling Lynton *was* the intruder.

Kelly got out of the car and smoothed down her top. Stuttering badly, she nervously explained the situation to the officers. "I had a roommate, but he returned my keys. However, I've got a feeling it just might be him if someone is inside."

Surprised that her thoughts actually mirrored his, Houston was astonished. Her comments meant that she thought Lynton capable of invading her personal space without permission. Kelly *was* onto his deviousness, a good sign. It pleased him to know she wasn't as gullible about Lynton as he'd believed.

The front door opened and the officers immediately drew their guns. Taking Kelly by the hand, Houston hurried her to the rear of the car. Both stooped down to shield themselves from possible gunfire. If it wasn't Lynton, the intruder could also have a gun. As much as Houston distrusted Kelly's friend, he didn't think he toted around a weapon.

"Don't move! Put your hands up, sir," one of the officers commanded.

"Sir," Houston aped in disbelief. "How polite are the police supposed to be to someone guilty of breaking and entering? We *do* know the person is guilty since they shouldn't be in Dr. Charleston's home."

"Please don't shoot! It's all a misunderstanding," Lynton called out. "This is my friend's house and I came back to get something I left here, something important."

Exchanging troubled glances, Kelly and Houston stood at the familiar sound of Lynton's voice. As he squirmed around on the front porch, looking totally out of his element, Kelly saw the fear in Lynton's eyes despite the distance.

Kelly walked toward the officers. "It's okay. He is my friend. I'm sorry we took up your valuable time. I can handle it from here."

"Lady, are you saying you gave this guy permission to be here?"

"Yes. He was living here but moved out before I went on vacation. It's fine."

Houston looked at Kelly like she'd lost her mind. That she wasn't having Lynton arrested was beyond all understanding. The guy should be locked up. Throwing away the key was a nice, evil thought. She had been under the impression he had given her keys back and no longer had access to her place. Lynton had deceived her for the umpteenth time and she was letting him off the hook yet again. *Would wonders never cease?*

Houston couldn't hang around for this madness, not without reacting to it in a negative way. Calmly, he opened the trunk and began removing Kelly's bags. After throwing the garment bag over one arm, he took the suitcase by the handle and wheeled it up the driveway. The front door was open so he just set her belongings in the foyer and went back to his car, where he got inside, fired the engine and drove off.

A look in the rearview mirror gave Houston a glimpse of Kelly looking at his car, yelling and flailing her arms about. He couldn't hear what she was saying, but he could imagine. Figuring what she was going through, his heart went out to her, but this was all about self-preservation for him.

Unfortunately, this was the only way Houston knew how to handle this situation. Had he stayed around to hear Lynton's B.S. excuses, he probably would've found himself facedown on the concrete while the officers restrained him with handcuffs.

Houston wasn't about to take Lynton's place in a jail cell. He'd never been arrested before and he wasn't about to start a life of crime now. He had too much going for him and Kelly's friend was not worth losing his freedom over.

The thought of losing the woman he loved over this hurt Houston like hell. Until Kelly came to the conclusion Lynton meant her no good, she'd have to deal with him all on her own. The two friends obviously understood each other way better than he did.

"The woman I love," he said softly.

Houston didn't have to ask himself where the confession had come from. He already knew. It had come straight from his heart. Even when he'd told her he loved her on the cruise, he'd had moments of doubting himself capable of being everything she needed and wanted despite his feelings. Thinking about the upcoming season's road trips had caused him to go back to second-guessing his ability to fully commit himself to her.

Houston was in no doubt he could be everything Kelly needed... and much more.

It was up to Kelly to figure out if he was exactly what she desired and needed.

The eye Kelly was giving Lynton could only be described as *evil.* She was seething, yet she tried to choose her words carefully, even in the heat of battle. She knew all too well words could not be taken back, hurtful ones or otherwise.

"I know you're upset with me, but I had no choice but to come back here. I had nowhere else to go," Lynton said.

Kelly looked bewildered. "That makes no sense to me. When you moved your things out, you told me you were able to move into the Green Tee property early."

Lynton's shrug was nonchalant. "I lied. You wanted me out and I didn't know what else to do to save face. The lease fell through. The owner decided not to lease the property out. His son had just learned his wife was pregnant and they needed a bigger place to live."

"You knew all that before I left on vacation?"

"Kelly, what do you want me to say that I haven't already said? I lied to you because I was ashamed of my circumstances. Your merciless grilling won't solve or change a damn thing. I still would've been homeless."

Kelly's eyes burned white-hot. "How dare you take that insolent tone with me? I'm trying to understand this huge mess you created. When did you make an extra set of keys? Before or after you found out the lease was off?"

Lynton glared back at her. "What are you trying to say?"

"That I believe you made those keys before you ever found out about the lease. In fact, to take it a step further, I doubt a lease ever existed. You never showed me one shred of paperwork. I don't think too highly of you right now."

"I know. Your boyfriend has seen to that. His jealousy and insecurities have influenced you more than you realize. He cared so much about you he didn't even stay around to make sure you were okay. He ran off like the yellow-bellied coward he is."

Kelly jumped to her feet. "The *all man* you refer to as a *coward* left to keep from ripping your head off and handing it to you. What you did is what I call cowardly. You've been in my home for several days without my knowledge, when you could've gone to a hotel. Now that's what I consider an act of cowardice."

"Whatever you want to say to me, Kelly, I can accept it. I know I didn't go about this the right way. But I'm not as devious as you're making me out to be."

"You're worse. You have money, Lynton. And don't try to tell me otherwise. The so-called house you were supposedly leasing was three thousand dollars a month. There are too many brand-new apartment buildings and condos you could've moved into for far less. Nothing you can say to me can condone any of what you've done."

"If I recall correctly, you made an offer for me to stay here. I didn't ask for this. Whether you know it or not, but I think you do, you've been sending mixed messages."

Kelly didn't know what to say to that, even though she knew it wasn't true. She'd never given Lynton a reason to think she thought of him as more than a dear friend. The fact he saw it the way he did was disturbing to her, but she considered it nonetheless.

He ran his hand through his hair, aware he may've gone too far. With the most pitiful expression on his face, Lynton was slow to rise to his feet. "Look," he said, "just let me stay here tonight and you'll never have to see me again. I'll leave at first light. I'm sorry if I took advantage of our friendship. I really don't want to lose you as a friend. Losing you will hurt me terribly. I'm trying hard to see things from your POV."

The look of regret on Kelly's face let Lynton know her heart was softening. His "woe is me" demeanor was getting to her. She felt sorry for him, just how he wanted her to feel. He was so madly in love with Kelly he didn't know how he'd face life without her now that they'd been reunited. He had loved her for so many years.

Why didn't she know that? Why couldn't she see his true-blue feelings for her?

"Tomorrow morning is D-day, Lynton. Please don't tax our relationship any further. You must leave in the morning. No more excuses."

Lynton watched Kelly as she left the room. He couldn't believe he'd totally misinterpreted her reactions. Resigning himself to the inevitable, he knew there was nothing he could do to change her mind. Plain and simple, he had lost the battle.

Kelly had come out the victor. More than that, he'd lost her to a mindless jock.

Dressed for bed, Kelly slipped between the fresh sheets she'd put on the bed the same morning she'd left on the cruise. As she reached over to turn out the nightstand lamp, she stared at the phone. Calling Houston was the right thing to do, but she knew there'd be hell to pay when he found out she'd let Lynton stay on for the night.

Houston wouldn't believe that her friend planned to leave in the morning. She was having a hard time believing it herself, but she wasn't backing down. No matter what lame excuse or pure bull Lynton tried to feed her, he was a goner. It was up to him to decide their future as friends.

Houston had been tossing and turning in his bed ever since he'd shut down for the night. Although he was concerned about Kelly he knew she could take good care of herself. If he thought she was in danger he would've never left. She and Lynton had a history he wasn't entirely privy to. He figured she was terribly torn between loving him and staying loyal to one of her best friends. There was no comfort for him in that.

After plumping his pillows for the hundredth time, Houston threw his head back onto one and pulled another into his abdomen. Holding Kelly instead of the pillow would've been much better, but she was unavailable to him at the moment, he thought, as he did his best to tamp down his anger. The last thing he wanted was to be upset with her. Reaching over to the nightstand, he flipped on the radio, which was set on his favorite easy-listening music station.

Nearly a half hour later Houston fell into a troubled slumber.

The delicious breakfast smells hit Kelly's nose the moment she turned down the corridor leading to the kitchen. The divine scent of freshly brewing coffee couldn't be ignored. If Lynton was preparing breakfast for her, she believed it was his way of apologizing. It was all well and good, but he still had to go. She would stick to her guns.

Kelly had hoped to hear from Houston last night, but to no avail. Once she got Lynton on his way, she planned to go to the man she loved, prepared to beg for his forgiveness and understanding. It was up to her to make things right between them. She was the one who'd wittingly allowed Lynton to get between them in the first place.

The note propped up on the toaster was the first thing Kelly saw upon entering the kitchen. After tearing open the envelope, she read the note penned by Lynton's hand.

I'm so sorry, Kelly I never meant to hurt you. I'll constantly pray that we can remain close friends. Good luck with Houston. Despite the things I said, I know he loves you. How could he not? Blessings, my dear friend. I'll always love you, Lynton.

Only Lynton would fix her breakfast and then disappear. "Apology accepted, dear friend. I'll always love you, too," she softly whispered, her emotions rising, "as a friend."

* * *

Houston had awakened before the crack of dawn. After showering and dressing in haste, he got into his Mercedes Benz and headed straight to his parents' home. With the memories of last night fresh in his mind, he found it hard to escape this harsh reality. Since his brothers weren't available to him, he knew his mom and dad would be.

Angelica set in front of Houston a plate filled with eggs, sausage and wheat toast. After retrieving the apple butter and two hot mugs of coffee, she placed them on the table. She then took a seat across from her son. "I'm sorry about what happened last night. However, son, I believe you should've stayed to make sure Kelly was okay. I hope this Lynton fellow doesn't bully her mentally or physically."

"I can assure you none of that will work. Kelly is pretty steel-headed and stubborn. That's one of the things I love about her. She doesn't allow people to make decisions for her. Her parents tried to choose her field of medicine…and failed."

Angelica raised both eyebrows. "You've sparked an intense interest here. You mentioned one of the things you love *about* her, but are you *in* love with Kelly?"

"Very much so." The stunned look on his mother's face wasn't lost on him. "I can only imagine what you're thinking. I'm every bit as astonished as you look. Love was something I never dreamed would catch up to me, at least not like this. I've been on the run from this deep emotion for what seems like forever."

Tears filled Angelica's eyes. "For me, this is wonderful news. I wish your dad had been here to hear it. Knowing you love Kelly is a beautiful revelation to me."

"I heard it, all right." Beaumont popped into the room. "You couldn't have chosen a better lady, Houston. She's a walking dream." He sat down at the table. "Now let us get down to the real nitty-gritty. You say you love her, but how much do you love Kelly and what are you willing to sacrifice to prove your love and earn and keep hers? Is it the forever kind of love?"

Houston set down his coffee mug and reached for a hand of each parent. His heart was so full he thought it might burst. "It's the forever kind, Mom, Dad. I came here to ask a favor. It's time for me to let Kelly know how much I really love her."

After composing himself, Houston made direct eye contact with his mother. "I know Dad buys you a bigger anniversary diamond every five years. Is it possible for me to borrow one until I can take Kelly to a jeweler? I gave her a promise ring on the cruise, but you'd need a microscope to see the diamond. Think you can help me out, Mom?"

Leaning forward in her seat, Angelica kissed her son's cheek. "The rings range from one carat to four." She wiggled the ring finger of her left hand. "This is five carats. And I can't imagine wearing anything larger." She smiled at her husband, hoping he understood she didn't want a bigger diamond ring. "A lovely diamond bracelet or necklace for our next anniversary would be a welcome gift."

Beaumont smiled broadly. "I hear you, my dear Angelica. I know it's a worn-out cliché, but your every wish is my command."

Angelica smiled back at her husband and winked. "Thanks for understanding."

She looked back at her son. "Houston, I have to say this, but I don't think borrowing one of my rings is the right thing for you to do. You are no pauper and you shouldn't start acting like one. Kelly deserves so much more even if you are feeling desperate. I have a great idea. Will you hear me out?"

Knowing his mother was right, Houston nodded and settled in to hang on to her every word. Angelica was a wise woman, he knew, wiser than he'd ever be.

Once Angelica told Houston what she thought would work, Beaumont felt it was time for him to give his young son more sage advice.

"Son, marriage is a beautiful thing, but it's something you'll both have to work at every single day. When each partner gives the same amount of love and attention given during the courting stage, the romance will live on. There are many creative ways to keep a marriage fresh and exciting. Look at Ashleigh and Austin. They're perfect examples. And I do believe they'll end up just like your mother and me after years and years of wedded bliss.

"Are you prepared for the possibility of her not agreeing to marry you?" Beaumont's query was serious and sobering, yet his tone was gentle. "Don't propose if you're not sure you can handle Kelly rejecting your proposal."

Houston scratched his head. "I hadn't given any thought to being rejected. Perhaps that's arrogant on my part. It's clear that I should think about it. Maybe it *is* too soon for her. But if I don't ask her to marry me, I won't know her answer. Dad, you just threw me a curveball. Where's Dallas when you need him?"

"In and out of baseball, Dallas gets a fair share of curveballs thrown his way. You three are replicas of one another, but you're each unique in your own right. You boys always deal with your problems but not necessarily in the same way. Dallas can't catch curveballs for you. Slip your own catcher's mitt on your hand, Houston," Beaumont advised in a loving manner.

Angelica was worried that Beaumont's remarks might have an adverse affect on Houston. Her son looked conflicted. "Houston, this is all about love," she said with heartfelt emotion. "It isn't about curveballs or any other mumbo jumbo. If you love Kelly enough to marry her, go and tell her exactly what you want. I've never known a time when my four men haven't risen to any challenge thrown their way. Go to her and handle your business. If you want Kelly, it's time for you to shout it out to the world."

Houston reached over and wiped away Angelica's tears. "Thanks, Mom. I needed to hear what you just said. Dad, I also appreciate your words of wisdom. I have a lot to think about. I know I'll make the right decision."

As Kelly stepped into the garage, she was caught off guard by the absence of Lynton's car parked right next to hers. Since Houston had picked her up and had driven her home, her car was already put away. *Had Lynton kept the garage door opener or had he raised it from inside?* Thinking about the letter he'd written to her made her doubt it.

Deceit in any form was strongly disliked by Kelly. What had upset her more was Lynton playing her for an idiot. He'd known all along he was coming back to her place after she'd left town. They might've discovered his presence a lot sooner had she come right home after the ship had docked in Galveston. Instead, she'd wanted to see her parents as soon as possible. The intended brief visit had turned into a long one.

As the music on her cell phone came on, Kelly looked at the caller ID. She smiled. "Hey, Mom, what's up?" She had greeted Carolyn enthusiastically, still very determined to continue healing the broken relationship.

"I was just calling to see how you are and to thank you for coming by yesterday."

"You're welcome. We had a wonderful time with you and Dad."

"I'm happy, darling. When can we look forward to another visit?"

Kelly sighed. "We'll try to make it real soon." She saw no reason to saddle her parents with her and Houston's problems, especially not after they'd seen how happy they were just yesterday. "I really need to get some rest."

"Is everything okay? Is there something you're not saying?" Carolyn asked.

Kelly blew out a stream of air. "I need to talk to someone about this crazy situation I got into with Lynton. Houston is at serious odds with me over it. Can I come see you at the clinic? I really need some sound parental advice."

"I'm not in the clinic. Dad and I took off the entire week. You're welcome to come to the house. Or do you want me to meet you somewhere?"

Kelly blinked back her tears. "I'll come there. Love you. Bye for now."

As he paced the floor in his bedroom, Houston wondered if he'd taken too long to get everything settled in his mind. A week was a long time to leave things idling, but he was the kind of man who had to be sure about every step he took. Kelly hadn't called him and he hadn't called her, but he had expected her to take the lead since Lynton was her problem. "Grow up," he loudly scolded himself. "You can't keep blaming others because of your bonehead failures. You're as much to blame for this mess as anyone."

However, Houston had finally taken his mother's great idea to heart, which was very similar to something he'd already done before. He recalled Kelly saying she wasn't too fond of surprises, but he hoped one more wouldn't hurt. Houston hoped she wouldn't see him as being too sure, because he was anything but that when it came to her. Kelly was an altogether different challenge than any he'd ever meet on the hardwood.

Deciding it was time to take the bull by the horns, Houston dialed Kelly's home phone. It was the weekend, and she should be off, unless she was on call. She answered on the third ring and he heard the hesitancy in her tone. *She must've seen the caller ID.*

"Aren't you going to tell me it's about time?" he asked, feeling terribly nervous. This wasn't how he'd meant to start out, but his nerves had got the best of him.

"About time for what?" Kelly clearly had no desire to get into a play on words with him.

The comeback was sobering for him. "Listen, let me get straight to the point. I need to talk to you desperately. Can I get you to come over for dinner this evening?"

Kelly hesitated. Maybe she didn't want to come off eager, especially when she didn't know what his intentions were. He could be desperate to end it with her. "I don't know. Do you think that's a good idea when we always seem to end up at odds with each other?"

"It's not going to be like that, I promise. Kelly, I just want us to sit down and talk and get all our issues out in the open."

"I thought we'd done just that before the cruise, Houston. I don't know how you are with your friends, because I haven't met any of them, but I'm loyal to mine. Yes, even those who betray me and pull fast ones that I may not understand. You just mentioned desperation. Have you ever thought that Lynton might've felt desperate?"

Houston *had* thought of Lynton as desperate—and on more than one occasion.

"I know he's a grown man," Kelly continued, "but he's in a new city and he doesn't know many people here. I can't help being compassionate. I don't think I'd make a very good doctor if I wasn't. Can I take a rain check? I really don't feel too well."

"Sure, Kelly, but you have me worried now. Can I do anything for you?"

"I'll be fine. You can look to hear from me in a couple of days or so."

Houston wanted to ask her if she was sure, but he knew better. It would only add more insult to all the injury he'd already caused. "I'll talk to you when you're ready, but if you need me please don't hesitate to call."

"Thanks, Houston. I'll keep it in mind." She disconnected the lines without a farewell.

Kelly felt more miserable than at any other time she and Houston had been at odds, but she just couldn't take any more risks with him. The idea of going back to her parents' home for the night came to her mind. How quickly things had changed in all directions. Who would've thought she'd find solace with the very people she had accused of abandoning her. It had taken her far too long to see she was wrong. Her parents had told her to follow her heart where Houston was concerned, but to Kelly it was a risky proposition. Maybe the man she loved had bailed out on her one time too many.

Tossing out the decision to go back to Sugarland, Kelly thought it was high time she ate something. Everything she'd touched after the disagreement had tasted like cardboard. Normally she ate when she was upset. Not this time. Houston had taken away her appetite for just about everything she loved to do. Kelly felt sad, lonely and a little hopeless, too.

The summer league was to start in a few days. She'd have to see Houston then. All the players normally took another physical after being off a couple of weeks. After all, she'd signed a contract with the Cyclones, and Houston was one of their superstars.

It was far from Houston's realm of understanding that Kelly hadn't called him back after he'd left so many messages. Several more days of silence had the man stark raving mad yet clearer about his feelings for her than ever before. One other thing was for sure: he'd see her today. Unless she'd canceled her contract with the ball club, she'd be at the training center this rainy Monday morning. No mention of Kelly jumping ship had come down from Max, whom he had talked to every day over the past week. When he needed anything from the generous Cyclones' owner, Houston had been strongly advised to call upon the man who had secured his future right out of college, so he'd done just that.

The team meeting lasted nearly an hour and a half. Much to Houston's surprise, Kelly wasn't there. So much for a sure thing. Dr. Jacoby Quinn was present, but he hadn't mentioned a word about his colleague. Houston wasn't too prideful to ask where Kelly was, but he felt he'd come off too obvious by a simple query. He sat there fidgeting, hoping another teammate would ask about her. He also believed his concerned voice would give his true feelings away. No way could he keep the inflection of love out of his tone. Kelly meant that much to him.

Max walked up to Houston once the meeting ended. "Is everything okay, Champ? You don't seem like your old self."

Houston nodded. "I'm not, but I'll get through this rough spot."

"I've never seen you like this. What's happened? Have you gone off and fallen in love with some pretty face?"

Houston's mouth fell agape. "She's more than just a pretty face, sir, much more. You and I have always been candid with one another. I'm in love with Dr. Charleston."

Eyeing Houston with open curiosity, Max took a couple of steps back. "I think every player on this team imagines he's in love with the sienna stunner, as the guys love to call her." Then Max saw the telltale signs in Houston's eyes. "But I think you're for real. Have you two been dating?"

"Yes, sir, we have. I'd like to keep that between us for right now. The truth of the matter is, I want to marry Kelly, but because of a few misunderstandings on my part, that may never happen. I'm afraid I've been arrogant and foolish."

Scratching his head, Max studied Houston even closer. "This is a miracle. The confirmed bachelor until retirement has been bitten hard." Max laughed. "Never thought I'd see this day, but now that it's here, what are you going to do about it?"

"Do you know why Kelly isn't here today?"

"I believe I do. But you haven't answered my question yet."

"I have a plan, but I'm no longer sure about it. Can I run it by you, Max?"

"You already know the answer to that. Anything that affects you affects me and the entire team. We're all family, Houston. I know, you're not ready to include the rest of the family in this. I can understand that. Let's go to my office."

As Kelly began to back out of the garage, Houston's car suddenly loomed in her rearview mirror. She quickly braked to a halt. Although she was happy to see him, she was sure he had a few choice words for her for not getting back to him. Unable to calm the nerves in her stomach, Kelly exited the car, but left the driver's door open.

Houston was already heading toward Kelly. As soon as she was within reach, he put his arms around her shoulders. Once he closed her car door, he hurried her into the open garage. Taking the keys from her hand, he activated the alarm on her car and deactivated the one to the house.

Taking charge of the entire situation, Houston directed Kelly into the family room, where he sat down on the sofa and gently pulled her down next to him. "I love you, Kelly. I can stand here and say I'm sorry for walking out on another caustic situation, but I did what I thought was best for everyone. I've missed you so much. I've had a rough time of it, and I can see by your eyes that you haven't had it any easier. I need to know something. Do you love me enough to work this out?"

Before Kelly could respond, the doorbell rang. Even though she hadn't heard from Lynton since he'd called to say he was taking up practice with another orthopedic group, she feared he may be at the door and the madness would start all over again.

"May I get that?" Houston asked. "I'm expecting someone. Before I go will you please answer my question? Do you love me enough to work through this?"

A liar Kelly wasn't, so she merely nodded her head.

Although Houston would've loved for Kelly to verbalize her response, it was what he saw in her glistening eyes that allowed him to move toward the door and get on with the business he'd gone there to handle.

This was either the first day of forever for them—or it was the last.

Closing her eyes, finally feeling the kind of peace that passed all understanding, Kelly waited for Houston to return. She was too exhausted to continue wondering who was at the door or even care anymore. Her man had seemingly come to make up with her, and she couldn't deny him the opportunity. He'd been right when he'd said her eyes told him it hadn't been easy for her, either. It had been harder than he could ever imagine.

Kelly looked up when Houston came back into the room, but it was the lady and man following behind him that highly aroused her curiosity. She watched in utter astonishment as the man worked the combination on the large briefcase he held. Kelly's heart nearly stopped when the man handed Houston an oversize blue velvet case.

Houston slowly opened the lid on the case and sat it on Kelly's lap. Surprising the daylights out of her were dozens of sparkling, near-blinding solitaire diamond rings and multidiamond wedding sets. Muffling her cries, Kelly held on tightly to the case as she tossed her head against Houston's chest. "I'm so glad you're here. I love you very much."

Houston dropped down on one knee. "I always want to be where you are." Looking up into her eyes, he appeared hopeful rather than self-assured. "I love you, Kelly, and I know it's the forever kind of love. Marry me. Please say yes so I can make it official by slipping one of these sparkling gems onto your finger."

Houston would later tell her how Max had arranged for him to get the jeweler to come to her home, after Houston told Max just how he desired to make it extremely special. Angelica had suggested a private viewing at a premier jeweler, but Houston couldn't fully embrace it until he could make the idea uniquely his own. Max had also suggested a private viewing. As was arranged, the jeweler and his wife had slipped out quietly and unnoticed by the woman he hoped to marry.

Trying not to be the least bit presumptuous, Houston had asked his parents, Dallas and Lanier to come to Kelly's home and bring bottles of champagne, but only after he called to say the proposal of marriage was sealed. If there was to be a celebratory fanfare, Austin, Ashleigh and baby Austin would join the celebration by speakerphone.

Kelly set the case aside and dropped down on her knees. As he eyes connected with her lover's, she held out her left hand and extended her ring finger. "I love you, too, Houston. Yes, please make it official. Just the thought of being married to you is an awesome feeling. I want it to become a reality. I'd love for you to choose the ring."

Houston had chosen a favorite, but he'd wanted Kelly to make her choice. As it stood now, she had made him an offer he didn't want to refuse. After plucking his favorite ring from the case, Houston kissed his bride-to-be passionately, slipping the ring onto Kelly's finger at the same time. "You have once again been kissed by the Carrington who will love, honor and cherish you forever."

Tears fell from Kelly's eyes. "I will love, honor and cherish you, too. I've just been kissed by my very favorite Carrington, my future husband."

The happy couple kissed again and again, sealing their official engagement.